Stones of Blood

DAWN J BRAITHWAITE

For the dreamers

One

THE CHOICE between life and death often left people to make irrational or hasty decisions. I made both kinds when I chose life, when I chose to escape Lord Rorric and the torment of being one of his Maids. Three years of being a god's plaything was enough for me.

Over those years, I often remembered sitting in wonder as I listened to the tales Gampy spun around the fires at night about the Five Lords and the fall of all the good in the world when Lord Rorric cast his curse and stripped the world of its now long forgotten name. Stories of a remarkable world we could barely imagine. One where people lived freely and everyone had access to food, water, and the technological marvels Lord Rorric hoarded for his own. The shadows danced across the ground and across our faces, giving an added eerie feeling to the tales. The deep scent of the wood burning beneath flames wafted through the circle as simple, sweet cider was passed around in an old, tinny canteen. The chilled air threatened to freeze our bones, despite the fire, as the story climaxed when Lord Rorric stole the powers of his brethren and enslaved humanity. A chill that reminded us the story was our reality. The tales, passed down for centuries with barely enough information to teach us to fear our ruler, only that we must fear him, frightened me. They also moved me, stoking embers in my heart that desired to see a better world.

Gampy always ended his stories with a controversial ray of hope. "There are those that say some of the Fallen Lords survived Lord Rorric's attack," his graveled voice inflected upwards. "That they're in hiding, biding their time to when they can claim what is theirs and correct his wrongs."

For me, believing in that particular legend was difficult to do. I thought it merely fanciful wishing, a pretty story to keep us going. I felt certain he added the possible survival of the Fallen Lords so we'd have good dreams to fight the darkness we lived in. After all, what were children without hope?

"Where's your hope, Grainne?" Gampy questioned when I expressed my thoughts to him.

"Hope isn't strong enough to get us through anymore," I'd shrug. The world needed something stronger, built of resolute steel and forged in fire to do more than just endure the rule of Lord Rorric.

In time, I grew to hate that legend. It made me see red; hot, glowing red. Even more after Lord Rorric's hired muscle, men willing to betray their own for money, came to my village, hauling me away with them to be one of his many personal play things. If there were surviving Lords out there, they were pretty damned cowardly, staying in hiding for centuries and prolonging the suffering of mankind. If they were alive, they were taking too long to save the people they once cared for. For me, that particular crime of cowardice, was unforgivable.

There were days since my enslavement that I'd have given anything to have the same kind of hope Gampy's stories had given me before I realized how dangerous and painful that kind of hope was. Even just the barest thread of it. After becoming a Maid of Rorric, hope became a myth. Especially on nights when I'd been summoned to Lord Rorric's chambers to fulfill my Maiden duties. On nights where his rancid breath crept over my body as he satisfied himself within my flesh. I died a little every time, a piece of me consumed by his insatiable appetites. Every time the fire in me that wanted to end him raged a little hotter.

Lord Rorric's Maids lived on a rotating schedule. Each one of us required to spend time appeasing every single one of his needs. Every need. The slightest hint of displeasure or disrespect would lead to punishments that varied from isolation to death, depending on his mood. That had been my life since being ripped away from my village, an endless cycle of fear and torment, of shameful obedience, and waiting for it to come again.

Too many years passed, my days and weeks repeated monotonously, the only changes were the faces of my fellow Maids when Lord Rorric bored of them and brought in new ones. I suffered in silence until I couldn't bear it any longer, until I saw my death written in his cold eyes, and I made the decision to change my situation.

He'd grown bored of me. It had taken him much longer to tire of me than others. I'd seen dozens of girls come and go over the years, and not one of the Maids that had consoled me my first day remained. Neither did most of the ones that came after me. There was no telling why he clung to me the way he did, and I didn't know whether or not to think it a blessing or a curse. Either way, I didn't want to die like the others he grew tired of had. It was then that I decided to escape.

I bought myself some time to come up with how I would do it by doing the one thing I knew he couldn't resist. I begged for pain with his pleasure, a plea sure to reignite his interest. He delighted in the sadistic freedom, leaving me mottled with black tulip bruises for a week. Thumb shaped bruises temporarily dotted the dip in my throat. My skin raised with angry red welts where he'd used his powers to hurt me. The move disgusted and pained me. It saved me from death while I plotted.

An outright attack would be impossible, I knew that. My escape needed to be one of cunning and deception. Something he wouldn't see coming, something that he'd walk right into. I mulled over various plots for days until inspiration struck, thanks to a sweet Maid named Shyah. She was new, had just finished her first rotation in Lord Rorric's bed. She returned to our quarters quaking, wailing like a banshee. Our nurse needed to sedate her to stop her screaming cries that threatened to echo through Galter and bring our master's wrath to our door. As I watched the girl swallow the pills the nurse urgently encouraged, my plan was set.

I would drug Lord Rorric.

I stopped the nurse as she left, "Could I have some of what you gave Shyah?"

Her eyes narrowed at my request, "So you can hurt yourself with them? Lord Rorric will kill me."

"I wouldn't dream of it," it wasn't a lie. I didn't want to die, I just wanted freedom. "I can't sleep lately is all."

She bought my story, one I repeated nearly every night for the next several weeks. It wasn't quite a lie, there was no guilt there. Sleep was rare in the three years since I was forced from my village to live in Lord Rorric's fortress, Galter. Complaining about it never occurred to me until I hatched my plan to escape. The nurse who oversaw our health was more than happy to give me the drugs to aid sleep. Only, I never used them. I hoarded them until there were enough to kill me, that way they were sure to at least knock out Lord Rorric. With his immortality, I was only guessing how much I needed to use.

Once my stash piled up, I ground the dozens of pills into a fine powder that I combined it with my lipgloss, mixing it with sweet, pungent berries to hide whatever flavor the drugs might have left behind. My lips, doused in the gloss, would become a weapon once applied. A weapon which he'd devour willingly.

I didn't tell a soul of my plans. The risk was too great. If someone ratted on me, I'd only live moments enough to regret it. If another Maid decided to use it on herself before I got the chance to, and got caught, my escape would never take place and guilt would be my lifelong companion. If she succeeded, I'd never get another shot. So, I kept the plan and the gloss hidden, placing it in my broken bed post in our quarters until the night I intended to use it.

I shook with nervous excitement as I readied myself when my turn came up again, hopefully for the last time. The gossamer dove colored gown felt different as I slid it on, not like a weight around my neck as it usually did. It felt like armor. I applied the gloss after every other part of me was made up to perfection, hair coiled in loose ringlets and an artificial blush on my cheeks. I had to fight from appearing too giddy as what I imagined would happen, wanted to happen, played out in my mind.

Careful not to lick the likely deadly dose from my lips, I couldn't wait to go to him with lips painted pink and plump. Just the way he liked them, innocent and alluring. A tempting shade that perfectly matched other parts of my anatomy he enjoyed so much. Only, I'd added one more thing to the pink gloss he loved me to wear. My lips were loaded with sedating drugs.

Despite being eager to let my scheme play out, I fought against a nervous tremor in my muscles that became increasingly difficult to fight the closer I got to his chambers. My plan was dangerous, even attempting it was courting death. If he caught me there'd be consequences to pay. He'd boil me alive, have me flayed, and turned to dust. All after he'd toyed with me in ways his darkest fantasies deemed. I'd gladly flirt with dying if it meant there was a chance at living free.

He wasn't waiting for me when I got to his room. He hardly ever was. Lord Rorric loved an entrance and had a real flair for the dramatic. Anything he did was more than necessary, especially when it came to punishments.

I sat on the edge of his bed, my sheer white nightgown a stark contrast to the deep reds and blacks of the satin bedding, waiting for his entrance. The time alone allowed my mind to wander, to remind me why I decided to try to escape, something no Maid had ever accomplished before. I was taken back to the first night Lord Rorric summoned me to his chambers.

I'd been innocent and untouched by any man then. The more experienced Maids prepared me before hand, giving me advice on how I should behave as they twisted my ginger curls with more definition and applied light make up to enhance my springtime eyes and full pink lips. Most importantly, they warned me not to show him anything but compliance. He didn't like it when his Maids fought against him, when his Maids showed any emotion other than what he expected. It was the same with anyone he dealt with, whether it be his soldiers, mercenaries, or the people.

I tried so hard to listen to the guidelines the others bestowed on me, but I couldn't control the tears that flowed freely that night. There was nothing to be done to keep the fear the other girls instilled in me from showing on my face. It was only because I didn't fight against him that Lord Rorric didn't punish me then. I'd gotten lucky.

The longer I waited for Lord Rorric to arrive, the more my thoughts circled around to changing my mind, to just doing my duty until I died, or came up with a foolproof plan. Was it worth the risk, I wondered.

The reality of what would happen should he realize what was happening before he passed out hit hard. If he didn't pass out, I didn't know what I would do. I decided to abort until I was better prepared.

As I reached my hand up to wipe the concoction from my mouth, and attempted to figure out a new plan, he entered. His raven wing robes flowed loose around his half naked body, the dark stone he wore always on display around his neck. My hand dropped immediately on seeing him. I had no choice but to go through with the plan. Whatever the outcome, I had to accept it.

Lord Rorric approached me, vile lust lit his gaze as his eyes slid over me. "You've healed nicely," his tongue dragged over his bottom lip. Our last encounter had left me more marked than ever, grotesque bruising encircled my throat and the welts from his magic had transformed into blood filled blisters. The nurse wore a grim expression when I went to her, and the guards wouldn't look me in the eye when I passed them in the halls. A hand shot out from the robe encircling him, wrapping around my neck. He pressed his thumb deep into my throat, the nail digging into flesh, "Good."

From there, it didn't take long for him to comply with my secret plan. His mouth was on mine the moment he stopped talking, licking and sucking with greed that would have had me fighting illness if it weren't for knowing what would happen soon. What I hoped would happen soon. The seconds ticked by dangerously slow as I waited for the drugs to take effect.

His mouth began to drag, his tongue lapped sloppily every time it passed his lips, leaving more and more drool with each passing. The sedatives were working. Desperate to be done, a prayer filled my mind for the drugs to work even faster. His movements became slower and slower. When his kisses finally stopped, my eyes snapped open.

"What have you done?" he staggered back with wild and sleepy eyes, Lord Rorric struggled. I'd won. With smug satisfaction I wiped the remaining gloss from my mouth, driving home my victory with constant eye contact. The wrath that etched his face at the realization of my betrayal held lethal contracts, a pledge to kill me, for the moments he remained upright. Lord Rorric's power flickered sleepily with his desire to end me, bringing a wide smile to my face. The drugs were more powerful than I hoped if they nullified his powers. One last gasp escaped his contorted mouth and his eyes rolled back, signaling the final effects of the sedatives falling into place.

The moment Lord Rorric's body crumpled to the ground, I ran. Wasting time on checking to see if he was truly out could have been a monumental mistake I wasn't about make. I didn't know how much longer I had before the drugs I gave Lord Rorric wore off. His immortality, his otherworldly powers, had to have an effect on how well they worked. I just prayed to whoever listened, if anyone listened, it was long enough to get me far away from Galter.

I padded through the stone lined halls, dimly lit by the dancing flames in the sconces hanging on the dark walls. As I traveled further from his chambers, I began to feel a hum deep inside my bones. A call so siren-like, I could not ignore it. The sensation tugged at me, directing my path to make turn after turn, every corner drew me further from the exit I truly wanted to get to. When I reached a darkened dead end, it stopped. Fear swelled in my chest. Had I just followed an unconscious call from Lord Rorric meant to trap me?

As fast as the worry came, an answer was delivered. A warm draft flowed from the seemingly blank space before me and the tugging began again. On closer inspection the shadows before me concealed a hidden door, perfectly concealed. Certainly one had to know it was there to find it.

The moment my feet crossed the shadowed threshold, a single shaft of light appeared and chased away the darkness. The light was a savior, showing the dangers that otherwise wouldn't be seen. The floor gave way to an endless black pit that took up most of the small space. In the center of that vast emptiness, connected to the entrance by a bridge barely two feet wide, a single platform of stone stood, and on that platform sat a pedestal of glass.

Something winked in the light on that pedestal, and I knew it was the something that called me there. There was no ignoring it, no matter how much I wanted to run from Galter. The call would not be ignored.

With careful steps I traversed across the simple bridge, making my way to where I came face to face with what beckoned for me. A large marble sized ruby sat on the pedestal before me. Noumenon, the stone trapping the powers of the fallen Lords for Lord Rorric to use as he pleased. I heard it's energy, felt the low vibration trembling through me. Its call mesmerized me. *Take me, take me.* The stone whispered in my mind, demanded my attention and obedience. My head pulsed in time with the silent chant, *Take me.* Over and over it repeated as my fingers twitched to heed the call.

The stone would be so easy to take. All I had to do was reach out and grab it. No one was there to stop me. I licked my lips and stretched my arm out towards Noumenon.

My hand hesitated, and pulled back inches from the stone. Fear ricocheted between muscle and bone, brain and action, reminding me of the consequences of what I was about to do. If I took the stone, danger would follow me. I would have to be on the run for the rest of my life, unless I found a safe haven Lord Rorric could not reach. As far as I knew, no such place existed.

On the other hand, a life tethered to Lord Rorric was no life at all. It was death, a dangling sword of certainty that threatened to fall at any moment. That was all I needed to understand I had to do this. It was a risk worth taking.

I grabbed the stone, making a fist around it. As I did, I knew this had to be the dumbest thing I'd done in my twenty years on this world.

The large red gem warmed my hand, like it was happy to be freed from its prison too. Grateful to escape Lord Rorric's possession. Or, perhaps it was warning me against taking it. A warning I'd willingly ignore.

My feet flew back across the stone bridge separating the stone's podium from the rest of the secret room and they didn't stop. Mere steps outside of the secret space, with the addition of the magical artifact, I realized I didn't actually plan anything more than drugging Lord Rorric and running. No idea how to get past the guards or the drones. No bag of belongings stashed away. No shoes on my feet. Only the white nightgown, lighter than air and sheer as dragonfly wings, hanging loosely on my body. So many things I should have considered were overlooked. I only had Noumenon, and the thin dress on my back. My desire to be free trumped any additional plans I should have made, and there was no time to stop and properly prepare. Now that I was in possession of this stone, I couldn't hesitate even if I wanted to.

The halls echoed with the faint sound of my bare feet slapping on the cold floor as I ran. Every step felt like a thousand needles being jabbed into my soles. I didn't care, I'd run until my feet bled if it meant getting away from Lord Rorric. I didn't want to be one of his Maids anymore, to me that was all that mattered. Being free.

Sneaking through the dreary and dank corridors of Galter, I paused at every corner and junction, cautiously searching for any sign of guards. By some strand of insane luck, I didn't encounter a single one. If I thought some actual higher power existed, I'd have sworn it was looking out for me, because it sure felt like someone or something did just that.

My confidence heightened as I approached the entrance hall, grand and dark even in the daytime. Stupidly, I forgot to keep caution on the forefront of my mind. As I rounded a corner without scouting, I barreled right into a guard. I froze in fear.

He stumbled backward, lifting his helmet that dipped down over dark hooded eyes, "Who goes there?" he shouted, spinning about. Sweat beaded on his furrowed brow and fear crossed his face. He couldn't see me, but how? After a moment he shuddered and continued on his patrol, obviously spooked.

Noumenon vibrated hotly in my hand, pulling me from my daze and reminding me to move. I opened my hand, staring at the stone. It pulsated once before going silent again. Had it kept the guard from seeing me?

I shook off my surprise and resumed running, this time keeping my guard up just in case whatever that had been was a fluke. I wasn't going to take any chances. Not even with Noumenon on my side.

Two

THE NEW DAY broke hours ago, bringing with it a raging storm instead of a promising sunrise. A storm possibly caused by Lord Rorric's anger when he finally came to and remembered what transpired and realized something else was amiss. I had taken power from him in more than one way.

The wind howled around my tired body. I hadn't stopped running all night, except to steal a cloak from a clothes line in the tiny village beyond Galter. I only paused long enough to yank the garment from the line and wrap it around my shoulders. That moment was long enough to catch interesting gossip streaming from the windows of the home. There were rumored rebels, united under the banner of a knotted serpent eating it's tail, far in the wilderness preparing to rise against Lord Rorric. They called themselves The Rising. I knew the moment I heard of them that I needed to find them.

The force of the gale wind threatened to topple me as it snapped the cloak, lashed debris, and splattered fat raindrops across the skin of my arms and face. Every impact threatened to break me open. The gossamer nightgown clung like tissue to every inch of me it touched, revealing me to the world every time the wind blew the cloak open. I couldn't rest yet, there was nowhere to seek shelter in this wide open space before the forest edging it in the distance. No where to hide. At least I knew the drones couldn't find me in the torrential weather pounding away at the world. Despite all of Lord Rorric's magic, anything electric still didn't mix with water.

That didn't mean that I couldn't be caught at any moment. There had to be quite a bounty on my head already, and plenty of men willing to face anything for the reward. A silent bid amongst his most trusted to capture me and drag me screaming to him. All I knew was Lord Rorric would never announce to the world that a lowly Maid bested him, let alone stole an artifact that few outside the fortress knew about. He couldn't be seen as someone who could be defeated, especially not by a mere mortal. People might get ideas. He simply couldn't allow that.

Sure, he might widely declare I'd gone missing. But whatever he told the masses, if he told the masses, wouldn't be accurate. It would be spun as something else, told with a lie of worry for my safety, a cry to make an example of those who stole from him. All to get his precious stone back.

Then there existed the biggest threat to me. The possibility he sent the beasts out. The very real possibility. The beasts were Lord Rorric's personal hunting companions, and trackers. Tall as a man with bodies of pure muscle rippling under their sleek mirrored fur, the beasts were perfect hunters. Nothing escaped them once their eyeless, heat based vision, and strong senses, locked on their targets.

I had to remain vigilant.

Four hundred feet separated me from the edge of the trees that lie at the end of the plain. To my aching, battered body it seemed like miles of fighting against the elements that wanted to keep me from getting there, a battle I didn't think I had the strength for. I had to hold out, though, even if my body didn't want to. With all my might I pushed against the wind, taking another strained step. My stolen cloak whipped around my forward leg like it wanted to hold me back, trying to stop me. I fought against it, taking another slow and calculated step. Then another, and another.

"I have to make it," I sputtered to myself against the wind, which filled my throat every time I opened my mouth. "Just a little further."

Lightning flashed high above me. It streaked across the ever graying sky, the clap of thunder that followed seconds after, split the air and shook the ground. I flinched, the shriek that escaped from me became lost in the wind. The storm was on top of me, and intensifying. I tried to move faster, only succeeding in adding a handful of inches or so with every difficult step. At the rate I moved, I'd be black and blue from head to toe, again, by the time I reached the sheltering woods.

As I got closer to the forest's edge, I began to feel something tugging at me just as I had in Galter. Something urged me on, told me I had to enter the densely packed trees. It felt like the same siren song Noumenon sang to lure me to it, to take it. An indescribable pull that I had no choice in responding to.

Another gust of wind whipped the hood of my cloak off and around my neck. Frantically, I ripped the strangling fabric away. Lord Rorric, if he was controlling this madness, was truly out to kill me.

Long minutes passed before I reached the tree line and ducked between two large conifers as I entered it. The branches danced over my head, groaning and threatening to break with each gust. Thunder rumbled the earth again, and rain pattered on the leaves, a few breaking through to reach the forest floor. The semi-safety of the trees was a welcome relief from the howling wind and rain, the trees acting as a shield.

The lure coming from the trees didn't die under the swaying branches, it intensified and pulled me deeper into the forest. Whatever called for me to find it, lay deeper within. For all I knew, I was about to get hopelessly lost in the forest. I wouldn't have minded, I sort of wanted to disappear and slip away from the world. I wanted to let the wild swallow me and the stolen gem that burned a hole in the pocket of my stolen cloak. Somehow, I knew that within the densely packed flora I'd be safe from Lord Rorric's clutches for at least one more day.

I trudged through the foliage until I came to a large tree, knobby and twisted with branches burdened with numerous black bulbs that smelled like they were rotting, the sickly sweet scent had me gagging. Covering my nose and mouth with my elbow did little to keep the smell at bay. An unease settled over me as I stood there, my stomach turned sour and my skin crawled with invisible insects. The feeling that something bad lie beyond that tree became overwhelming. All logic screamed for me to turn the other way and find another path, that if I continued something awful would happen; but the siren song had other ideas. Ideas that simply couldn't be ignored. It reminded me how hard I fought to make it to this point and demanded I continue beyond the gnarled tree.

Ignoring the bad smell, I reached out and braced myself against the tree, hoping a few deep breaths would soothe the nausea welling in my stomach. The rough, gnarled bark scraped my palm, which burned like fire against the prickled wood. It felt wrong. No comfort came, no ease in the queasy feeling in the pit of my stomach. I straightened my back, squared my shoulders, and took the first shaky step past the dark tree to head deeper into the forest.

Ten steps beyond the black fruit tree my ears began to ring. Four more steps; the ringing intensified making my ears thrum and pulsate. Twelve steps; a sheen of sweat covered my brow despite the cool air. Six steps; the crawling sensation on my skin became unbearably itchy, causing me to twitch and shake. Cramps attacked my whole body after another seventeen steps. My body doubled over, racked with pain so intense I felt like I was ripping in half.

The ringing in my ears became so loud at this point, I could barely hear my own breathing. Even most of the noise of the storm dulled in comparison to the high pitched ringing tone in my head. A headache settled in a few paces after the cramps came, like an ax had been wedged into my brain, the pain radiated over every inch of my head. My eyes watered and stung from the intensity of the pain; I could barely see enough to keep moving on.

Yet, I had to. The call insisted.

Three more steps, and my heart began to race, beating erratically against my ribs and stopping every few seconds as if to rest. Twenty steps; I stopped and retched. The meager contents of my stomach spilled on the ground, the smell of it wafting into the breeze made me heave more. I felt no better. In fact, I felt worse. My body, wanted to give up.

I collapsed, falling into the puddle of sick, and sobbed. The pain raking through my body was unlike anything I'd ever experienced before. I'd never felt so sick or helpless. I wanted to die. Part of me debated doing just that, giving up and lying in this spot until whatever this was killed me. At least then, I knew I'd never be in Lord Rorric's clutches again. I'd have died on my terms, not his. Free. The morbid thought raged with frightening truth.

I lay there, contemplating my death, the lure tugged harder at me. It annoyingly urged me to fight the pain and sickness, and continue to follow it. Weakly, I looked up and scanned around until the tug lashed violently in my mind. I stopped. Something beyond the trees in front of me caught my eye. A shape in the distance took hold of my gaze, a dark smudge that stood against the verdant life of the forest. The siren song wanted me to go there. I couldn't tell for sure what it was, it could've been a really big rock or a wall of bushes. Though it seemed very unlikely, it could have even been a house. I couldn't see clearly enough through the water gathering in my eyes, through the pain tearing my brain in half. I hoped it was a house of some sort. A house that maybe someone lived in. Someone who could help me.

My body didn't want to move anymore, but I had to reach the distant object just on the chance it was a house. Why else would what-ever called me insist I head toward it? Maybe it knew that once there, I'd be helped. I willed myself to get moving, even if I had to drag my ass across the dirt to do it. My arms trembled, weak and tired, when I stretched them before me and clawed my fingertips into the ground. I pulled with every ounce of energy I had left in me. My body dragged forward, towards the structure. Dirt, pebbles, and sticks scratched along my body with every pull, and every movement ate away at my waning strength.

Soon, the structure began to become clear, it was a house, a lonely house in the middle of nowhere. I nearly broke down in exhausted, rejoicing revelation. A dim, light flickered against the structure, a light in a window! Someone lived there. The dying embers of my hope sparked back to life, renewing my resolve.

With a last, tiny rush of adrenaline, I pushed my body harder and fought against the worsening pain and nausea to reach my goal. Those last few yards were arduous. The effort to get there should have been more than what I had in me. By the time I reached the house, I was in hysterics. Animalistic howling cries of pain and determination came out of me. No doubt the person inside thought me to be some terrible beast stalking their home.

The side of the house I dragged myself to had no door, but there were a few windows that sat mere feet above the ground. A small sigh of relief passed my lips. I was thankful I wouldn't have tow my battered and weary body any further to try to find the door. I didn't have it in me to do it. I barely made it up to the house as it was. All I had to do was let the person inside know I was there.

The house's large stone foundation perfect for my fingers to grip and hoist myself up. I sat and rested against the stones, giving myself a chance to rest before trying to yank myself up to the window. I needed every ounce of fight left in me to do it.

After a few minutes of ineffective respite, I turned my aching torso and reached up to feel my way to the window ledge. Every dip and dimple of the dusty gray foundation slowed my progress by seconds that felt like hours. When my fingers finally met the ledge, I grasped onto it for dear life and strained to lift myself from the ground. My arms gave out on the first attempt. I slipped, scraping my elbows on the stone foundation on the way down, adding to the roster of pain wrecking me. I stamped my foot in weak frustration before trying again. With another deep breath, I tried again. This time, I managed to pull myself into a hunched position, resting my elbows on the window ledge to help support my weight.

The windows were filthy, crusted with years dirt and moss that obstructed me from clearly seeing inside. Only vague shapes could be seen through them, even then, just barely. The filth didn't bother me. I was just as dirty if not more, covered in my own layers of dirt, sick, and blood.

Shifting my weight so I didn't fall, I tapped the window with the heel of my palm with everything I could afford to give. My hand thudded weakly against the pane, the hollow rapping was barely loud enough to be heard. It had to be enough. The effort of holding myself up became agonizing, taking up all of my energy to maintain. I felt fainter by the second. My body would give out soon, making the need to get whomever lived there's attention was urgent. I hit the window harder.

A figure emerged from the shadows of the house and began to move toward the window, just as black dots begin to fill my vision. I closed my eyes and rested my head on one arm while the other hand continued to rap on the panes. A muffled shout met my ears right before a I heard something behind the window click. A warm wooden scent washed over me as the window opened.

I lifted my face, straining to open my eyes more than a slit. The figure before me blurred into itself and the widening black spots in my vision. "Help me," the hoarse, whispered plea managed to escape my lips right before I lost consciousness.

Three

I WOKE OVERHEATED, under layers of thick, soft blankets. My pain had dulled to a bearable sear. Sore muscles and stinging wounds were all that remained. The nausea and whatever else had been afflicting me before were completely gone. I wondered why and what had caused it. The only thing I could think of was that strange knotted tree had poisoned me somehow, since I hadn't felt ill until after I'd touched it. It had to be toxic.

I didn't feel like I was dying, that relief alone made me not question it too much. I had better things to focus on anyway, like trying to figure out where I could find the rebels I'd heard about back in the village. I stretched and ran my fingers through my tangled red curls, finding bits of twigs and leaves in the near matted knots caused by the winds, before sitting up to take a look at my surroundings. Between my hair and whatever bruises marred my body, I must've looked frightening.

I continued to run my fingers through my hair, picking out debris as I surveyed the room. The space I found myself in appeared to be a workshop of sorts with random pieces of furniture thrown in for comfort. The warm aroma of sawdust, oil, and heated metal filled my nose. Every wall was lined with shelves that were absolutely packed with an agglomeration of contraptions, some I recognized and some I didn't. Despite the cluttered shelves, it had to be the cleanest tinker's shop I'd ever seen. I assumed its isolated location had something to do with it. That, and the strange, sickening atmosphere of the woods around it. Both of those were good reasons the place didn't get much business.

A man sat on a dilapidated and hideous green couch across from the one I was on, his dark head of hair bowed as he worked something in his fingers. They slid and twisted whatever he held in them with an impossible dexterity. The tops of his eyebrows furrowed in concentration at the task.

"Excuse me," I interrupted after a minute of watching him work.

"Huh," he grunted more than answered, looking up from his project. Dark eyes under thick eyebrows met mine briefly. A flash of a closed mouth smile nestled above a stubbled chin, more of a polite greeting than a sign of happiness, accompanied the look. He went right back to his work after a moment. "Feeling okay there?" he asked without looking back up.

"Remarkably, yes. I have no idea what came over me out there."

The guy moved his head back and forth in a manner that indicated he had a general idea, but wasn't going to share. "Seems to me you've been traveling hard, a long way too. Don't see much of provisions on you, bad move on your part. I'd say exhaustion."

That was not exhaustion. I knew exhaustion. Days of being Rorric's current obsession, waiting on his every whim at all hours of the day led to exhaustion. No time for real sleep, no real rest given, always doing something. That was exhaustion. I had no idea what that episode in the forest had been, but I didn't tell him that. He didn't need to know how I measured being tired. "Maybe."

He started to whistle some tune I wasn't familiar with, but it sounded old. Not old, ancient, full of history and violence and love. A living thing. Every note hit me, and sunk into the depths of my being, becoming part of me. I felt it resonating in my bones. No, deeper. In every cell. The melody seemed to lasso my heart and lock my eyes on the stranger.

"Thank you, for helping me," I interrupted again, not worrying about being thought of as rude. "I'm Grainne."

"Uh huh," he started to whistle again.

The wind continued to howl outside. The storm raged on, harder than it had all day even. By the sound of it, I wouldn't be leaving anytime soon. I didn't like that. I wanted to keep moving. I had to. Sitting still was the best way to get caught. Even in a remote place guarded by some unseen force that made people ill. I wouldn't be convinced otherwise that wasn't what happened to me.

"Hey, do you have a holo-caster or something? I want to see if they know when this storm is blowing over," I half lied. Besides the weather report, what I needed was information. What I truly wanted was to attempt to pin down the rebel broadcast I'd heard about in the village when I stole the cloak. I thought they sounded like the people I needed to get Noumenon to. If anything, they were people I could hide with.

The guy grunted, using his head to point to some shelves in the back of the room. I followed the nod to the dimly lit area. The shelves were a mess, piled with seemingly random bits of rusting junk, tools, and stacks of papers. It took me some time to find the holo-caster I looked for. It was an ancient model, probably one of the first ones made. The left antenna bent forty-five degrees and the right one was half missing. Even if I managed to find the rebel station with the analog dials, I wouldn't be able to see half of it. Hopefully there wouldn't be important memos in the margins to see, the clues I needed to find these guys and hide away with them forever.

"Is there a battery for this thing? An on button?" I asked rotating the old thing in my hands.

He grunted again and stood. My eyes widened at the revelation of his huge frame as he lumbered to me and yanked the box from my hands. For the brief moment his fingers grazed mine, a spark of calm shot through me.

I could tell he was tall when he sat, but his hunched over frame belied his true height. Well over six feet, maybe close to seven feet tall. It was possible he was taller than Lord Rorric even, who towered over everyone else in Galter. He opened a compartment on the side and pulled out a long cord attached to the inside, a round rubber block sat at the end with metal prongs on it.

Then he moved along the shelves to where they met the wall. He flipped open a little metal door that rested just above the chipped wooden counter, revealing a circle set into the wall with holes in it. The rubber, pronged block fit in it perfectly.

A plug. I'd never seen one in person before. Almost everything that required energy was powered through the sun or battery, even the discarded and outdated tech that weren't deemed fit for the powerful or powerful adjacent folks anymore. Plugs were ancient, rarely seen relics. It was a miracle he even had a source to power it.

In moments the holo-caster crackled to life. The knobs and dial lit with a white light and the broken hologram screen popped up displaying blue static, sparking a few times.

"Is it safe?" I eyed the old device suspiciously.

"Probably not," he said, his voice low and graveled. He said nothing more, just ambled back to the beat up couch, sitting down to continue his task. It seemed my striking host was a man of few words.

I shrugged to myself, it was better than nothing. I bent eye-level with the dial and began to fiddle with one of the knobs and discovered it controlled the volume when the static shot from muted to ear splitting as it turned. The man grumbled, annoyed by the sudden burst of noise, I responded with an apologetic grimace.

Turning my attention back to the holo-caster, I began to turn the other knob. This one was much harder to turn, probable years of not being used caused it to get stuck frequently. The little, red bar in the dial moved back and forth across the white hashmarks slowly as I struggled with it. Every time a hint of image appeared in what was left of the holo-gram projector, I'd stop. At first, all I got was static with blips of images that gave way to fuzzy lines faster than I could blink. Then, after ten minutes of trying, I got a flash of something more. Finally!

I turned the knob back carefully until the flash settled into an actual, partial, image. The broadcaster's head looked like it'd been put on sideways thanks to the bent antenna.

"The missing Maid..." an image of a Maid, although distorted and lacking color, came on the screen. I couldn't even be sure it was an image of me.

Nope, not sticking on that one, just in case. This guy didn't need to see this one. Or even know it existed. I didn't know whether or not this man would turn me in if he knew my whole story. Moving on quickly, I turned the knob more until I got another hit. Just propaganda encouraging men to join Lord Rorric's forces. I moved on to the next station, landing on what I pretended to search for; weather. I paused briefly and made sure he wasn't paying attention. Seeing his intense focus on the project in his hands, I felt it safe to keep looking for what I was really after.

I continued on.

Soon, I neared the end of the dial. What if I passed it up, or the stupid box was too old or damaged to receive the signal? Or the gossip I overheard was just that, idle and hopeful gossip? Shit.

When all seemed lost, I got one last solid hit. It didn't seem like anything at first, a static laden image, and then it changed. No audio came from the station, only a floating symbol, a snake wound into an intricate knot. The symbol I'd been looking for. The symbol of The Rising, distorted by the broken screen. After a minute of silence, the audio crackled on. I lowered the volume in an attempt to hide what I listened to.

"Whispers from Galter, indicate there is more to this missing Maid than officials are letting on. Our sources say Lord Rorric is desperate for the young woman's return not because she is a precious Maid, not because he is concerned for her, but because she has stolen an object of value from the fortress. Something important. Whether or not she knows how important the item is, or if she stole it simply to fund her escape, is not known at this time. Whatever it is, it has Lord Rorric shaking in his boots. My bet is that it is some artifact that could possibly lead to one or more of the Fallen Lords. As you know, there is legend that says not all of them died..."

"That's not the weather. Shut it off," the man interrupted with a booming voice.

I ignored him, I wanted to hear this. I needed to hear this, just because it was the rumored rebel station. All I had to do was wait for the coded location to air again. I turned down the volume one more notch.

"... I say, we certainly need someone like the Fallen to fight for..."

"I said, shut it off."

"It's interesting."

"It's drivel. They are gone. If they aren't dead, they just want to be left alone," he marched towards me. "Now, turn it off, Maid of Rorric."

The world snapped around me, like the jaws of a beast, strong, jagged, and threatening my life. My pulse picked up and my breath hitched. He knew, he must have seen the broadcast. Crap, crap, crap. I shook my head vehemently, "You have me confused with someone else," hoping to deflect his suspicion.

"No, I do not," his hand came down on the counter next to the holo-caster, making me jump. His dark eyes flared blue. It had to be a trick of the light, that they reflected the hologram display. Either way, it frightened me. Almost as much as Lord Rorric. He yanked the holo-caster from the counter, the frail, old cord snapped at the base of the plug, leaving it in the wall, and the display fizzled away as the voices died. Leaning in and putting his face inches from mine, he sniffed, "You got the stink of Rorric's power all over you."

The stink of Lord Rorric's power? What?

I stared at him, half bewildered and half afraid. I didn't want him to expose me or turn me in for whatever reward there was. I figured continuing to lie would not help me. "All right, you got me. I'm the missing Maid." The man continued to glare at me, unblinking. I shifted uncomfortably under the scrutiny. "Please, don't turn me in. I can't go back there. I can pay you for your silence." I looked to him, pleading, hopeful, and ready to hand over Noumenon for payment. Losing the stone meant I had nothing to offer The Rising if I found them, but if it kept this guy's mouth shut it was worth it. All I knew about him was that he was kind enough to have let me in from the cold, cared for me while I lay unconscious, and he had a huge chip on his shoulder. That didn't mean anything. Even with his obvious hate of Lord Rorric, there was a chance he's betray me for the right price.

"I know as well as you do Maids do not have money." His blazing eyes studied me, harsh and judgmental before suddenly softening. The tenseness in his body melted, and he sighed, "I'm not turning you in. You can sleep here tonight, in the morning you get on your way. I don't need the trouble that's following you."

Without another word, he went back to his seat.

I pressed my lips together and nodded, staving off the tears that wanted to flow despite the relief that filled me when he said he had no intention to turn me in to Lord Rorric. However, he'd also cost me. I had no idea where to find the rebels that could help me permanently. The holo-caster gave me nothing that I didn't already know before he forced it off. Broke it. I was no better off having listened to it. This man probably wouldn't let me use another holo-caster if he had one.

The tears behind my eyes burned away as fear gave way to anger. What was this man's deal? Every word or grunt out of his mouth had been indifferent. He got far too bent out of shape over a holo-cast about the Fallen Lords, a story that, more often than not, inspired hope to the downtrodden people. There was something strange about him, and not just that brief blue flare in his eyes. He said he could smell Lord Rorric on me. A smell I was all too familiar with, but most didn't pick up on that. Only Maids would. The sharp and sour earthy scent that washed over me every night in his company would haunt me forever.

But this man had specifically said he smelled Lord Rorric's power. His power. As far as I knew, that had no specific scent of its own. If it did, only someone like him would have been able to smell it, right?

Someone like Lord Rorric.

His words boiled in my mind, *"If they aren't dead, they want to be left alone"*. The words replayed over and over in my head until it hit me. I stumbled against the counter, gripping the edge until my knuckles whitened.

He was like Lord Rorric. He was one of the Fallen.

But which one? Obviously not Orah or Blix, he was definitely not female. That left Hux or Raidyn. I dug deep into my memories for any trace of the stories Gampy spun that would help me identify my host. Identifying him would've been so much easier if I knew what the Fallen Lords looked like. Images of the Fallen had been banned since their fall, which was too long ago for anyone alive to remember. There may have been a few in existence somewhere, but I had never seen any. All I had to go on were word of mouth stories, which were vague in their descriptions.

From what I remembered, both of the two male Fallen were described as formidable in their own ways. Raidyn had been slight and agile, moving like a whispering wind. His weapon was an extension of himself, able to follow commands, possibly his thoughts. Hux had been an unstoppable, explosive force, larger than life. He was smart and cunning, an inventor.

My eyes roamed over the workshop and studied my host with a new perspective. He was definitely larger than life. Bigger than any man I'd ever met before. His build suggested a natural strength, something that came from just existing rather than working for it. He'd barely stopped working on the project in his hands since I woke. This guy wasn't just any tinker. He was *the* tinker. Hux.

With that realization, I couldn't seem to take my eyes off of him. I took in every detail, amazed that Hux sat feet away from where I stood, hunched over a pile of scrap metal and wires. As I watched him, the awe filling me shifted. Anger took over. How did he just sit there, hiding in his scraps while the rest of the land suffered under Lord Rorric's hand?

Perhaps he just needed the right incentive.

Four

"I WANT you to escort me on the rest of my journey." I cornered the man I suspected to be Hux the next time he ventured to the work counter. Pretending to be interested in investigating the shelves of junk, I hadn't moved from the spot since I realized who I was with. In reality, I watched him, studied him while I formulated a plan that would keep me safe and possibly help save the world.

"You what?" his dark eyes batted in disbelief and his mouth hung open.

"Come with me, protect me. I promise I'll keep your secret."

"My secret? You know me all of a few hours and you think you have dirt on me?" he pushed past me and went back to the ugly green couch. I followed, plopping next to him and releasing a cloud of wood scented dust. I did, in fact, have dirt on him, big heaping mountain sized pile of it.

"Yes, I know your secret, Hux," I deadpanned, keeping my cool and pretending it wasn't that big of a deal. His ruddy pallor paled ten shades. That all but sealed his identity as the Fallen Lord, not that I needed confirmation again. He couldn't be anyone else. I smirked, "That's right. You are Hux."

He leaned back against the back of the couch for a moment,

cupping the back of his head in his hands, his options tumbling through his head. When he leaned forward again, keeping his hands clamped together, it was with a heavy sigh. "And if I don't, you'll rat me out?"

"No. It's not my place. Even though the people need you, Hux, I won't tell. That is a decision you need to make on your own." I didn't think there was any mortal that could make him do anything he didn't want to.

"So, nothing to gain and nothing to lose. Tell me then, what incentive do I have to help you?" he cocked an eyebrow up. Surely, he thought he had me there. He didn't know how determined I could be. How determined I was to stop Lord Rorric now that I knew it might be possible to do. He had no idea I had something he needed.

I let out a breath. I had really good leverage. I knew I did. But, I hoped that with Hux escorting me, he would see the deplorable state the land was in, that seeing how close it was to dying completely first hand might move him enough to help. To take on Lord Rorric and claim his rightful place. Help rebuild. I couldn't tell him that, though. I had to offer something.

"Like I said before, I can pay you."

"With what? You're a Maid. You have nothing." That part was mostly true. Maids had no personal belongings, no personal anything. But this Maid had something.

"I have treasure. That holo-cast was right, I stole something from him." More than treasure.

"I can't be bought with treasure, I don't need it."

"I think you do," I dug Noumenon from the cloak pocket, wrapped in a piece of my nightdress I'd torn off. Shoving aside stray wires and scraps, I placed the bundle on the small table before us and unwrapped it. A soft glow emitted from the stone, something I had yet to see it do. Not even in the presence of Lord Rorric on the rare occasion he'd bring it out and flaunt the power within. "I'll give you this," I stated triumphantly. There was no way he could resist it.

Hux's eyes widened as he stared at it, a reverent breath escaping from his lips."You stole that?" he gasped after a moment of awe-filled silence. "Do you know what this is?"

I nodded, " Noumenon. It holds the powers of the Fallen Lords. Your powers. Lord Rorric showed it off more than once."

"Of course he did," he said, rolling his eyes. "You're wrong about it, though, about it holding powers. It doesn't hold all of them. Most, but not all. We were left with some, otherwise what would be the fun in defeating us." Hux picked the stone up with reverence; a loving disbelief. I barely made out the crystal-like tear running down his right cheek. The glow of Noumenon brightened in response to his touch. "How did you get it?"

"I was already on the run when it called to me. I followed the call and took it."

Hux arched a heavy brow at my response, "Interesting. You just stumbled on it while already escaping, having already escaped him? How?"

"I'd been planning for weeks. I drugged him," I replied simply, and pushed the stone a little closer to him.

His eyes darted back up to me, "Are you insane?"

"I might be," I shrugged. "I know I have a huge target on my back now for sure."

"That's the understatement of the century, literally," his eyes locked back onto the stone.

"Hence, why I'm asking you to escort me." I added. Even if he wasn't one of the Fallen, I might have considered asking him. He was a big guy. Intimidating. Surely, no one would mess with me if he were by my side. There was also something else, tickling the back of my mind, that made me want him around. I didn't know what it was, just a strange feeling of needing him there.

Silence filled the room, I let it settle. I didn't see any reason to break it, even though I had questions. So many questions. I wanted to know more about what really happened all those years ago. Why he hadn't done anything to stop Lord Rorric since. Those questions needed to wait. There was one more, much more important question I wanted an answer to first. Whether or not he would help me if I gave him the stone.

After quite some time had gone by, Hux put the stone back on the table. He ran his large, rough hands over his face and then raked them through his hair. His breath vibrated over his lips. "I think I have no choice but to go with you," he said after another minute of heavy silence.

"It's all yours," I said, motioning to Noumenon. I felt victorious. Not only had I escaped from Galter with Noumenon in tow, I'd found one of the Fallen Lords and got him to agree to coming with me to find The Rising. Sure, I found him by accident, although, part of me doubted that too. I'd noticed since obtaining Noumenon that things seemed to work out in its favor.

"I'm not doing it for the stone. I don't need it, but you, you need me. You won't make it a day out there unguarded. I'm sure there isn't a soul out there not looking for you, fewer still that won't turn you in for a reward."

His refusal of the stone astonished me, deflated me even. Why wouldn't he want it? Part of him was stuck inside it. Didn't he want his powers back? Didn't he want to stop Lord Rorric? I folded the cloth back over the stone, hiding the glow under the light woven material. It felt heavier as I picked it back up to put in my pocket again. A trick of my mind, surely, related to what the stone represented. Knowing that one of the Fallen Lords stood before me and refused to take back what rightfully belonged to him, was disheartening.

"If you don't want the stone, then why agree to help me?"

Hux studied me intensely, an amused smirk painted on his face, big enough to reveal a deep dimple on his cheek. "You've got massive balls, Maid. You're mad enough to poison Rorric and steal Noumenon. Least I can do is help you keep it out of Lord Rorric's grasp."

"But, you can use it. Take the powers. Then it's useless to him anyways."

"No, no, no," he waved his large palm in my face. "Bad idea. No one needs that much power. It's dangerous. Even he knows that. Besides, the only real reason Rorric hasn't taken the powers in it into himself is because he can't. Powers can't reside in any being unless they are willingly given by the true bearers. He can tap into them, sure, but not keep them."

"Oh." The idea of Lord Rorric having all the powers of all of the Lords terrified me. The power failsafe comforted me. There would've been no hope without it. Lord Rorric would have been unstoppable. "Then why not take your powers at least?"

Hux chuckled, smiling broadly and unleashing his dimple once more. It changed his whole face, or seemed to anyways. He looked warm and friendly for the first time since he let me in. "There is much you don't understand."

"Enlighten me then."

"It's my business, not yours. Not the world's," the warmth drained from his face and he turned away, shame hung in the air. There were things he didn't reveal that haunted him deeply when it came to the stone and Lord Rorric. I wasn't about to push for them. The look on his face warned me not to.

I didn't feel bad for him, though. No, not one bit. My blood boiled from his refusal to do more. Sure, he had the right to not talk to me. He owed me nothing in that matter. That wasn't the problem. The fact that he seemed to turn a blind eye to the deplorable condition the world sat in was what got me riled up. Whatever trauma or story he didn't share, shouldn't outweigh the needs of everyone else. It was wrong, selfish. It mattered to the world that he wasn't willing to regain his powers and fight for us. He owed the world.

I decided in that moment that I didn't need him or his protection. He was wrong there. I got this far on my own, I could get further. Sure, the decision was childish, immature even. I didn't care.

"We leave in the morning," he decreed before I could take back my request, giving me no choice in the matter. Hux got up, taking the device he worked on with him. He made his way to the workspace counter at the far end of the room, placed his contraption down, and began working on it. I watched him work for a moment or two, his frame hunched with the weight of his past.

"Fine," I agreed to his back. Inside I formulated my own plan. I had no intention to wait until morning. I planned on leaving that night, even if the weather still sucked. Without Hux. Screw him.

Five

A ROGUE SPRING dug into my back as I lay on the couch, eyes closed and breathing steadily. Hux believed I fell asleep sometime ago. In reality, I was listening closely to my surroundings. It was something I'd mastered back at the fortress. We weren't allowed to leave Lord Rorric's bed until dismissed, which was usually as the sun set the next day to make way for another girl. So I adapted to protect myself. Many nights were spent lying prone, in his bed, slowly breathing and waiting. Listening. Preparing myself for the inevitable, for when Lord Rorric's carnal cravings surged again. It was better to be awake when they did. Sleep on those nights never came. I was forced to hide my weariness until the next night, when I slept in my own cot. Even then, I barely slept.

My ears stayed trained on the sounds Hux made as he milled about the small space, shutting down for the night. Luckily the storm subsided as night came on, and the sounds of his n nightly routine weren't masked by thunder overhead. His feet shuffled over the floor, sawdust grinding under every step. His breath came out heavy with exhaustion and, undoubtedly, stress from the disruption my presence brought to his hidden life. The muffled clatter of tools and such being put away told me bedtime had to be soon.

As he went about his business, my anxious need to head out grew in my chest like ivy, choking out everything else for survival. I needed him to move faster. The sooner he fell asleep, the sooner I'd get out of there. I didn't need him, or his protection. Not if he, the only living being that could, wasn't going to do something about Lord Rorric. Coward. All his greatness siphoned away by the rock in my pocket, his tail permanently set between his legs. How disappointing.

The lamp clicked off, finally, and Hux's tired heavy steps echoed away to his private room, the only room other than the bathroom that was closed off from the rest of his workshop. The mechanism in the door whispered into place. I waited a moment, to be sure he wouldn't come back out for some forgotten task. Silence persisted. I opened my eyes and sat up, pulling my knees to my chest, waiting for the light under the door to go out. My breaths seemed too loud, too alert, and I feared he could hear them and the deafening ticking rhythm of my heart, which skipped impatiently. Minutes passed, the light stubbornly stayed on. Did this man ever sleep?

The buzzing of my anxious body couldn't take the waiting. Risking being caught, I began getting myself road ready. I slid my feet off the couch and onto the cool floor. The clothes Hux gave me for our journey sat in a neat pile on the table before me. A thick pair of brown canvas pants, a basic white shirt, a pair of socks and a pair of boots. Discarding the cloak and thin nightgown, I began to dress quickly and quietly. I even took the time to rip strips of the nightdress to bind my breasts. The attempt was poor, being cursed with being buxom, but it was better than nothing.

As I pulled the shirt over my head, I checked under Hux's door once more. The light was out. Finally. I yanked the pants on and shoved my feet into the socks and shoes. Almost forgetting, I gathered up the cloak, taking Noumenon out of the pocket and putting it into the one in my pants. After rolling the cloak up to take with, it was time to get going.

I moved like a ghost across the room to the supply packs Hux had prepared after he decided he'd accompany me. Every step I took was carefully calculated to make as little noise as possible. The last thing I needed was to wake the god in the next room. He'd likely tie me to one of the couches until morning to fulfill his own sense of chivalry. I made it this far without him. I'd make it all the way to the rebels of The Rising too. Somehow. I only wanted him along when I thought he'd do something about Lord Rorric. Since he wouldn't, he'd wake alone in his workshop yet again and go on with his life.

The provisions bags were large, heavy looking, and one was about half the size of the other. I didn't know what he packed in them, though. I'd pretended to fall asleep before he filled them with supplies. Looking through them wasn't a priority at the moment, I'd rummage through when I put some distance between me and this place. Whatever they were packed with, Hux had to be better at planning being on the road than I proved to be. Not that this adventure was planned, but I had a feeling I wouldn't have thought of everything he had.

Hux's reluctance in helping me as more than a protector made me feel certain he would not follow once he realized I left in the night. I imagined he'd have a sense of relief when he found the responsibility of my safety was off of his shoulders, and breathe easier with me out of his hair. Saved from having to step up and face his cowardice. Hux would probably go back to tinkering with his scraps and hiding away from this horrible world. Hiding from the responsibility of caring for it.

I selected the larger rucksack, knowing full well it was meant for Hux so it had to have the better supplies. With all the strength I had left, I slung the bag onto my back. The weight of it immediately threatened to buckle me, to crush my knees and ruin my get away. Gritting my teeth, my body pushed back against the weight and righted itself. Just wearing it for that brief moment felt excruciating. It was too much for me, I wouldn't get far with it on my back and could be easily caught. I slipped it off and every joint sang in relief to be rid of the extra weight.

With the decision of which pack I'd take made for me, I opened the smaller one and shoved the cloak in without looking and closed it back up. I prepared my arm for the heft of the smaller of the bags. It was much lighter, though still had good weight to it. I'd possibly regret not toughing it out with the larger one down the road, but my body was at least able to move under the weight of the smaller one. I shrugged the bag on and took a deep breath. I was ready to go.

As I tiptoed past the worn bedroom door, Hux's soft snores were the only sound coming from behind it, the only sound that could be heard other than the rhythmic sounding one my heart in my head. That silence broke with a single step, a groan of the flooring snitching on me. A deep guttural moan replied from the closed room. With a gasping inhale of breath, my feet froze on the spot waiting to be caught and forced to stay. Forced to let him act as my guardian. That wasn't happening if I could help it. I regretted even asking him in the first place.

Heartbeats passed, there were no signs of Hux waking coming from his room. He must have reacted to the squeaking floorboard in a dream. What did gods even dream of? Was Hux haunted by the ghosts of his past? Did he have a nightmare of his defeat by Lord Rorric? Or perhaps regret chased him with shadowy fingers that clawed at his conscience, horrific monsters with fangs dripping with the blood of the people he abandoned. Did he dream of the cowardice that kept him in the darkness and the world in tatters? I hoped so. I hoped it ate away at him every time he closed his eyes.

I waited another beat, still there was no sign of stirring behind that door. The breath finally left my lungs with a relieved sigh. I moved again, my steps lighter than before to avoid another worn floorboard. Anxiety riddled my every thought and movement as I approached the exit, breathing another sigh of relief when I reached it too many seconds later. My hand trembled on the doorknob, worried it too would groan and complain, actually wake the sleeping giant in the next room and end my disappearing act. I pushed it gently, slowly, millimeters at a time. After tortuous minutes the door opened wide enough to make my exit and I stepped through into the night. The sight of the inky green darkness of the woods welcomed me, cool night air kissed my face, and the crisp smell of nature called out to me. The freedom it promised left me exhilarated despite the threats that lurked out there.

I faced a lot of unknowns and possible dangers being out in the world on my own, being constantly vigilant was imperative. Every muscle in my body tensed as stubborn bravery settled into every fiber of my being. Night embraced me and I slipped away into the dark, becoming one of its shadows.

Thankfully, I didn't have to worry about becoming sick again. Hux explained about the strange illness that overtook me before, once he was aware I knew his true identity. A security measure cast into place that only worked on those heading towards his secluded home. A means to drive trespassers away. Traveling away from it, there would be no ill effects. At least I didn't have to worry about becoming unbearably sick again, I didn't think I could take it.

There was no silence in the forest at night. Life sprung forth to replace the day dwellers who slept in their nests and burrows, the nocturnal animals prowled through the underbrush and flew through the inky black sky in their stead. Insects sang in the tall grass and toads called from their watery homes for mates. Nothing malicious nor vile to be heard. Yet. Still, I jumped at every innocuous snap of twig and rustle of branches swaying with the night air. It was more what I didn't hear that had me truly on edge. Mechanical eyes of whispering drones, or the drooling maws of the beasts as silent as the grave they brought with their powerful bodies. These were what made the fear rise in my heart like ocean tide, strong, unforgiving, and drowning me in its depths.

I didn't mind the tremble in my step, it had use in keeping the adrenaline pumping through my veins. It guided my steps, swift and quiet, around and over the obstacles nature set. Sleep didn't claw at my mind or add heft to my eyes because of the watchful state I was in. The cold failed to pierce the clothes on my back. I felt warm and alert. I needed to be until I put enough distance between myself and Lord Rorric, myself and that coward Hux. There was no telling how long the adrenaline would carry me. I hoped it would last until I felt safe, because rest had to be a stranger until I did. I intended to make the most of it while the adrenaline still coursed through my veins.

Through the canopy of the forest around me, I tracked the time by the moon's flight. I watched through the branches as the inky blue sky gave way to washes of pink and orange, eventually brightening as the sun woke from its own enviable slumber. The night song was replaced by that of morning birds. The toads finished their mating calls and the chitter of small forest animals began to take over. Morning had come, that meant I had to be even more alert.

After the sun had warmed the world, my muscles began to seize, protesting the long night of vigilant hiking. I knew the time to give in would come sooner rather than when I wanted it to, but I forced myself to continue on just a little longer. There had been nothing but trees for miles, nothing suitable for shelter. Not a secure one anyways. Finding one shifted to the top of my list of things to do as weariness began to drag across my limbs.

It was nearing mid morning when roaring splashes echoed through the forest. The sound gave me little hope of finding a resting place. All it told me was that a rare, raging source of water sat somewhere nearby. There was no way I could rest in water, let alone raging water. It couldn't be used as a means to cover my tracks either, the water sounded as though it moved far too swiftly to walk in without falling.

I followed my ears anyways. All I'd seen for hours was greenery and the occasional forest animal. Plus, I thought the water would be a welcome change of scenery, and perhaps if I followed it long enough I'd be able to wade in it at some point. My feet throbbed at the thought of naturally chilled water enveloping them. The idea of the cooling water easing the night from my weary feet put a spring in my step.

It didn't take me long to reach the source of the noise. Instead of the flowing body of water I expected to find, I came to a small body of water at the base of a high rocky wall. The surface danced with ripples and foam generated from the disproportionately large waterfall tumbling from the top of the wall, at least thirty feet above ground.

The hope of a hidden pathway folded in on itself, leaving only the chance for much needed relief for my aching feet. A chance I was delighted to take, if only for a few minutes; I'd earned a short respite. I sat on the shore, unlacing the shoes that kept my feet captive. They seemed to vibrate in excitement to be released from their bonds and soak up the sparkling coolness of the water before me. Every tug at the laces only excited them more. The moment the shoes and socks were off, my toes stretched and popped, they delighted in the moist earth while I slipped their leather cages into my provisions bag. I dipped my aching feet in the water, allowing it to lap over my toes and up past my ankles. Relief sighed through me. That small allowance of rest invigorated my spirit.

I waded around, the water lapping at my calves and soaking the legs of my pants, thoroughly enjoying the cool water. The rest of the lake didn't look too much deeper. The water only got darker towards the waterfall. There weren't any streams coursing away from it either. The peculiarity of it swam around my head. How was this body of water not either bigger or deeper, constantly fed by a waterfall? It made no sense. Where did all that water go?

Exploring the oddness of the lake, the waterfall began to call to me. It had to be the biggest piece of the puzzle. Perhaps there was a small stream behind it, winding its way through the stone and coming out on the other side.

I sloshed lazily across the body of water to the waterfall. The noise of the crashing water became deafening and hollow the closer I got to it. A few feet away, the fine mist spray tickled my face. I relished in it, throwing my arms wide and my head back to soak up the light moisture in the air. Sunlight and shadows swayed over the face of the falls, giving the place a slightly magical feel. I needed to absorb that magic, that peaceful mystery of the place.

The waterfall reminded me of the river near my childhood home. All the children in the village would play there. The braver ones would sneak farther up river to where the river began. There was a small water-fall there, it ran down a gentle mud covered slope. There, the kids would splash for hours on hot days, turning the waterfall into a muddy slide, screeching in mud covered joy. Those days were full of innocence. I would have treasured them more if I knew then what was in store for my future.

As I inched closer to the falls, the thick silty bottom suddenly fell out from beneath me. I lost my footing, a surprised gasp escaping me as I slipped under he surface. Inky blue water surrounded me and the turbulence of the waterfall threatened to shove me deeper. My wits came together in a need to survive. I may have been willing to give up when the mystery illness left me in tortured pain, but not anymore. I wasn't going to have escaped Lord Rorric to just drown. It would be an insult.

I kicked hard against the onslaught of water to resurface when I noticed a current, sucking around my body and towards the stony wall that bordered the lake below where the waterfall met with it. A current laced with the same call I'd felt running through the forest; the same one that urged me to take Noumenon. The current slipped like silken ribbons running over my arms and legs, curiosity and the call demanded

I follow it. My lungs already burned from the fight against the water-fall's onslaught, there was no way they'd hold out without another breath. I surfaced first, to fill my lungs, and then I dove purposely.

I took a minute to let my eyes to adjust to the low light under the surface and get my bearings. When I did, I noticed a patch along the stone wall that looked darker. I headed towards it. Up close, I realized the dark spot was actually a hole in the wall, big enough that I could swim through unimpeded, as long as it didn't narrow further in. All I wanted to do was follow it, learn its secrets. But I wasn't about to leave my provisions bag on the shore unsupervised.

I kicked my way back to the surface one more time, and pulled myself up into the shallows to make my way to the shore. The pack waited for me where I left it. Before going back in, I searched through the pack for a portable light of some kind. Surely Hux put one in, preferably one that wasn't reliant on fire and would survive the water. After some searching I found a makeshift flashlight, it was clunky with various scraps of metal welded together in heavy seams and a thick discolored piece of glass protecting the bulb. It was obviously built from salvaged parts. Whether or not it would survive the water was yet to be seen. I fiddled with it for a moment, searching for the on switch, a small lever on the bottom proved to be the ticket. Leaving the light on, I closed the bag back up, and hoisted it onto my back, my body groaning in protest at the added weight.

The third trip into the deep of the lake was the least disorienting of them all, the most arduous too with the addition of the hefty pack that threatened to drag me down. I knew what to expect, up until entering the hole. Admittedly, the plan was flawed. I had no idea if the hole went all the way through, or if it was a dead end. I didn't know how long it was and hoped the tunnel in the wall played in my favor, and that I'd be able to reach air again in time.

I swam directly for the hole and paused at the entrance. Prayer filled air bubbles floated around me while I steadied myself. Finally, when I knew delaying any longer would certainly end with my lungs filled with water, I entered the wall, and swam towards whatever lay on the other side of it.

Every second felt like minutes. The fear I'd made a horrible mistake sprouted roots in my soul. Would my breath hold out long enough to reach the other side? I swam on and on, it wasn't long before my lungs burned for air. Just as I felt certain my lungs would give out before the tunnel did, the flashlight, which thankfully proved to be waterproof, illuminated on what appeared to be the end, an edge with a watery field beyond it. I propelled myself, kicking desperately towards my goal and reaching the surface at the other end within another minute. As I breached, the gasp that filed my lungs with sweet oxygen echoed off the cavern I found myself in.

Treading water, and sucking in lung fulls of air, I surveyed the place I'd just risked my life getting to. Vents high in the rocky ceiling cast dim rays of light throughout the space. It wasn't much, but it made it possible to see. There was little to see other than water, rock walls, and a crescent shaped dirt and pebble packed shoreline that provided a dry place to rest. Only one wall was without a small beach attached to it, the one I just came out of. I was thankful for the difference. Without it, leaving this cave could have been difficult.

From somewhere deep inside me, I pulled out one last reserve of energy and swam to shore. My body dragged onto the pebbly beach, collapsing in sheer protest from the long night I'd just endured. I felt entirely made of limp and, contradictory, leaden noodles as I star-fished, gasping to catch a long awaited restful sigh.

I wasn't sure how long I lay prone on that tiny beach. It could've been minutes. Hours. Sheer exhaustion had a tendency to make time inconsequential. Eventually, I rolled to my side and into sitting position as I took off the pack. I immediately opened it and checked the contents, happy to find the bag was waterproof for the most part. Only a little water seeped through, but nothing appeared completely damaged or soaked.

I took another look around, there appeared to be no other entrance to this cavern, and the beach was pristine other than the marks I'd made. No one had been here in some time, if ever. It was well secluded, a perfect hidden place to stop and rest for more than a few moments. I would even be able to make a small fire, if I could manage to find the right tools to do it. Looking around, I doubted I'd be able to. The beaches were made of rock, dirt, and small pebbles, clear of grasses or driftwood, and had a few larger stones jutting upwards sporadically.

If there was anything in the provisions bag that could start and maintain a fire, I couldn't tell. I couldn't make head or tails of many of the contraptions packed inside, and was too tired to even try to guess at the simpler ones. There were, however, easily identifiable packages of dried foods, a tube, the flashlight, two rolled blankets, a bottle of clear alcohol, and some small cooking tools. I'd have to be satisfied with what I knew.

I settled in, replacing everything in the pack except for a pack of food and the blankets. I swirled the canteens tied to the pack to check their water levels. Both were still partially full. Not knowing how clean the lake water was, I didn't want to refill them. The water in the canteens would have to be rationed to last.

Once I figured how much water I had left, I ripped into the package of food. Inside I found smaller packages; a serving of dried fish in a honey glaze with some dehydrated plums, marinated yellow beans, and sliced crusty bread that was more like a thick cracker. My stomach rumbled eagerly when their combined scents wafted to my nose. I didn't realize how hungry I was until that moment.

My fingers raced get the food to my mouth. The fish, I expected to taste overly salty and fishy, tasted a perfect combination of sweet and salty. The plums were perfectly chewy and the yellow beans had been soaked in something vinegary. The cracker, though a little bland, was crisp and flaky, despite its thickness. I regretted eating so quickly the minute the last bite passed my lips. I wanted more. The rumbling in my stomach demanded to be fed more. I couldn't. With no idea how long I'd be traveling, I couldn't afford to eat more than one package of the prepared food.

The adrenaline coursing through my veins ebbed away during my little meal. True weariness followed, filling the spaces left behind. I felt confident enough in the secrecy of this cavern that I decided it was safe enough to finally rest. I saw no point in using one of the blankets as ground cover. A fine layer of grit and dirt already covered me. Instead, I left one rolled to use as a pillow and covered my body with the other.

Sleep came the moment I settled.

A FAINT NOISE interfered in my dream, like the grinding of a shoe in dirt. At first, it integrated itself as a background noise, growing louder each time it sounded. Then it became unnatural. Jarring. Then the noise sounded like it came from right by my ear. I realized then it was not part of my dream-scape. The noise really happened. My eyes jolted open.

I must have slept for hours. The light dimmed considerably since my arrival, my eyes had to adjust for several seconds before I was able to see. Before I could even turn to observe the cavern, the grinding sound happened again, followed by a heavy sigh.

My body, reflexive as a cat, twisted towards the sigh. A shadowy figure loomed over me, a low chuckle coming from it. "Now, you didn't think you could actually give me the slip, did you?" I recognized the voice attached to the figure, Hux. My vision cleared further with the realization bringing him into focus. He stood over me, dripping wet and scowling.

Dammit.

"What part of me sneaking out in the night are you misinterpreting as me wanting your help still?" I huffed. He offered me a hand to help me stand, but I refused it. He was blowing my plans. "I don't need you."

"You do."

"No, I don't. I think I've managed just fine. I found this place all on my own, didn't I?" I paused, squinting my eyes at Hux in study. It didn't seem very likely he knew about the hidden cavern, being the shut-in he was. I had felt completely alone when I made the discovery, certainly he hadn't been nearby when I found it. He couldn't have followed me. "How did you find me anyways?"

He screwed his mouth around and clicked his tongue while preparing his answer, "Well, I had the darndest suspicion you might go and do something stupid. From what I know about you, you don't think things through too well." His reference to my theft of Noumenon stung. It was right, but it still offended. "Of course that meant I had to sew a tracker into your provisions bag. Both of them, actually, just in case you were crazy enough to take mine." He tilted his head, scratching the dark stubble on his chin, pleased with his cleverness.

"I hate you."

"I have to live with that, I guess," he replied casually.

"No, you don't. Go home, back to your hidey-hole and junk piles. Forget you ever met me. It's not that hard to do. You've forgotten about everyone else." I brushed the dirt clinging to my hands onto the brown pants I wore. Hux's eyes bore into mine, challenging my request silently. His dimpled half smile tried to disarm my annoyance. Tried. He didn't know me well enough to realize I was immune to godly persuasion. "Well?" I implied when he didn't make any sort of move to acquiesce.

"You got grit, Maid. I'll give you that. But your steely glares and insistence that you don't need help won't send me back to my shop. I'm more stubborn than you are." He paused as if to prove his point, "You need someone on your side. You landed on my doorstep, might as well be me. It's the right thing."

The irony of his words just proved how moronic he was. "The right thing. That's rich, coming from you," I snorted. "You wouldn't know how to do the right thing if someone showed you how. You've been hiding out all these years while that poor excuse of a deity has been running the world to extinction. Where was doing the right thing then? When the so called droughts he caused started? The famines? When Lord Rorric began slaughtering whomever he pleased? Entire families and towns were taken out for the offense of one person daring to stand up to him. When he took me to his bed, practically still a child?" I screamed at Hux, unleashing every last ounce of hurt ever put on me, onto him. He didn't do these horrendous things, but his inaction facilitated them to some point. The weight of my fury crushed me back to the dirt, where my screaming morphed into heaving sobs and then into tears. Each drop burning drop blazed trails down my cheeks.

Hux squatted next to me and lifted my chin with surprising gentleness. There was sympathy there, not just in his dark eyes. It manifested across his body and touch. For all his size and strength, he was remarkably gentle. I didn't hold his gaze though. It felt too painful, too raw, to look at him. I hated him seeing me so broken, though I wasn't sure why. "I. . ." he started then paused as though he changed his mind as to what he wanted to say. "I'm sorry for what he has done to you. To all of you. His actions are embarrassing and deplorable, and not at all what we stood for. But the truth of it is, I can't stand against Rorric. You can't possibly understand."

His sympathy became empty to my ears the second those words left his mouth. He was right, I didn't understand. I'd never be able to understand how someone could allow such things to happen, to continue to happen. Turning a blind eye made him just as bad.

My eyes tore into him, shredding him apart. I jerked away from his touch, which started to feel like acid on my skin. Anger rose beyond explosion in my soul, soundless and without end. It burned me even deeper that I had to be stuck with him for the rest of this journey. He was a persistent pebble in my shoe. There was no way I could shake him now, not without a miracle, that infuriated me more than anything. I didn't bother hiding my displeasure at his intrusion. "I don't want your help," I averred. "You're a useless coward."

He glowered back, his dark eyes inquisitive and intense. "I know you don't want me. You need me. You're underestimating what you're up against."

"I think I was clear about how well I know Lord Rorric."

"It's not him you're underestimating. You underestimate what desperate people will stoop to doing to help themselves. Even if you have a common enemy."

I hated to admit it, but there was truth in his words. People were selfish and self serving at their worst. The people of the land, so ingrained with pain, were desperate and had been for years. Many would jump to their deaths if it meant their families were provided for. I imagined that whatever Lord Rorric put on my head would make any decent human weak with need. Perhaps having Hux with me was for the best. That didn't mean I had to like it.

"Fine. Do whatever you like, then. I don't care. Just do what you feel you must then leave me be," the concession killed me, but less than admitting he was right would.

His provisions bag hit the dirt next to me with a thud, splaying dirt in all directions. He soon followed, carving miniature canyons in the ground as his feet pushed out in front of him. It reminded me of digging in the hard earth as a child. How the hardy sticks cut through the dirt like knives to make grand rivers that I'd fill with water. The leaf and stick races against the other children in the village in those small and mighty waterways were part of the few good memories I held. Those innocent days disappeared the moment Lord Rorric claimed me from the village. Washed away like leaves in water, and crushed under tyrannical heels.

The sound of Hux's droning voice shook the memory from my mind. It dissolved into air as his face came into focus, becoming just another ghost of my past. His expression was curious, with dark eyes expectant and eyebrows wrinkling his forehead. "I'm sorry, you said something?"

"Did you not think to build a fire or something to help you dry?"

"With what?" I twisted my torso with my arms out indicating the lack of kindling anywhere in the cavern. "No kindling, and no matches. I'm not a god like you, can't just summon fire from nowhere."

"If you'd not been a pig-headed fool, you'd have known what's in your pack." His meaty hand grabbed my pack, dragging it across the dirt to him. The contents rattled against one another in quiet chaos. "Just for reference, making fire out of nothing was never in my scope of powers."

"I was doing just fine figuring it out." I huffed defiantly, again unable to admit defeat to him. I had no intention of bowing to any god ever again.

"Okay then, what's this?" Hux's hand dove into the pack, rutting around for a treasure. It came up brief moments later wrapped around its bounty. His fist unfurled revealing the tube, he held the slim silver cylinder out toward me like an offering. Even without a lot of light it glinted there on his hand, taunting me to grab it. It made me not want to. I did anyway.

The metal was cool against my fingers as they wrapped around it, and flipped the tube between my fingers and hands. It seemed to be nothing special, but I knew better. He wouldn't be testing me otherwise. I looked through one end, little light shone through. The light was being obstructed by something at the other end. I turned it over and peeked inside once more. Sure enough, a sheet of something black sat lodged in the other end. At first the blockage appeared solid. A closer inspection revealed tiny holes, almost too tiny to see. There's only one thing I thought this metal tube could be. "Easy. This is a straw," I said confidently and tossed it back to him.

"Okay, I'll give you that. But, it's not just a straw. This straw filters the dirt from water. Makes it safe without boiling it."

"Huh, neat I guess." Inside I was impressed with it, a handy tool for traveling long distances for sure. It could've been better though, "Wouldn't it be easier to just place a filter on the canteens? Filter more water faster, without the need to search for a little tube in a big pack every time you needed a drink?"

The dimple on Hux's cheek exploded into existence with the broad smile that appeared on his face. He nodded and blinked his sleepy eyes, "A really good idea, Maid. Thank you."

"Could you stop calling me that? I'm not one of his Maids anymore." The title was vile to me. Poison. It scooped out my insides and laid them bare on the ground. Every time Hux called me Maid, it reminded me of all the things I'd been forced to do as one. I died a million little deaths at the word. "I'll die before I'm called Maid again."

"You got it, Grainne. Maid you are not." He tossed the straw aside and dug around in the provisions bag once again. This time, he pulled out a cubed device about seven inches wide, made of mis-matched metals both shiny and rusty, and tossed it to me. "How 'bout you give this a go?"

I expected it to be heavy, but was surprised by its lightness when I caught it. The smooth and rough textures of the box were a sensory mish-mash against my palms. There wasn't anything special about it that I could see. Running my fingers over each side carefully, I found a few of the panels were looser than others. Some of the panels gave slightly when I pressed on them. A faint scraping sound emitted from one particular panel I pushed in; a rusty piece the size of a man's thumbnail. Each thing I discovered, though, revealed nothing of the cube's purpose.

I was in no mood to play "guess what this is" for the rest of the day. I caved, instead of continuing to examine the device in my hands. "Yeah, I dunno. Why don't you just tell me what everything is?" I held the thing out for him to take, which he didn't.

"You said you had no problem figuring these out."

"I lied," I admitted. "Just didn't want you to be right."

Hux nodded, chuckled wryly, and took his contraption from my still outstretched hand. I knew he knew already, he just wanted my admission. "This is a fire box."

"Let me guess, it makes fire?" I replied, my voice leaden with snark.

"No. Better than that. It simulates fire, creates the warmth without the hazard. No worrying about your fire getting out of control. No worrying if your fire can be seen by anyone. And the box cools quickly, allowing swift camp pickup if you're in a rush." He showed me a dark panel on the box that was slightly depressed and pushed it in. A blue glow appeared from the fine seams, along with a projected timer. He ran his finger along the top edge, making the timer change. "See, you can set how long you want it to stay on before it cools," he explained. He left the timer set for thirty minutes and set the fire box on the dirt before me. Within seconds the air shifted around us, becoming the same glowing warmth one would get from a small camp fire. I had to inch back from it to keep from getting too warm.

The firebox was incredible, and I never would have figured it out on my own. It was obviously made for adventures like the one I was on. Where staying as invisible as possible became key to survival. Hux must have invented it to keep himself hidden on hunting trips and supply runs.

"There's two of them in the bag," he added after a minute or two of silence, "so you can warm food up faster." He shoved his boots off one at a time, one knocking the firebox over. Instinctually, I began to scramble for the metal box, worrying that it'd stop working. Hux's hands caught me and pulled me back, his work roughened hands felt like sandpaper on my pampered skin. "You'll burn yourself, Grainne. The box is hot."

"Won't it malfunction or something?"

"No. The beauty of it is that it works no matter its position. Designed to take a beating. It'll damn near work in any weather too." His fingers rubbed across where he held my arm, casual and familiar. Something about his touch felt so comforting and natural, I'd forgotten he held onto me until that moment. My eyes widened in shock and curiosity as I slid my arm from his grasp. "I'm sorry about that. I get it if you don't like to be touched. Rorric..."

"Its fine," I cut him off. There was nothing in this world that made me want to have any sort of conversation about that man touching me. He occupied my mind far too much as it was. Had his own private island there, it seemed, no matter how hard I tried to evict him from my thoughts. His greedy eyes and licentious hands still stole away my dignity every chance they got. I probably would never be free of the ghost of his touch. Hux, practically a stranger, didn't need to know that. "I'm fine," I insisted, rubbing my arm where he had.

He gave me no prying response, only raised a quizzical eyebrow over a dark eye full of what he, smartly, didn't verbalize. What I didn't admit. I wasn't okay. He understood. The conversation was closed, nothing more to be said. I liked that he didn't insist on making sure I truly was okay, it would only turn me into an angry crying mess. Somehow, Hux knew and respected that boundary.

My respect of him rose a hair, though I was still sorely disappointed and incredibly angry with him. Nothing would change that.

I curled back up, not exactly trying to get rest, even though weariness branded the deepest parts of me still. Curling up was my way of not interacting with my uninvited guide. With his intrusion, part of me was more than ready to thread my way through the forest and over roads. I'd have preferred to do that on my own. That wasn't happening, not with the trackers in the provisions bags. I needed at least one of those if I wanted to survive out there. Hux and survival were now a package deal.

Hux on the other hand, still had boundless energy. A benefit of his godliness. With nothing better to do, I watched him. He sifted through the provisions bags, pulling out two fireboxes from his bag and enough meal packages to feed us both for two days. He followed up with the small pans from both bags, then emptied a few packets into them before setting them directly on top of the fireboxes. While he waited for the food to warm, he became a flurry of arms, legs, metal rods, and swaths of dark canvas. Then it registered what he was up to.

"Who said we needed to make camp?" I bolted upright faster than lightning. I had zero intention of staying put long enough to need anything more than a light meal and a few more hours rest. The more distance I put between me and Lord Rorric, the better. That wasn't going to happen sitting in this cavern for who knew how long.

"Who said we didn't?"

"Me. I'm ready to keep moving. So pack it back up." Dirt clung to my clothes and skin. Brushing it off with my hands proved pointless and only coated my palms in grainy particles.

"I just got here, had to track you pretty far. I'm impressed, actually, you got this far before stopping."

"How far?"

"I'd say near sixteen miles, maybe more. Considering your exhaustion level and all, that's mighty impressive by my standards." Hux kept working on the tent, never stopping for one moment. He just continued going like I hadn't said anything. Jerk.

"Not far enough by mine." I kicked at the dirt with the toe of my boot sending small clods flying everywhere. Still Hux didn't react. He remained level headed, no sign of the man that lost his cool over a radio broadcast. That was the man I needed on this journey with me. A man with fire in his soul, ready to spring into action, not mild mannered camping boy. I couldn't stand being near him. Reasoning with him was impossible.

I needed space between us.

Seven

MY FEET CARRIED me around the edge of the water as far as they could take me from him. It wasn't far enough, but it would have to do. The heated energy building in me had all of my focus, I wasn't paying attention to where I went. Only that I was putting distance between myself and him.

I didn't see what my foot hit, but it sent me flying forward into the gravely dirt. My hands stretched out fruitlessly to catch me, a lost cause before there was even a chance at recovery. They slid along the ground, allowing my knees to hit hard as well. The left side of my face followed suit, dragging on the rough beach. The impact felt like dozens of shards of glass ate at my palms, knees, and left cheek. Quick footsteps crunched in the dirt behind me.

I quickly jumped up, wiping my hands on my pants.The action burned, and left splotches of blood behind. Turning, I saw what I already knew; Hux was making his way around the water to me. I groaned at the sight of his tall form speeding toward me. Why did he insist of playing hero all the time when he wouldn't do the truly heroic thing?

Heat rose from my chest into my cheeks and eyes, releasing angry tears. I wiped them away, not surprised when my fingers come back wet with both tears and blood. Those ended up on my pants too.

My heated glare stopped Hux in his tracks, his concerned look melting into something close to disappointment. Maybe confusion. Hurt. Who could tell with him? His emotions were hard to read, mixed up with that iron curtain he shielded himself with. He took another cautious step towards me. I answered with more heat in my glare, like hellfire consuming every ounce of my soul and exiting from my eyes right onto Hux. It could consume him, and he knew it. He took a step back, turned on heel, and went back to his tent construction. Message received.

Good boy.

My attention turned to assessing my wounds and cleaning myself up. My hands were a complete mess. Bits of rock and dirt, probably some shell, embedded themselves into my palms, lodged snugly under my skin in a few places. There wasn't much to do for them at the moment, other than rinse them off. What I needed was a first aid kit to get all the bits out. My pants were shredded at the knees, which were scraped but not enough to actively bleed. They'd scar up a little for sure though. Not wanting to take off the pants, I cleaned the scrapes as best I could with water from the lake before turning my attention to my face. I cringed with every handful of water I splashed onto my wounded cheek, both from pain and cold. Hopefully it was clean enough that I wouldn't get an infection or parasite. Perhaps when my head cooled I'd see if Hux had something better, just in case.

The water lapped at the shore gently, near imperceivable, its slap on dirt lulled my mind into wandering deep into itself as I cleaned my wounds. The sound triggered memories I'd rather forget of when I first arrived at Galter.

The guard led me through Lord Rorric's fortress. We turned countless times through the dim halls until we came to an open space. Inside there was a man-made pond fed by a fake waterfall. Precious water he'd stolen from the people so he could have an oasis. He lounged there on hot days, surrounded by his Maids in their wispy pastel dresses, soaked and as useless as tissue-paper. Every inch of their bodies on gossamer display while they feign delighted play in the cooling water. Beneath their giggles and smiles, they were terrified.

That was my first memory of Galter, being introduced to Lord Rorric with another new Maid, when I was just seventeen. The Maids swarmed us, a flurry of giggles and sheer cloth, their wet hands grabbing at our arms and hands to pull us into their play. Their smiles didn't quite light their eyes, which were empty of promises that everything would be all right. The other girl resisted, her body thrashing against the Maids pulling at us. She shrieked, loud, piercing cries of distress. Yet the Maids persisted, some shushing her, one attempting to stroke her hair. My heart raced faster. Not from my fellow new Maid's panic, but from the quiet fear that obviously cascaded through every set of eyes before us. I knew instantly they were afraid for her.

Lord Rorric's shadow crept over us like a blanket of terror. Most of the Maids dropped their hands from our bodies, stepping back and bowing their heads. Two wrapped their arms around me, forcing me into their ranks. I tried to follow their cues and bow my head as well, squeezing my eyes closed as tight as possible. Based on their reactions, the other new girl had created a bad situation for herself. I didn't want that happening to myself. My mimicry was undone when cold fingers lighted under my chin. My eyes snapped open at the chilling touch. The fingers guided my face upwards. All I saw before me was a dark, blood red robe, embellished by ropes of golden vines. My vision tracked upwards, the red robe ended at Lord Rorric's face. His eyes, like molten rock, glinted with vile pride and his dry cracked lips were posed in a disturbing smirk.

He removed his fingers from my chin, gently raising them to caress my cheek in admiration. "My Maid," his voice crackled with possessive glee as he slid his fingers from my face and stepped back, "let your sister be a lesson." Only then did I notice the girl struggling against him. His other arm wrapped tightly around her. The belled sleeve of his robe draped over her shoulders reminded me of a trap, bloodied and dangerous.

The girl's eyes were pools of tears complete with waterfalls tumbling down her sun kissed, freckled cheeks. Her dark hair trembled in satin sheets, and her lips, painted a glossy burgundy for this introduction, quaked silently. Her hands clawed fruitlessly at the arm beneath the robe sheathing her neck. Watching her affected me. My heart transformed from muscle to ice, her distress became an ice pick striking at it with the force thousands and cracking it beyond repair. Yet, it didn't shatter, staying intact to keep the pain there as a reminder to behave.

I didn't know her, but she could've been me. I might have been her.

Lord Rorric raised his free hand and lay it on her face with a gentle touch, much like how he had on mine. Only this touch wasn't admiring his new Maid, it was maliciously tainted with an orange glow that matched his eyes. She gasped the moment his hand lighted on her skin, her face frozen in a horrific, pain filled silent scream. Slowly, her clear blue eyes lost their color, becoming slates of murky white. Grey veins shadowed on her skin, creeping towards Lord Rorric's hand. They grew darker, becoming inky as night when they met their goal. Her golden complexion faded under his touch, turning her skin the color of dirty water. The darkness spread in opposition to the direction the veins traveled. It didn't take long for her sunny skin to become like charred bark, flaking off in horrific chunks. At the same time, Lord Rorric's skin brightened, as if sucking all the light from her. The life from her.

I forced the memory to fade then. I couldn't relive the moment when he pulled his hand away from her husk of a body. When her bright ink colored eyes completely dulled into goopy pools of dirty water. When she fell away from him and crumbled, literally, to the ground at his feet, becoming a pile of human debris. That was the moment when I witnessed Lord Rorric's monstrosity first hand. The moment I knew the bleak future in store for me. That a girl with any sort of fight in her would die.

It took years for me to realize that fighting, that dying, was better than a life under his control.

I brushed it all away, scrubbed it from my mind once again as I stood and rubbed my hands on my pants. My palms burned against the coarse fabric, reminding me of the wounds there. I'd been so lost in that memory, I nearly forgot my injuries.

The smell of Hux's food wafted across the cavern. The savory aroma, rich with herbs, made my mouth water. My stomach reminded me I'd neglected to eat my fill, and that I'd left my pack with him. The meaty aroma of his meal was too tempting to ignore. I had no choice but to suck it up and return to Hux's camp.

I slunk back at a reluctant pace, and sat down a few feet away from one of the fireboxes. The warmth immediately comforted me. The chill I hadn't noticed before seeped away from my bones. I had nothing to say to Hux, I just kept my gaze on the firebox in front of me, displaying my wounded pride like a flag of surrender. Words weren't needed for him to know exactly why I came back.

Minutes after I sat down, a small shallow bowl hovered near my face. Steam rose from the stewed meat and chunks of potato in a gravy-like sauce, tantalizing my nose and sending my salivary glands into over-drive. My fingertips grazed the rim of the metal bowl just before Hux's rough hand stopped me from grabbing it. The bowl hovered away, my eyes following in disappointment until it settled on the ground. My gaze flicked to Hux's face, irritated again. He held a finger up, indicating to give him a moment. Whatever made him take the food away better be good. My patience with the man waned faster than a hornet's temper could flare.

I watched him go to his tent and dig around in his provisions bag sitting just outside of it. His hands came up with the first aid kit, and a bottle of clear liquid. Of course he had packed those in the bag intended for him. Like he had said earlier, he knew deep down what actions I planned to take. How well he seemed to know me was more than a little creepy. At the same time, it felt comforting in moments when he knew I was furious and hurting. He had patience beyond measure there, and deserved credit for that. Credit I'd so far failed to grant him.

He settled near me, sitting with his legs crossed, placing the bottle next to him and the first aid box on his lap. His hand raised chest level, palm up, and waited expectantly. He wanted to help and wouldn't move until I let him. Half of me wanted to suffer in stubborn silence, and only seek out the first aid if an infection settled in. The other half of me reminded the other half that Hux deserved some credit.

"You can talk to me, you know," I placed one of my hands parallel to his, my skin barely touching his.

"You sure? My mouth seems to piss you off a great deal," his crooked smile let me know he took no offense at my anger. We both know it was misplaced. He lifted the bottle of liquid in his free hand, "Rum."

I salivated at the offering. More than once alcohol had played a large part in my survival at Galter, the effects of the drink made aspects of that life more bearable. "Yes, please," my other hand shot out like a snake, eager to get the libation into me to dull the pain; not to mention take the sharp edges off of the world around me.

"Hmm. It's not for that," Hux yanked the rum out of reach. After a moment he added, "Yet." He lifted the bottle to his mouth, his perfect teeth gnashing around the stopper. It popped, sending light echoes of the sound bouncing around the cavern. The rum splashed against the glass walls, some escaping the long neck of the bottle. Hux took a long swallow, his Adams's apple bobbing, "For nerves."

"What do you have to be nervous about?"

He didn't answer, only gave me another amused, yet serious look before taking a deep breath. Got it. I made him nervous. Lifting the bottle, he poured the rum over my hand. Fire laced needles assaulted my hand and open wounds. They weren't actually there, but that's sure what it felt like.

"Shit," I screeched, pulling my palm back. Instinct wanted me to lash out more, kick at Hux, spat on him. I quelled those feelings, shoving them deep down. He was just trying to help. "You could have warned me."

"Would it have helped?"

"No." It wouldn't have. Nothing could prepare you for alcohol on open wounds, not even knowing it was coming.

Hux took my hand back, cautiously. He flipped it over, pressing a fresh white bandage on it to absorb the excess alcohol. His rough hands were gentle when he used sharp ended tweezers to remove the embedded bits of dirt and rock from my palms. He looked over my hand carefully, ensuring every piece of debris got removed. Another wince inducing round of rum followed. Then, he duplicated the process on my other hand, along with quick treatments of my cheek and knees, which suffered far less damage than my hands.

Finally, my patience allowing Hux to tend my wounds was

rewarded. The bowl of stew was returned to my newly bandaged hands and Hux placed a mug of rum on the ground next to me. The warmth of the dish still stung my hands through the thin bandages, but I didn't care. The food before me made it worth it.

As a Maid our diets were carefully curated to keep us nourished enough to live, but not enough that we'd flourish. Fed like we were small children, except for when we were invited to dine with Lord Rorric. Those meals were sumptuous enough to make one's head swim. While they were delicious, the decadence often left many of the Maids feeling unwell.

The first bite of the stew was pure comfort. The rustic meal reminded me of what I once had. A home. Warm fires in a hearth and four walls so close together that the love inside of them threatened to break them down. A mother's gentle caressing hands soothing away nightmares. Those ideas, nestled in this small bowl, were enough to bring a tear to my eye. That was what I wanted again, what I'd probably never have again. I didn't want to be brave or join a resistance. Fighting wasn't my strength. I had to, though. I had what they needed.

If I sought out my childhood home, the one place I really wanted to be, I would not be welcomed with open arms. No matter how much they loved me. They knew my presence there would be a death sentence for them all. They'd turn me away the moment I set foot in the village. If they didn't turn me in for a reward that is. Like Hux reminded me, desperate people would do anything to survive. Even to the people they loved.

I ate voraciously, savoring the homey comfort of the stew. Between bites, I took hearty gulps from the mug of rum. The harsh flavor burned deliciously from the inside. By the time I finished the meal, I felt lit from the inside; heavy and warm from the stew, and fuzzy and light from the rum. The combination turned my eyelids to lead. I couldn't help but drift off into a deeper sleep than I'd known for years.

I woke inside the tent, not knowing how long I'd been out. Or when I'd been moved there. Between the heavy meal, rum, and exhaustion, I'd slept hard.

Hux could be heard outside, whistling low and somber. A rich, dark, nutty smell seeped in through the canvas walls. The aroma was hypnotic, tantalizing, and unmistakable. Coffee. The scent drew me from the tent with the promise of erasing the remnants of sleep that lingered in my head.

Bright spots of light speckled the inside of the cavern, and danced off the water's surface blindingly. Hux, stood near the waters edge. He gripped a tin cup by the rim with his fingertips, letting it hang lazily by his side. The steam rising from the cup filled his hand and coiled around it, escaping into the open air. His solid stance looked like a ghost of the god he was supposed to be, strong and unmovable. Yet, I could almost see the weight from his troubles bearing down on his shoulders with every breath that heaved them. A vulnerability that kept that god locked down.

A void opened in my stomach watching him. His kindness and patience with me was too much. I'd been almost nothing but indignant and demanding of him since our meeting. I didn't deserve it.

I shuffled up next to him, but couldn't bring myself to look at Hux. Instead I stared out over the water. The light on the surface was beautiful up close. It had a hypnotic promise of good weather on a beautiful day waiting outside the cavern. "I'm sorry I'm so difficult. I don't. . ." he cut me off before I could finish.

"You have nothing to apologize for Grainne. You're angry, hurt, afraid. Human. Your emotions are real and raw. You deserve to have them with the hand you've been dealt."

"But, I don't. Not towards you. You took me into your home and offered me help. You followed me to make sure I'd be all right. Most others would've written me off to deal with whatever lay on the road on my own. You endure my verbal abuse and tantrums, and still mend my wounds with patience. You're kind in the face of adversity." I looked over at Hux, who still watched the water. Wordlessly, he raised the tin cup to me in offering; and I noticed his other hand held another cup at his chest. I accepted the tin cup, it warmed my hands with the same promise the sparkling water gave. "Thank you."

"You're welcome," he replied with a twinkle in his sleepy brown eyes.

His graciousness chipped away at my dislike for him just a little more. Perhaps I'd never fully forgive him for his inaction, but that didn't mean I couldn't be nicer.

56

more. Perhaps I'd never fully forgive him for his inaction, but that didn't mean I couldn't be nicer.

Eight

A TENUOUS PEACE formed between the god and I once I decided to try not to get pissed off at everything he did. If I was going to be stuck with him for the unforeseen future, being angry the whole time didn't sound practical. Not when we had to deal with potential threats.

After a hearty breakfast of bacon, grits and eggs, Hux made short work of breaking down his camp. Our camp. Even though I'd been against it, camping in the cavern had been exactly what I needed. The much needed rest left me less on edge, and probably less likely to rip Hux's head off for nothing.

As we readied to dive back into the lake, to make our way through the underwater tunnel to the outside world, Hux handed me another of his inventions from the depths of his provisions pack.

"I bet you didn't know about this," he chided, handing me an oblong, silver object with tubing coming from it. At the end of the clear tubing was a small prong with rounded ends. The object was much lighter than anticipated, weighing no more than a feather.

Fighting the knee-jerk reaction to get mad, I chose truthful sarcasm instead, "Of course not, I'm too impatient for that." I studied the palm sized metal device briefly, trying to beat Hux at his game and figure out what it was. I didn't know what exactly it was, although I figured its purpose was tied to what we were about to do.

"This is a breather. The chamber holds ten or so minutes worth of oxygen." My gut instinct proved right, the pod would make the swim through the tunnel much easier. Hux truly had packed for every situation.

"How did you know to pack this? Psychic abilities?" I asked as he attached the breather to my provisions bag strap, instructing me on its use. Put the pronged end of the tube in my nose, keep my mouth shut. Easy enough.

"I've learned to be prepared for everything," his late answer came with grim notes. Ghosts of his past mistakes haunted him. What not being prepared cost him drove his actions. That was why he prepared the way he did.

Everything in me wanted to scream at him again. Rail on him for the most obvious thing he could have done to amend those mistakes. The one thing he kept telling me he couldn't do. I controlled myself, though. What I wanted to happen depended on it.

While Hux broke down camp, I had devised a plan. A plan to wear him down and persuade him to take action. He probably wouldn't, especially if I berated him over it the whole time.

"We should get going," he stepped into the water's edge, not bothering with a breather of his own. He didn't need one. He didn't need the flashlight either, but he still lit it because I did.

The water rose up to his waist when he stopped to look back, before I bothered to follow, affixing the tube to my nose as he'd instructed. The rounded ends fit snugly in my nostrils. There was no way water could get past them. I had to test it, though before I trusted it. Hux may have been a genius, but I wasn't stupid either. Inhaling through my nose, sweet, odorless oxygen filled my lungs.

First test passed. Next one would be in the water.

We dove under together. My body panicked moments after diving as natural instinct fought against taking that first breath under the water. I surfaced, sputtering uselessly and gasping in fear. Hux followed a few moments later.

"I can't do it."

"Sure you can. Moxie it up like you usually do," he goaded. His dark eyes met mine, holding my gaze steadily. His surety seeded confidence back into me, a sense of calm washed through my body. "You got this."

When we dove this time, he stayed with me, keeping his eyes locked on mine. He nodded, and I mimicked him. My mind and heart still raced with worry, but with Hux before me it wasn't enough to send me racing back to the surface. He wasn't going to leave me until I was ready.

Without breaking eye contact, I took that first underwater breath. I didn't drown. The breather worked. Completely sure that I'd be safe going through the tunnel I gave one last sharp nod. Hux's dimpled grin replied. We swam toward the dark hole in the stone wall and beyond to the world outside.

The sun beat down on the shore, warm and inviting. It would have been idyllic, resting on the edge of the water while we dried from our swim, if it weren't for the threat of Lord Rorric looming over us. From the moment our heads broke the surface, we had to be vigilant once more. There'd be no more sound rest until we found what I looked for. The Rising. If all went right, Hux would remain with me, with us, if and when we found them.

"You should let me take care of those," Hux nodded to the bandages.

I looked at the blood stained, soaked wraps that covered my injured hands. Keeping them clean and dry hadn't crossed my mind. In fact, I hadn't thought about them much since the breather incident, and hadn't noticed the sting that settled over the scrapes."Probably," I shrugged, holding them out for him.

He chuckled, digging through his pack for the first aid kit. "You're remarkably compliant today," he commented while setting out the supplies he needed.

"You have a problem with it?"

"No, not at all. Just curious what changed. Last night you wanted to strangle me every time I opened my mouth."

"Understatement," I held my gaze on his a few beats before cracking a wry smile that he returned. "I don't know. I guess I felt a little bad about how I treated you when all you've done is be nice to me."

"Okay," he nodded, returning to taking care of my hands. This time, the cleaning didn't sting as much. A good sign that the swim didn't contaminate them. He dabbed at the alcohol, keeping his focus on my hands, "I was thinking about Lord Rorric," he offered.

My heart stopped. Had he changed his mind without me having to persuade him? A glimmer of hope niggled at the back of my mind. "Oh?" I didn't dare show any feeling about his revelation.

"Noumenon really." My hope deflated, a small ember of anger taking its place. I forced myself to squash it, for the sake of sanity. "He wouldn't have kept it somewhere easily accessed by others. It would have been somewhere only he could go."

"What are you saying? He let me take it? Like some sick game?"

Hux shook his head, "Hell no. Rorric wouldn't play games with power." There was no denying that was true. Lord Rorric enjoyed the games he played with everyone and everything around him. But power, that's what he truly valued. He wouldn't just let someone waltz in and take it from him. "I think it was Noumenon."

"Noumenon?" At first, I wanted to reject the idea. It didn't make sense for a rock to be able to allow someone to steal it from a magically guarded room. But the more I thought about it, it made perfect sense. Noumenon wasn't some ordinary stone. The magic of the Fallen had been imbued into it. Who was to say that those powers didn't want to be free and manifested a will of their own to get someone to help them? I just happened to be that person.

"Yeah," Hux interrupted my thought process. "I think that stone wanted you to take it. Led you to find me. I can't think of any other way you made it past the wards around my place." He finished re-wrapping my hands, holding onto them. "Noumenon chose you for a reason."

Noumenon pulsed as Hux said those words, like it understood them and confirmed them. The hairs on the back of my neck rose in response, but not from the tug coming from the magically enhanced stone. From Hux's words themselves. The way he'd said them, like I was special. Soft and hopeful, like I was more than the annoyance he'd been burdened with, out of duty. I wasn't sure I liked it.

I slid my hands out of his, sighing. "Maybe. Maybe it has been looking out for me." I shared with Hux details of my escape, particularly when I ran into the guard and he acted as though he hadn't seen me. The call inside me that I followed. The way Noumenon warmed in my hands the moment I stole it. All of it did make it seem like it was meant to be.

"Maybe," he agreed somberly. "Our powers. . ."

"What about them?"

Hux opened his mouth to answer only to be interrupted by a sudden hush falling over the lake. Every sound in the area died out. Everything except a whirring that grew as the seconds passed. A sound I'd heard more than once at Galter, which came from something Hux surely was all too familiar with too. He made them after all. He made them and Lord Rorric corrupted them. Drones.

My stomach dropped, from the look on Hux's face he felt the same dread coiling in his own. We'd sat too long, distracted by our theories.

We scrambled at the sound, rushing to get everything back in the packs and on the move. I cursed under my breath as I slung on my boots, not bothering to tie them. Our slackened vigilance, our stupidity, was about to get us caught.

The buzz of Lord Rorric's mechanical spies grew closer and closer, a knot formed in my stomach. The clearing the waterfall sat in was too open. There were few trees to offer protection from robotic eyes, or from the nets the drones would launch when they got me, us, in their sights. It wouldn't be long before Lord Rorric's men followed the tracker built into the net and find us.

If that happened. . .

I couldn't even think about it. This wasn't just me on the line this time. Hux was in danger too. That put any chance of hope for the people in jeopardy. If Lord Rorric caught the only remaining Fallen Lord left and killed him, that was it. The end.

Just as we started for the trees, the drones appeared over the waterfall. Shit.

We kept going, hoping to outrun them into the denser forest, only to be met with more drones coming from above the tree-line. Turning to run the other way proved just as useless. Drones were circling in from every direction. There was no time to dive back under the water to the hidden cavern. They'd found us, and trapped us.

"I'm sorry," the words broke from me in a sob, not only an apology for Hux. It was an apology for everyone I'd doomed by getting him caught.

"It's not your fault," Hux pulled me to him. I curled against his chest, not caring about the closeness. I was desperate for a last moment of comfort, even if it meant nothing. His strong arms wrapped around me, as if he could hide me from the drones and be taken by them alone.

The drones circled overhead, swooping lower and lower with each pass they made over the clearing. But they didn't attack. Not even when one hovered within inches of Hux's head, not even when it's scanner swept over us to confirm its catch.

"Why aren't the drones striking?"

"I don't think they can see us," he said. Just like at Galter, the guard who didn't see me when I was right in front of him.

"How?"

"It's Noumenon," Hux whispered in my ear. "I told you, it's protecting you from being seen. It has to be."

"Then why aren't they moving on?"

"Just because the drones can't see us, doesn't mean they can't sense us."

It wasn't hard to figure out what that meant in regards to being captured. The drones were programed to signal to Lord Rorric's men in two ways. If the nets were deployed, or if they needed assistance. "We should make a run for it then. They'll have notified someone by now."

"These drones are smart. They'll follow our presence, even if they can't see us." Hux unwrapped his arms from around me, stepping back and pulling off his pack. "I have to destroy them." He knelt to the ground and began rifling through the bag. When he stood he held a breather and a small black disk. "Get this breather on," he ordered, "then get in the water. When I tell you to, dive to the tunnel. You'll know when to come up."

"What are you doing?"

"Just listen to me," he snapped, bringing a flare of blue into his eyes. This time the glow didn't subside in seconds.

The small display of Hux's remaining powers was enough to persuade me not to question him. I dropped my pack and listened. Without bothering to remove my shoes, I quickly entered the water, going close to where the drop off was. There, I turned and waited for Hux's word while I affixed the breather into place.

Hux stood stoic along the shore of the water, watching the drones swirl in the air. He studied them, memorizing their flight paths. All the while, the thumbed the black disk in his hand, making slow, deliberate circles on its surface.

Once more, he looked the part of what he was. What he had once been; powerful god, unstoppable and fierce. I saw the cunning in his dark eyes, still flaming blue, while he watched his prey. His jaw tightened, every inch of him tensed. Suddenly, his thumb stilled on the device.

"Go," his eyes met mine, dulling back to their normal color. There was nothing demanding in his words. They were a plea.

His words were my release, freeing me from the tense stance I'd taken while watching him, waiting for him to make his move. Without hesitation I dove, only looking back long enough to catch a glimpse of Hux furling the disk into the air.

I kicked to the tunnel with all my might. I had no idea what that small disk did, but whatever it was I knew it was dangerous. I swam blindly to where I thought was halfway before I felt it.

The stone around me shook. The water moved, tossing my body along with the man-made current and pushing me into the tunnel walls. A thudding sound, like distant thunder pulsed through me. That disk, whatever it was, did its job. I only waited a breath before turning around and heading back to see the aftermath.

Nine

THE SCENE in the clearing was not what I expected.

I'd expected more destruction. The blast I'd felt in the tunnel had me thinking I'd surface to find the clearing in completely obliterated. Instead, other than the drones that littered the ground, entirely broken, the chaos was at a minimum. The surrounding forest survived. There were only a few broken branches and stones among the scrap metal.

In the middle of it all loomed Hux, shoulders heaving and head hanging low. His presence was larger than life, expanding out from his natural form to make him seem like a giant. Terrifying. It was my first real glimpse of Hux the god, he was impressive. Somehow he remained unscathed. There was no sign of injury to him, the clothes he wore were intact; as were the provision packs that lay at his feet.

He didn't hear me approach him. When my hand lighted on his shoulder, which still trembled with adrenaline, he jumped. I was met with wide wild eyes, a face that bore haunted lines. In a minute, he regained his composure. Everything in him relaxed, making him more the tinker I met in the woods than a god.

"Are you all right?" he asked, reaching out for me, but thought better of it and dropped his hands.

"I think I should be asking you that." I cracked in response.

"I'll take that as a yes then," he ran a hand through his dark locks, lifting a corner of his mouth weakly. He wasn't. I could tell, but I didn't think he would admit that.

"So, what was that?" I gestured to the heaps of scrap metal that were once the sleek drones.

He looked around, as if just becoming aware of the destruction around him. "Sonic bomb," his answer came out emotionless, detached.

I toed at a smoking hunk of metal and wire, the burning smell wafting over me. "I've never seen anything like it. I don't think Lord Rorric has these." Nothing could stop him if he did.

"He wouldn't. I invented them after, when I was alone."

The sonic bomb was an impressive invention. A powerful weapon I was thankful Lord Rorric didn't have.

I simmered with the knowledge Hux had this, and had no intention of using it. Not to mention whatever else he had hidden in his private, mechanical arsenal. It was more proof that I needed him to fight. We, everyone, needed him. I had to persuade him he had to act.

"How are you not hurt?" I avoided thinking about fighting Lord Rorric by changing the subject. Avoided getting angry all over again.

"I can still shield against explosions. It's weak, though. Risky. I could't risk it failing and hurting you. The packs, are pretty much indestructible, I wasn't worried about them. Only you."

"Why? I'm not that important."

Hux stared at me, his face weary and soft gazed. He didn't say anything for a long time before sighing, "Noumenon. Noumenon chose you, so you are." His answer felt forced, like an excuse. A lie. I didn't push though, keeping the peace with Hux was more important.

"We should move," I suggested instead of calling him out. Half of the day had already wasted away, "If those drones sent out a signal for Lord Rorric's men, they won't be far behind. I gathered up my pack from near Hux's feet, "Which way do you think?"

"You're the boss, Grainne. You tell me."

I had no idea which way to go. We didn't have a set destination other than to find the rebels. Their location was completely unknown to me. For all I knew, I travelled in the opposite direction of wherever they were camped. All I'd been doing is following my gut.

Or maybe. . . maybe I'd been following something else.

Hux insisted that Noumenon had been leading me from the moment it called to me at Galter. The stone had kept me safe and led me to Hux, it gave me the strength to get past his wards. Noumenon hid us both from the drones, for the most part, and it kept us from being caught in their nets at least. Maybe it had been leading me silently in the right direction.

It was a long shot, but I was going to trust it. It couldn't hurt.

I closed my eyes. The world around me filled my senses. The air was heavy with the smell of hot metal and wet earth. The waterfall crashed and bubbled, drowning out the hum of the forest beyond. A slight breeze whispered over me.

Concentrating, I tried blocking it all out to feel for anything that might suggest which way we needed to go. Everything blurred together until all I became aware of was my heartbeat and breathing.

Then there was a tug, barely perceptible telling me which way to go.

I opened my eyes, smiling broadly at Hux. I pointed just to the left of where he stood, "Noumenon says to go that way."

It was easy to fall into silence as we traversed through the forest. Silence was our friend. Hux and I didn't have much to say to each other either. He'd been brooding since the drone incident, back to communicating in mostly grunts like when we first met. I didn't mind the silent company at first, he didn't make me mad nearly as often without his mouth running. I didn't even mind the silence that night when we made camp. I was able to enjoy the cool night songs of the creatures that lived there. It conjured up memories of younger years and quiet nights lying in tall fields of dry grass and dreaming of a better world.

Those nights, so long ago, were some I cherished. Lying alone in the grass, staring up at the stars, I felt like I could breathe. I didn't have to worry about keeping my head down or doing as I was told. I didn't have to worry about being pretty. Hiding in those blades of grass, I was small and insignificant. Something no one would notice.

Midway through the following day, though, the silence became too heavy. No sounds between me and the forest left only room for a light paranoia to settle in. Every little noise became suspect of being from one of Lord Rorric's various means of hunting me down. My muscles were constantly poised to launch my body at its highest speed all of the time.

At sundown, when we made camp for the night, I'd had enough of his silence and the anxiety it brought with it. "So, Hux," I began making awkward small talk, not knowing what else to say, "it's been good weather for us so far."

He grunted his reply, striking tent posts into the ground.

"Rain might be nice though. Cool things off a bit." The weather had started to get warmer, but not unbearably so. That didn't mean it wouldn't soon become stifling. Still, I was just making small talk, trying to pull conversation out of Hux.

Nothing.

"A swarm of beetles could liven things up," I offered the ridiculous in hopes of anything. "Or a freak snow storm." Hux finally looked up over his shoulder at me, eyebrow cocked as if to mock me. I looked him right in the eye, "A fire tornado even."

Amusement filled his eye with the light chuckle that came from him, "Do you really want to talk about the weather so badly that you hope for natural disasters?"

"No," I scoffed with sarcasm, "maybe I'm just so bored with the company I'm in, I need so me excitement."

"Now I'm boring? I thought I was an ass?" the joke that slipped from him washed me with relief.

"That too."

"If you're bored you can set up the fireboxes and make our meal," he turned his attention back to setting up the tent.

"I don't know, do you think I can handle it? I might not know what food is." I joked.

Hux shook his head, his shoulders lifting with silent laughter. Standing, he turned around and walked up to me. His towering height made me feel small right next to him as he looked down onto my face. "Grainne, shut up and do it," he face brightened with a dimple inducing grin that sent laughter into his eyes and had me feeling a bit better.

"Fine," I shrugged, sticking my tongue out before doing what he suggested. Hux returned to tent building.

I set up the fireboxes, turning them on so they'd be ready to cook by the time I got the pouches and cooking utensils from our packs. I realized, as I rifled through them, the pouches weren't exactly labeled, not that I could see anyway. The only difference in them was size and weight. I grabbed three pouches that seemed like they were the same, two canteens, and a couple of small pots to cook with.

My judgment was way off. Each pack contained something different. The first one I opened was some sort of fowl with roasted potatoes. The second one contained the stew Hux and I shared in the cavern. The last one, held nothing but a mixed assortment of nuts, berries, and dried meat. A lot of it.

I screwed my mouth and stared at the packs briefly. There wasn't anything I could do about it, and didn't want to waste anything. I'd probably just make it worse going back for more packages. With a shrug I put the stew, chicken, and potatoes on to cook.

As I watched our meal simmer on the fireboxes, Hux's shadow fell over me. "When you said you didn't know what the food was, I didn't think you were serious," he laughed.

"I blame you. They weren't labeled."

"But they were," he countered, sitting next to me.

"Bullshit." He didn't say a word to my challenge. Instead, he reached for the bag of mixed nuts, berries, and meats. With his thumb, he highlighted the utterly tiny printed letters on the bag, *Protein Mix*. To my credit the small print was close to a seam and in a color close to the packaging. Anyone could have missed it. I rolled my eyes at him, taking the bag and popping some of it's contents into my mouth, crunching loudly on the mix.

Silence settled back over us as we ate. I worried that brief interlude had been just that. I was prepared for another stretch of only my thoughts for company. The food, though delicious, seemed like sandpaper to me because of it. It probably would have been better if Hux hadn't joined me.

I finished my meal, cleaned up my dishes, and started to ready to sleep. Before I entered the tent, Hux stopped me with his words, "I'm sorry, Grainne. I'm not good company. Spending as long as I have isolated, I haven't had to be. After the drones the other day, I don't know how to feel. I haven't been that man in a long time."

I turned back, taking the spot next to him again. "How long has it been?"

"Far too long. I've been alone for nearly a hundred years, with only my tinkering and maintaining my home to keep me busy. My kind, we aren't meant to be that way. We aren't meant to be alone."

"What are your kind? Where are you from?"

"This world, before humans evolved into imaginative and intelligent beings. We cultivated them, led them. They saw us as gods, terrible and merciful. We were worshiped. As they evolved further, it was decided they no longer needed us. We decided to disappear, hide unless we were needed. Many of our kind left this world entirely, sought out new places to influence. We five, Blix, Orah, myself, Raidyn, and Rorric, we stayed here to keep the promise to watch out for you all.

Our culture was built on unity and companionship. We all needed each other, relied on each other because without connection we were less than. Corruptible. That's what wrong with Rorric. He never quite fit in, thought he was better than the rest of us. Isolated himself because of it." He paused, lost in memories of his past no doubt. "Anyway," he started again, "we should get some sleep."

He wasn't going to say anymore on the matter. I wanted him to. I wanted to understand his kind and what had actually happened to us.

I let it go, too tired myself to argue, and wrapped myself in my cloak. I only hoped he'd open up again in the morning.

Ten

THE TUG OF NOUMENON STOPPED.

A sea of black stretched out before us, cracked, with some tiny, solid waves jutting into the air. A pile of red and brown bricks cascaded out over the hard ground to our right, from a structure made of them. Other crumbling buildings dotted the area sporadically. Years of obvious abandon had begun to turn man made stone to dust. A faint acrid, bitter smell rose from the ground, with the smallest hint of earth. These were remnants from a time before Lord Rorric. From before the reign of the Five Lords even. A tiny patch of a life fighting to hang on to the world it knew.

I'd never seen any thing like it before. I only knew how things were since.

"It's blacktop. The world was covered in places like this when it began to fail. That's when the others and myself came back from hiding, showed the people that lived here how to adapt and live better, simpler while maintaining some technological advancements. How to keep the world from completely dying. We tried to help them save this world. For them, it meant regressing to simpler times for a while. For us it was a redemption." He'd been quiet, but not completely silent since we talked over dinner. The trek much more bearable because of it, I found I somewhat enjoyed his company. My opinion of him was still marred by the unknown of if he would stay with me when we found The Rising and help us with Lord Rorric, though. Only time would tell on that one.

"What do you mean?" I prompted, in hopes it would continue his tale from the night before.

"When my kind disappeared from humanity, we were forgotten for the most part. Remembered not quite accurately, woven into new tales and religions. Renamed. When we came back, it took some time to be accepted. Some saw us as returning gods, others as charlatans; snake-oil salesmen. There were some who even blamed us for the condition the world fell into. They thought we abandoned them to destroy themselves. When our methods began to work, to heal the broken parts, almost every human began to worship us again.

Raidyn, the girls, and myself, we weren't too comfortable with that. We knew we had to disappear again, or at least make it known we were no better than any human. We weren't gods. Nearly immortal beings, yes. Gods, no.

But Rorric, he loved being worshipped. It fed into his ego. He didn't like what we wanted to do. You know the rest, I'm sure."

I did.

"Here's as good as any place to make camp for the night."

"Yeah," I agreed distractedly. My mind busied itself trying to imagine a whole world covered in vast expanses of this, as far as the eye could see. Only small designated areas of nature left standing. I envied those people, not for the world they lived in. But that they lived in a world without Lord Rorric. Certainly, they had their own struggles, their own terrible rulers. But not Lord Rorric with his magic and unending life.

Hux tugged on my arm, a little call to movement, and together we crossed onto the blacktop. The surface of it felt strange under my boots. Similar to flooring, but not quite. Also not quite rock. The sensation hatched a flurry of timid butterflies in my stomach. Or rather, amplified the anxious feeling growing in me since laying eyes on it. More foreign than anything I'd ever encountered, this place was exciting and scary all at once. Anything could've been lurking inside the dilapidated structures; drones, Rorric's soldiers, beasts, or nothing at all. Perhaps even people. Every shift of bricks sent me rocketing out of my skin.

"For a girl with such moxie, you are jumpy." Hux paused for perhaps the hundredth time in the past ten minutes. He'd been immeasurably patient with me, as always. That didn't mean he wasn't amused by my well deserved paranoia, which hadn't lessened with better conversation. "At this rate, we'll make it to a decent spot to set up in by nightfall."

"You know, you don't have to wait on me. I didn't ask for you to come along." I retorted. Despite the small bridge of trust he'd built with me since the cavern, he still got under my skin too easily.

"But you did," he reminded me of my mistake of asking him. "I remember it clearly, you tried to bribe me. You didn't have to." He turned on heel and began to walk again. Watching him walk away, my mouth hung agape. What did he mean, I didn't have to? Of course I did. When I thought he wanted it, would want to set the world right. I didn't like the reminder of what might happen when we find the rebels of The Rising, Hux would leave. It reignited the annoyance I'd done so well to keep at bay.

"You know what I meant," I huffed after him, jogging to catch up and changing my pace a step behind him. He knew I uninvited him. My eyes bore holes in the back of his dark head. His head turned, giving me a sideways glance. Even from this angle I saw the impish snicker in his face. My eyes darted to the ground. Looking at him was going to make my top blow. A few days of peace, only to be thrown back into him chipping away at the thin relationship we'd built.

We came to a building that defied the test of time, standing taller and more intact than its brothers. The grayish stones around the base peeked through delicate vines that forced their way through the man-made ground and crept in defiance up past the gray stones and continued up the old red bricks, filling in the gaping holes that had fallen away. I was more amazed by the unexpected strength of the verdant plants than the fact the building still, mostly, stood. How something so small in comparison, so much more delicate, could overtake an immovable thing and bring it to its knees. The meek defeating the mighty. That rang home with me.

Leading into the building was a door, plain and gray with small flecks of the orange it once was, that rested askew from its hinges, barely hanging on. It also sat about three feet from the ground. The remnants of what had been the stairs below it were useless. We were going to have to climb in. Hux hopped up into the structure with ease, his long legs made the gap seem smaller. He offered his hand to help me up, I refused with a defiant stare that had him stepping back, his hands up in mock surrender. With my back facing the doorway, I braced my hands on the threshold. The cold surface stung my torn up hands when I put my weight on them to boost myself up into the building on my butt. I followed that move with an awkward turn onto my knees, and then got myself standing once more. My climb through the door took more time than I'd liked to admit to, and held all the grace of a newborn foal.

Hux stared at me, his hand curled over his mouth. Though he tried to hide it, my ascension amused him. "What?" I challenged. "Its not like I've got superhuman strength or agility like some people here."

"Nothing, that was great," he half chuckled, earning a pointed look from me as I shoved past him into the abandoned structure.

Silently, we delved deeper into the building. Even in the dimmed light, the effects of abandonment were glaring. More vines crept through empty window panes, bleeding onto the floor and up the walls. Thick cobwebs clung to nearly every surface, and there was enough dust lying on the floor for us to leave significant footprints. A staircase sat at the back of the open space; pieces of railing had broken out and fallen to the floor. The stairs themselves seemed sound from a distance, but I felt sure I'd find them rickety on closer inspection. I wasn't about to add testing those stairs to my list of bad and hasty decisions.

When we reached the center of the room, Hux dropped to a knee, taking off his pack and placing it before him. He rummaged through, coming out with a mis-shaped and modified red ball the size of his fist. He ran his finger along the thick black seam running its circumference, with was dotted with large shiny black spots every inch or so. Happy with his inspection he placed that on the ground and looked back in the pack. This time he pulled out a thick, white, plastic rectangle with a handle coming off one side. In one sweeping motion, he palmed the ball and rose to an upright position. He adjusted the sphere in his right hand until the seam ran parallel with him.

"What are those?" a question I'd become accustomed to asking him.

His inventions were always incredible, and mysterious. Though more often than not they looked like something pulled from the trash.

"Heat sensor and display," he wiggled the device in his left hand. "It'll show us hot spots in the building. If there are any other people hiding here."

"Do you have a gadget for everything?"

"Uh, yeah. It's what I do." My snide question was answered with an equally snide remark. He clicked something on the ball and tossed it into the air. Red lights flickered like lightning bugs, flying to every corner of the room. The light show only lasted a few moments before the ball fell, landing in Hux's waiting palm and the lights abruptly turned off. He promptly tossed it gently into his open bag, then looked at the display, a frown forming on his face.

"What is it?" My heart picked up. Had the sensor seen anything worrying?

He grunted, shaking the display and tapping it against his thigh. A high pitched whirring filled the room and sent Hux into a tirade of grunts and expletives. He hit the device repeatedly on his leg until finally the whirring stopped giving way to a low beeping noise. Hux laughed triumphantly, his easy smile bringing out the dimples in his cheeks that threatened to disarm me completely every time, despite my best intentions. Those were his weapons against my heart completely growing to hate him.

"We're clear," he affirmed after a minute of scanning the results on the display. "There's nothing bigger than a large rodent here, besides us that is. Let's set up camp." While the idea of sharing the space with rodents sent chills down my spine, it was better than the absolute dread unexpected human guests that could possibly be threats brought on.

Setting up fo the night was easier. There was no need for the tent with the building over our heads. All we had to do was roll out our sleeping mats and set up the fireboxes. Neither of those things took long to do.

The crumbling brick walls warmed quickly once the fireboxes began running. The setting light outside seeped in through cracks and windows, making the room glow orange. As though we had lit actual fires. I didn't welcome the fading light. Once it disappeared, we were in the dark until sun up. No lamps allowed, just in case there were people out there. The wrong people. For now, we enjoyed the fading light in relative silence while listening to the songs of evening crickets.

"Noumenon stopped tugging earlier," I informed Hux between bites of some of the honey coated fish I'd enjoyed in the cavern. Finding it in Hux's pack sent peals of delight through my tastebuds. "When we reached the blacktop."

"I wonder why. There isn't anything special here."

"Maybe it agreed this was a good place to stop," I offered with a shrug. The stone still mystified me. There was no rhyme or reason why it would have chosen me to steal it, or find Hux. I wasn't strong, or a fighter. All I wanted was to be free of Lord Rorric.

"Maybe," Hux agreed, but there was no conviction to his words. He drained his tin cup of the alcohol inside, pouring himself a little more of the clear rum afterward and draining that in moments. It was a nightly routine for us since we joined up in the cavern. A little drink with dinner. A small reward for a long day's journey, and a small celebration for lasting another day.

The libation also helped me sleep. Even though we knew Noumenon offered some level of protection, we weren't entirely at ease on the road. There was always the chance that we'd be caught. After all, the magical stone had only been proven against two of Lord Rorric's forces: drones and soldiers. The effect it had over his beasts had yet to be seen. Hopefully, that test would never come.

Our meal finished just as the sun's last rays crept away. Left in the dark there was nothing to do but sleep. I made my way to the bed roll I'd made in a far corner of the empty space and forced myself to sleep.

Eleven

DARKNESS GREETED me when I woke up in my corner of the room. Except, there was faint reflection of light dancing on the wall next to me. My head steamed. We decided it would be safer with no lantern light. Why on earth had Hux lit one? Just to spite me? Irritate me? My body twisted, rolling into a sitting position; the sleeping bag slumped into a pool around my lower half. I shoved that away like it was a beast trying to devour me.

As I stood and turned towards the center of the room, I noticed Hux didn't sit alone. Five strangers sat with him. It was their lamps giving minimal light to the whole room, not Hux's. He'd stuck to our rule.

I approached with caution, rightfully wary of the newcomers. I didn't know who these people were. They could've recognized me, they might not have. They could've been working for Lord Rorric. They could've been like me, trying to find a path to freedom, or looking for the rebels. As I got closer, Hux seemed at ease. There wasn't a single ounce of tension in his large body. Whoever they were, they either had him fooled or they were all right. I stood back, watching, and tried to get a feel for the air between everyone. After a minute or two, I shuffled forward. My footsteps caught the attention of the group and every head turned to look at me.

A man with mahogany skin and eyes like coal stepped up, a friendly smile on his face. He pulled his wool cap off of his head revealing thick black curls matted by the hat. "Hey, you must be Ann. I'm Elden," his large squared hand, sheathed in fingerless, black gloves, shot out in search of mine.

I was confused by what he called me, "I'm not. . ." I saw Hux shake his head. He knew what I was about to do and warned me to go with the misnomer. "I'm not big on touching people," I recovered with a timid wave. It wasn't entirely a lie. After the last few years of my life, I really enjoyed the personal space I'd been getting the past few days. Not being fawned over, man-handled, or groped at any given moment was delicious. I liked keeping physical contact to a minimum.

"That's cool," he pulled back his hand and shoved it into the pocket of his dirty, ripped, blue pants. "We, uh, were passing through the black zone and heard your buddy Sly here whistling. Figured it didn't hurt to check it out, see if he, well you both needed anything." Hux once again gave a barely noticeable shake of his head. Elden lied about that. That was one mark against him.

"These fellas here," Hux nodded his head towards the whole lot, "tell me they know of an underground thing for people trying to get away from the oppressive state of things."

Something close to hope ignited in my belly, a warm ember of yearning began to take hold. "The Rising," the rebel name fell from my lips in a sacred hush. Could it really have been that easy? They just stumbled upon us by chance?

Elden put on a wily smirk and raised a single finger in front of it, topping off the expression with a wink of his coal-like eyes. He welcomed me to join them with his other hand, "Let me introduce you to the others." Still uneasy, my arms crossed over my body as I stepped into the midst of strangers; an ineffective shield, but it made me feel a little better.

The circle around the firebox felt crowded. Seven bodies huddled around seeking warmth, five I didn't know. All these strangers made me uneasy. At the same time, I wanted to be near them. These were the people I'd been looking for. The war between the two feelings raged behind my calmer facade.

Elden pointed to a tall man with long, wavy blond hair falling out of his wool cap. He had warm brown eyes and a sharp nose set in a slightly pinched face. A light mustache sat on his upper lip. His slender build and height combined made him look near emaciated. "This here is Lucas, and this lady here is Prue," he pointed over to a petite woman with silvery hair pulled away from her tanned, heart shaped face. Her quick blue eyes gave her an icy appearance. Lucas tipped his head in greeting, and Prue gave a smile that changed her face from ice to warmth. There was something familiar, but not quite right about the familiarity, about her.

From behind them, a boy stepped out with a haystack of copper hair sticking out in every direction and big green eyes framed by freckled cheeks. He couldn't have been more than 12 years old. "This hooligan is Trevor, our scrappy little tag along." Elden walked by him and tousled his hair, messing it up even more. The boy had an impish quality to him, which became even more so when he grinned with his disproportionately large mouth at his leader.

"I'm Cordee," a young woman with a strong build, sandy skin, and olive eyes waved before Elden could introduce her. Her mousy brown hair fell over her face, hiding half of it. On the other half I saw a mess of freckles covering nearly every inch of her skin. She looked tough, through and through.

After introductions everyone sat again, enjoying the warmth of Hux's firebox. I settled on the floor next to Hux, despite the remaining tension between us. I trusted him more than the group, but only because I didn't know them yet. Elden and his people sat across from us, a clear segregation of the two groups. They spoke in hushed tones amongst themselves. Deliberating about us, no doubt. It didn't take a genius to see that they too wondered if we were to be trusted.

"Why do they think my name is Ann?" I whispered close to Hux.

"The same reason they call me Sly, I gave them those names." He glanced warily on them, "I'm not dumb enough to announce myself to the world. Best you don't either." I couldn't tell if he was warning me or threatening me to keep his secret. Maybe both. They lied about how they came across Hux. They could've been lying about who they were too. Keeping our true identities close to the chest was a good idea until they proved themselves; though I doubted Hux would ever reveal his.

"They lied. They lied about how they found us."

"I know. I wasn't whistling when they came upon me. And their packs are too light for days of travel. I think they've been watching us from somewhere." Hux took his eyes off of the group and moved them back to me, "But they aren't lying about who they are. They're being cautious is all. Just like us."

"How do you know?"

"I know liars. Despite their cautious fib, they aren't liars. They can be trusted. Do you think I'd have let them close to you if they couldn't?"

To say I was taken off guard by Hux's question was an understatement. Yes, he'd been kind to me. That didn't mean he thought of me as anything more than an annoyance. A responsibility. The tone with which he made that statement said he actually cared on some level. I blinked away the thought rapidly. It made more sense he was simply covering his ass through the veil of keeping me safe. What would they do if they knew he's one of the Fallen Lords?

We turned away from each other to see the rebels all had their eyes on us. "So, Ann," Cordee piped up, "Sly tells us you're running from Lord Rorric."

My heart jack rabbited against my ribs, and doubt snaked its way into my mind. I wondered what exactly "Sly" told them about me. I licked my lips nervously while trying to formulate what to say.

"Oh, hey. It's okay," Cordee picked up on my panic. 'We've all been there. Dude's scary as shit. His men raided my town six years ago. I got lucky, they didn't want me. Not feminine enough. My brother, though. He's a big guy and they wanted him, wouldn't take no for an answer either. They beat him half to death before they forced him into their ranks." I wondered if I'd seen him at Galter. It was possible, there were soldiers always coming and going.

I spring boarded off of her story, "They took my sister as a Maid years ago. When they came back this last time, I ran away and hid. Being of Maid age now, I was terrified they'd take me too. I came across Sly here a few days later. Starving and exhausted, he took me in and promised to take me to the one place I knew I would be safe. To you guys."

The story wasn't far from the truth. When I came of Maid age and Lord Rorric's men came to my village, I hid. Tried to anyway. Buried myself in a pile of moldy, manure ridden hay, as far down as I could bear, at the edge of the village, well away from my home. The dry straw itched against my tender skin, and the smell had me wanting to escape the moment I dove headfirst into it.

The men who were looking for me though, knew I was of age. They only came when they knew what they were after, who they were after. Lord Rorric, it seemed, had them watch the villages for potential Maids and soldiers. It was likely they'd picked me for him well before I came of age.

They searched for me for an hour before they resorted to bribes. Threats. It wasn't long before my mother's screams reached across the village. I knew they were hers. I couldn't stand the thought of her or my father suffering at the hands of Lord Rorric's men. Dying. Escaping their plans would have meant nothing if I had no family left to be with.

I left my hiding place, reeking of shit and mold, to save my parents from being tortured. The guards sneered, fighting to hold their noses against the stench coming from me as they dragged me from the village. It was a bittersweet revenge, knowing they were being tortured by the aroma the whole journey to Galter.

"Well, you've found us. Or we've found you," Elden joked. "And we'll be more than happy to allow you to tag along with us to our place. Every person on our side is one less on his." He stood and brushed his hands on his pants while taking a few steps forward. "And we really should get going if we want to get back by sun-up. Night travel is safest." He was right, traveling at night proved safer. The drones were grounded, leaving only man and beast to contend with, although beasts were more often than not stabled at night, sometimes they were let loose. It wasn't much safer, but safer nonetheless. It had been my plan, until Hux found me. I didn't fear the dangers of the light with a god on my side. "But first, I want to hear it from you. Are you absolutely sure you're up for this?" he gestured around to his friends. "It isn't easy. Lots of hard work, and lying low. Maybe even some fighting, if we find that Maid before they do."

My palms twitched and my mouth went dry, "What Maid?" I played dumb.

"What Maid? Have you been under a rock?" Lucas's familiar voice scoffed, his whole body slouching in disbelief. His dark eyes twinkled playfully at the jab.

"Kind of. You don't get much news when you're traveling less taken paths."

"You're going to be well in the know soon. One of the jobs with us, keeping up on whats happening in Galter." It clicked why Lucas sounded familiar. He'd been the voice on the holo-caster that night at Hux's workshop.

"Absolutely, Lucas," Elden agreed with his lanky friend. "A Maid recently went missing from Lord Rorric's fortress. That's what they say anyway. We're pretty sure she ran off, and, according to our sources, took something pretty important from him too."

"What did she take?" Hux leaned forward, gripping his hands in his lap. He knew, of course, but they didn't know that.

"No idea. But why would they be putting so much effort into finding her otherwise? That or she has some pretty significant information they don't want getting loose."

Both, I thought to myself. If these guys knew who we really were, or what I had in my pocket, they'd pee themselves with excitement. That, and they might force us with them even if we didn't want to go with them. They'd try anyway. These five would be no match for Hux, if he were to use what power he had left.

"Do you know what she looks like? Maybe we saw her on the road?"

"Unfortunately, no. The image on the casts is never clear, or in color. Lord Rorric's way of keeping her to himself still, ensuring no one but his people find her, I'm sure. Keep others, like us, from helping her," Elden explained. I breathed a sigh of relief. "Anyway, why don't you two get packed up and we can get going."

Hux lumbered up, his huge frame shadowing everyone else. I guessed it had to be the first time Hux stood since their arrival, as their eyes became saucers at his full height. They might not have known his true identity, but it didn't stop them from seeing the power behind his size and demeanor. I could practically see the electric excitement as the idea of Hux joining them settled into Elden's mind.

There wasn't much to pack away, Hux had pretty much already done that. He kept a clean camp, putting things away when done using them. I left it to him to shut down the firebox, and I focused on getting my sleep mat rolled up and making sure my pack had everything. My heart thrummed as I rolled the mat, a mixture of excitement and nerves. My half-assed plan was coming through. I'd found the rebels and, in time, I would tell them the truth. I was the Maid they looked for. I had Noumenon. I just hoped I could reveal all before too long.

Even then, Hux's true identity would be protected. We didn't see eye to eye all the time, but I wasn't about to out him out of spite. That was his secret, not mine.

After clipping the mat onto my pack, I was ready to join my new people. I carried the bag in front of me, kicking it out with each step and setting it at my feet when I rejoined the circle. Hux wasn't far behind me. He set his larger pack next to mine and transferred a few things from his to mine.

Hux slung his pack onto his shoulders and gave me a long sad look, "Good luck. I. . . Take care of yourself, Ann." He looked like he wanted to say more, like he wasn't sure about what he wanted to do next. Instead, he turned without another word and began walking away.

"Hey, where you going, Sly?" Elden jogged up to Hux, using the fake name he gave them. "We could use all the able bodies we can get."

"I'm no able body, not for this. I've no claim in what you're doing."

"You're not even going to try now? After all we went through? We've come all this way." That tiny balloon of hope I allowed to form, burst. Hux still wouldn't stand against Lord Rorric. Even after all the things he did to him and the others. Even after all the time we spent together. My tongue soured with a deep bitterness about his stance. Even after all these days with him, he confused me more than anything. All I could do was glare to keep angry tears at bay.

"I never promised anything other than to get you to these people. I've done my end." Hux began to stalk away, his shoulders heavy with more than the bag on his back.

I chased after him a few steps, digging in my pocket. "Wait," I tapped his shoulder, "your payment." I held Noumenon out, still wrapped in the delicate fabric of my Maid nightgown. I didn't dare unwrap it in front of these people. It might have given away my identity, which I wasn't sure would be a good idea, yet.

Hux glanced over his shoulder briefly then starts walking away again, "I told you, I don't want it. That means nothing to me now. You need it more than I do, for protection. I hope," he broke off, looking at the group of rebels behind me, "I hope you find what you need." His eyes came back to mine, shining and sad, "Stay safe." With his head hanging ow, he lumbered away, hopped down from the building's entrance, and disappeared.

My heart twisted, angry and thrown by his strange goodbye, which stung more than I wanted it to. It hurt, like he brushed me off, handed me over like I was nothing. I thought we'd at least become friendly enough to treat each other better than that. That time together, I'd been sure it would change his mind somehow. That pierced deeper than the feeling of abandonment.

The anger welling in me would no longer be dammed up. My outstretched hand clenched around the stone and dropped to my side, the other clenched to match. Hot, angry tears filled the corners of my eyes until they could no longer hang on, spilling silently down my cheeks. I didn't think I could hate anyone as much as Lord Rorric, until now.

The group of rebels behind me shuffled awkwardly. "Good riddance, we don't need cowards like you," Trevor spat after Hux. I couldn't agree with him more. Good riddance.

A hand lighted on my shoulder, "Hey, I'm sorry your friend bailed on you. That's rough." My gaze flitted over my shoulder, following the hand to its owners face. Cordee.

I gave her a half smile, wry and full of vinegar. "He's not a friend. I barely know him. Just a means to an end to me." Her hand patted my shoulder a few times before sliding off. I knew she saw my disappointment. It filled me to a point of breaking. All I wanted to do was scream after him and tear this place down brick by brick until he turned around and listened. Until he did something about Lord Rorric.

A single last tear escaped my eye as I watched out the door. I wiped it away, like it would eat away at my skin if I left it to fall. My pack felt heavier than it should have when I hoisted it onto my back, as if Hux added the weight on his shoulders into it for me to bear. *Here you go Grainne, the world is on your small, mortal shoulders now.*

I spun on my heel to face Elden and his friends, the thin layer of dirt grinding under it loudly. I imagined it was Lord Rorric. I imagined it was Hux. Both deserved to be ground under the heels of humanity. One for treachery, the other for the worse crime of cowardice. "So, which way do we go?" I sniffed out, my arm dragging across my nose. I buried my disappointment under a fine layer of anger, "I'm eager to get started."

"Thats what I like to hear," Elden cheered, his voice filling the empty space. He didn't fear being heard or seen. Everyone gathered up their bags and lanterns, their feet as anxious as mine to get moving. "Alright, let's roll," he ordered when the whole group was ready. One by one, they headed out the door, jumping to the dark ground below. Nerves spiked in me at the thought of leaping through the doorway. It signified the true end of one part of my journey and the beginning of the next. It also meant I was at the mercy of these people that I wasn't entirely sure I fully trusted yet, despite having been looking for them for this very reason, to join them.

Lucas waited for me on the other side of the doorway. "Hey, Ann. Thought you might need a hand." He produced a crooked, thin smile and his eyes sparkled, it was easy to see this was a man whose soul hadn't been darkened by the harsh world we lived in. He was pure at heart, a rarity in our time. My hand hesitated to accept his, keeping to not wanting to be touched and also out of sheer habitual defiance. Doubt laced his dark eyes when I didn't make a move, wiping away the eagerness in his gaze. Something in his long face made me ache, reminding me that he wasn't the person I was mad at. He wasn't Hux. Lucas was absolutely nothing like Hux as far as I knew. He and The Rising were willing to lay their lives down against a god for the good of the people in an uneven battle. Hux didn't even entertain the idea. I had more reason to have faith in them, even if they hadn't earned my trust, despite how kind and good the hermited tinker was to me.

"Thanks," I slipped my hand into his and prepare to jump. As I leapt, his free hand caught my waist and he lowered me the rest of the way to the ground, settling me close to him. Taking his hand for help was one thing, that amount of closeness another. I took a step back, a looked at his face which was flushed and sheepish, and I learned something new about the man. He wore his emotions on his sleeve, and just then he thought he'd offended me.

"I'm sorry, I know you said you don't like being touched. I just thought..."

"It's fine. You're being kind, helpful. Thank you."

"Yo, Lucas, stop trying to have game you big doofus." Trevor teased his friend, effectively pulling our attention to the waiting group. The playful, light, slap on the back of his head he got in return sent him running to the other end of the group. I couldn't help but smirk at the interaction. It had been a long time since I'd witnessed such lighthearted behavior.

A trickle of something close to hope entered my heart.

Twelve

WE CREPT along the outside of the dilapidated building, going around two of its corners. The way the team moved, like synchronized misty spirits, showed how well they worked together. They'd honed their skills moving in the shadows to avoid detection, and it showed. Me, in my inexperience, made more noise than the lot of them combined with my nervous breathing and unsure steps on the still foreign blacktop.

Halfway across the back of the building Elden halted in a crouch, his fist up next to his head. The rest of the crew froze instantly, taking up the same crouched position their appointed leader had. I, on the other hand, stumbled into Cordee with my stomach in my throat, afraid of what had caused Elden to stop so quickly and suddenly.

The dark tree line at the edge of the blacktop didn't provide any clues as to what he saw, or heard. My eyes scanned it frantically once more looking for some hidden villain lurking there, all the while telling myself it could've been Hux. He left right before we did, after all. Unlikely, but I had to think it in order to keep from panicking. There was nothing but darkness and the sounds of crickets and a lone owl hooting in the distance. When my attention turned back to the group, hoping for a sign the coast was clear and we could keep moving, I wasn't prepared for what I saw.

Instead of standing on alert, the group relaxed and dropped their bags. Elden, Lucas, and Cordee crouched down. My eyes followed and watched as they came up with arm loads of tangled vines and branches they'd pulled away from the base of the building, revealing a large black, metal grate. Once the grate was clear, they worked together to pull the hinged grate up, silently despite the heavy metal that made it. I leaned over the edge and peered down. By the dim lantern-light I saw a ladder leading down to a gray floor about fifteen feet down. It appeared to be an underground tunnel system. Impressive.

One by one, we started our descent, Prue taking the lead with Trevor right behind her. It did't take long for the thudding of their feet landing on the ground below to echo up and out of the hole, followed by an all clear from Prue.

"You're up," Elden pointed to me and Lucas, telling the gangly man to go first just in case I needed help. He jumped to follow the order, giving me a crooked smile as he disappeared through the opening.

The first rung groaned under my foot as I began my descent and the wear and tear of its use continued to show with every step down. The rungs were rough under my hands, the paint flaked and stuck to my palms. I was certain it would detach from the wall and send me and Lucas crashing to the ground and into the waiting Prue and Trevor. The thought locked my lungs and shook my movements even more. When my feet hit the ground my breath shuddered in relief.

"Next!" I heard Lucas call up to Cordee and Elden as I spun to take in the small space. It wasn't what I expected. There was no tunnel leading away from the ladder and building to some unknown destination. Instead, we were in a small empty space made of concrete, perhaps ten square feet in all. The air inside felt warm and humid, almost too warm to bear. On the far wall sat a gray door that practically blended in with the concrete walls. A small square pad was mounted to the right of it. On the pad there were nine buttons with no designating numbers, letters, or signs.

Elden was the last to come down, going straight to the door and tapped the blank buttons on the pad in a pattern; each key lit green as they were pressed.

Cool air swept past us when the door swung inward, behind it a stairwell leading down. Just when I thought I had things figured out, they threw another curve ball. Suspicion niggled at my mind, and I began to wonder where exactly they were taking me. So far, we'd gone exactly nowhere, except down. From their own words before, they came upon us accidentally. I was beginning to truly understand that wasn't the case. Hux may have been right about them watching us.

Trevor and Prue led the way down the stairs, their lanterns filling the enclosed space with enough light that the others extinguished theirs. Elden, myself, and Lucas followed, and Cordee took up the rear. She allowed the door to slam behind her, which set off a quick buzzing tone.

The feeling of being trapped began to ice its way into my veins. I glued myself to the stair I landed on, refusing to go any further until I got some answers. Truthful answers. Lucas crashed into my back, nearly toppling me over. The commotion prompted the party to halt and take notice.

"You good there, Ann?" Elden came back up a few steps to check on me. "Not afraid of closed in spaces, are you?"

"No, I'm not. And I'm not fine. I have no idea who you people are. All I know is you lied when you met Sly and sold me on it too. Now, I'm completely at your mercy," my short rant ended with ragged breaths. Even though Hux assured me he could tell they were the rebel group they claimed to be, their actions had me on edge.

"I'm not sure what you're talking about," his coal eyes looked me dead in mine giving no hint he lied. He was good.

"You lied," I jabbed an accusing finger into Elden's chest. The rest of the group shuffled nervously, they'd been caught and they knew it. "Sly couldn't have been whistling while I slept. He knew better. We'd been quiet as mice all night. Heck, he didn't even want to light lamps just in case it attracted the wrong attention. He wouldn't have risked exposure. He may be a coward, but he's not stupid. Sly spent enough years hiding away to make that kind of mistake."

"Dude, she has you," Lucas piped in, leaning against the stairwell wall as he crossed his lanky arms across his chest.

Elden put his hands up and stepped back down one step. "Okay, you caught me. We didn't come upon you by chance. The minute you entered the black zone, we knew it. Our alarms went off. This building above us is the only shelter here for a reason, we keep it that way. We needed to check y'all out, so we did. Make sure you weren't here for trouble. Other than that we haven't lied to you."

I didn't feel satisfied with his explanation, but there wasn't much I could do. They had me outnumbered, and confined in a stairwell. "Fine," I huffed, "seeing how I have no choice now, I'll let it go. For now." One way or another, I was definitely getting more answers when we got wherever we were going.

The group remained silent the rest of the way, heavy with the mistrust I'd sown. I couldn't be sure how far down we ventured, but it made me uncomfortable to be this far from the stars and the sky. They alone comforted me on those long nights in that prison, especially on my nights with Lord Rorric. They were the dream then, to be free beneath them lying in a field of grass. Now that I'd had a taste of that, the idea of being unable to see them cracked my heart and dimmed my spirit. It made me feel like I was being imprisoned again.

At the bottom of the stairs the group gathered at a door, identical to the one above, at the base of the stairs, with the same panel to the right of it. The tones from the keypad were different from the ones at the top of the stairs. The lights came on, and my palms began to sweat. Elden turned the handle and cracked the door, sending my heart skipping while a lump the size of a grapefruit lodged itself in my throat. Behind that door was either exactly what I'd been looking for, or the worst mistake I'd made in days. With my luck, it'd be the latter. "Welcome to Sanctum, our little resistance base," he said.

In a streak of red and freckles, Trevor shoved his way past Elden, his little, dirt covered hands slammed into the door, too impatient to wait for the door to finish opening. The gray door flew wide on its hinges. The boy leapt over the three steps leading down and tore into the most astonishing sight I'd seen since fleeing Galter. I expected four dreary gray walls and a floor to match, littered with lean-to tents and dilapidated wooden tables. Lines of starving people waiting for their meager handouts, worn from day to day life. There were four gray walls and a floor to match, but that was all that matched my expectations.

The ceiling was painted dark with crisscrossing strung lights hung over the long fixtures that currently burned bright. I imagined they look a little like stars in the sky when they were lit. On the gray walls were patches of child-made paintings. Hand prints, flowers, rainbows, and puffy clouds brought burst of joy to the space. Happiness. A glimpse of what normal should have been. Would have been if Lord Rorric had never came to our world.

There were people everywhere. More than I anticipated. Children screeching with glee rather than terror, joined Trevor in his mad dash through the space, making his return a game of chase. Adults went about their business without a care in the world. They didn't have to look over their shoulders for danger that may or may not have been there. They didn't have to curb their voices in fear of the wrong people overhearing. These people were the beginning of what the world could be. What it would be when Lord Rorric was gone.

With the scene before me, I knew that I'd be safe as long as they didn't know who I really was, but I realized another thing that set a dark spot in this hidden world. They might not be safe with me if it was ever found out I was here. My mind was made up. I couldn't ever let them find out Hux lied to them. That I was not Ann. I was Grainne, former Maid of Rorric.

I had to be Ann to protect them, to protect this small haven where Lord Rorric didn't exist.

Thirteen

"LUCAS, CORDEE," Elden ordered the moment the automatic locking door shut behind us, "you know where I need you to take Ann. Ann, I'll talk to you later, explain everything. I promise. For now, I have reports." The vague demand didn't do anything to settle my nerves, even with the promise of explanations afterwards.

"I got broadcast duty later Eld," Cordee protested. "I could really use some sleep before hand." Elden studied her with a incredulous look. "Really?" she whined at the scrutiny.

"Sure, go on, kid," Elden burst out laughing after a minute, his stern look dissolving to mirth.

"I hate you," she teased in return before heading off to wherever she slept.

"You got this Lucas?" he asked, a trace of laughter still lingering in his voice though it also had a serious note to it. The way Elden eyed the spindly man implied more than asking if he could handle taking me wherever it was he had been ordered to.

"No sweat, Elden. I'll behave, don't worry."

Lucas led me through the open space, everyone glancing at me curiously. The new girl, a mysterious outsider in their ranks. I felt like they all saw through me, as if I had a large sign hanging over my head declaring me to be a liar. A sign that advertised the danger I brought in their sanctuary.

He stopped us in front of a door that read *Medic* and knocked. A tall woman with short dark hair and ice blue eyes opened the door before he had the chance to knock. Her eyes were a stark contrast to her dark skin, so smooth it looked like marble. She looked ethereal. "Lucas, don't tell me you got injured on a short surveillance outing," she joked, a bright and toothy smile lit up the air around her. She was a cool breeze and night sky; calming the nerves that had settled in my stomach.

"Not me Eileen," he ushered me forward, "this is Ann. She's been looking for us for some time now. Got a little banged up on the way, probably could use a booster too."

The statuesque, stunning woman turned her attention to me, her eyes pooling with sympathy as she took in my rough appearance. "Oh, you poor dear," she wrapped me in her lithe arms before I could protest and took a deep breath, as if to lead me to do the same. "Let's get you taken care of." She ushered me into her little room in a hurry. I took a quick and unsure glimpse over my shoulder at Lucas as the door closed, just in time to see him give an encouraging thumbs up and a crooked smile.

Eileen's medical room was a far cry from any that I'd seen before. Something between the sad, lacking healing space in my village and the cold, imposing medical suite at Galter. It was warm, comforting. The space was small, with three walls painted a soothing blue, not too different from a bird egg. The fourth wall, on the right side of the room, had been painted to look like a forest. Large wooden cabinets lined the back wall. On top are folded blankets and pillows. An actual bed lined the left wall, with linens cleaner than any I'd ever seen. Near the bed, a little green stool sat diligently, a place for Eileen to sit while treating patients. The air smelled clean and crisp, but not in a harsh medicinal way. More like lemons and lavender.

The confined space made me wonder what happened when she had more than one patient. When there were mass injuries to care for at a time. I guessed living here, I'd find out. I hoped I wouldn't be the cause of such need, ever.

"Sit over on the bed, dear," Eileen instructed.

I followed her order. The bed felt even softer than I imagined, cloud-like compared to the sleeping mats I'd used recently. A strong burst of lavender wafted from the linens as I sat on them. "What's a booster?" I asked while I watched her search her cabinets for what she needed. She popped the items she selected into a little woven basket she carried under her arm.

"A booster, is a couple of things," she said with her back still turned to me. Her body stretched up a little to reach a bottle filled with a pale, pink, clear liquid on the top shelf. It tipped dangerously close to falling just as her fingers got a firm grip on its smooth sides. She turned with a triumphant grin, shaking the bottle, "This is part of it. A vitamin and mineral rich drink. My own special recipe. The other half is a toxin patch. It'll draw out toxins from your body to help rejuvenate you. I almost don't think you need the drink, you seem well hydrated."

"No, my travel parter was well prepared for the trip. More food and water than we actually needed."

"That's good. I didn't see your partner. Did they not need any medical care after being out in the wilderness then?" she raised a perfect eyebrow with interest.

"He didn't come here. He left me with Elden and went home." The reminder of Hux's abandonment tasted like dried bile on my teeth.

"Oh. I'm sorry," she sounded truly dejected as she sat on her stool and placed her things on the floor next to my feet, "I'd have liked to have met him." She dug into her basket, pulling out what looked like scrap of mesh fabric filled with a dark substance. She waved it at me, "Toxin patch. And I do think I'll give you the drink too, just to be safe. I'm going to need one of your arms, so you'll need to undress your top half. Is that okay?"

I nodded, even though I felt a little unsure. I just got my bodily autonomy back not too long ago. Someone asking permission to see it, was weird for me, in a good way. But it didn't stop the quick flood of memories from the fortress drowning me from the inside out. Not to mention, I had to keep Lord Rorric's mark out of sight, which could easily be done with strategic placement of my shirt once off.

Upon acquisition, every Maid of Rorric was branded. A jagged circular mark with a sun in the center burned into the flesh, dead center of the chest, just under the breasts, forever scarring every girl unfortunate enough to be selected. His. Only his. That was what the mark meant. His, until he tired of you. Then you died.

The memory of my branding flashed in my mind. It was the same day I arrived, merely hours after witnessing another girl's murder. That horror fresh in my mind, I thought the worst when Lord Rorric's men escorted me to a darkened room deep inside Galter; instructing me to lie on a stone table in the center. A roaring fire blazed in a large iron bowl at the foot of it, a long metal pole jutted out from the flames. Attached to the table were heavy manacles at each corner.

The freezing cold stone bit through the sheer dress I'd been given as I lay on top as instructed, trembling, juddering. I fought against the tears that threatened to spill, the screams that wanted to unleash. There wasn't anything that would convince me to give in to them. The fear of what happened to the other girl dictated that I had to be strong, to behave.

The manacles weighed what felt like a thousand pounds each, cementing me to the table beneath me. The soldiers fastened them around each limb, pulling the chains tight as they secured them. I wouldn't have been able to move even if I wanted to.

Lord Rorric swaggered in, unweighted by his earlier actions. Why would he have been? He cared little for anything but his power. Inflicting pain on those he deemed beneath him was an every day thing. Everyone knew his truth. Everyone.

"Remove her dress," he ordered indiscriminately, yanking the metal pole from the fire. The end glowed hot and angry, the promise of pain etched in the flattened end. One of the soldiers complied, using a short dagger to slice down the center of the dress, leaving me exposed to the room.

Inside I was screaming as silent tears managed to escape, despite my best efforts.

Lord Rorric leered, greedy and possessive, "Remember Maid, you are mine." The searing hot brand sizzled against my sternum as he pressed it there. The scent of burning flesh filled the room, adding nausea to the the list of things I fought against giving in to.

All that existed was the smell of charring flesh and pain.

"It's okay, Ann," Eileen's hand lighted on my shoulder. Her touch was a life raft lifting me from the dreadful memories filling me. "We can do this another way. Are you terribly attached to that shirt?"

I looked down at the borrowed white shirt I wore. Dirt caked it, and it smelled awful. I probably did too. Frankly, I wanted to burn everything I wore. They were only reminders of Hux and his betrayal of mankind. Eileen's loaded question indicated its demise. I smiled. "I'm not sentimental. I could probably do with something cleaner."

She nodded and reached into the basket at my feet. A long pair of silver scissors appeared as her hand slid out. No time was wasted. The cool metal grazed against my skin and I shivered despite myself. "Hold still, hon. Don't want to nick you." The scissors sliced through the fabric with ease, a testament to their sharpness. The sensation almost sent me back into reliving the branding. I didn't let it.

In mere moments, the sleeve flapped open, exposing my arm. Eileen uncorked the vitamin drink and poured part of it onto the booster patch, which she fastened to my upper arm with a long bandage.

"Here, drink the rest of this while I tend to your injuries." Eileen coaxed the bottle at me, the liquid sloshing into the neck. I took a long draw from the bottle. It was thicker than I expected it to be, like honey. It coated my insides, making them warm and tingly. The sensation didn't dissipate either. It spread through me, making me feel heavier and heavier, calming me.

Eileen made quick work of assessing the scrapes on my cheek and knees, putting a cool ointment on them. "Your travel partner, they treat your hands?" she asked unwrapping the old bandages from them.

"Yeah, he did the best he could with what we had." The memories of him being so gentle and thoughtful while caring for me crept into my head. A flash of his deep dimples when he got playful, along with the lazy smile that came with them. The good memories of our trek together glowed fondly, like distant ones of my family. I chided myself for them, reminding myself he was probably halfway home already, unhindered by a slow human, not even thinking of any of this. Of me. He'd gone back to hiding instead of staying where he was needed most.

Her nimble fingers ran over the still healing scrapes and gouges on my palms, a whisper of a laugh on her lips, "He did good. What's he like?" she put the ointment on my palms and began to re-wrap them in fresh bandages.

"I don't want to talk about him. The coward."

"Coward, huh? Seems to me he might be very kind, considering the care he put into these bandages."

I ignored her dead-on statement about his kindness. "Don't get me started. He acts like he's this weak, old tinker and he's not. He has no practical reason to not help us, and every reason he should."

"Thought you didn't want to talk about him," she teased as she finished up with the last bandage.

"I don't," a large yawn escaped from me. "I'm sorry."

"Don't apologize, I should. I should have warned you the booster can make you drowsy."

"That's ironic." After she mentioned it, I noticed just how tired I really felt. Sleep beckoned me, a pied piper too powerful to ignore. The way Eileen watched me, her ocean eyes calm and waiting, made me think she knew the booster drink would make me sleep. She expected this reaction and kept it from me. Despite it, I couldn't bring myself to not trust her. I don't think anyone could resist trusting the calming air that hung around her.

"You can lie down in here if you like. No one will bother you." The suggestion vibrated inside of me, invading every cell. Suddenly, all I could think about was curling up on the lavender and citrus scented bed. I was incredibly tired. My body had been in some version flight or fight for what seemed like ages. The years of restless nights were catching up with me. I hadn't slept peacefully, of my own volition, since before Lord Rorric's fortress. The episode at Hux's workshop didn't count. I was practically dead on my feet from the strange illness that raked my body that day. He never expected anyone to force their way through it, let alone someone like me. He forgot how strongly a person would fight for freedom. For their lives.

The bed creaked under my shifting weight as I gave in to her suggestion. My eyes grew heavy the moment my head hit the pillow. Through my lashes, I saw Eileen start to leave. She turned at the door and gave me a look that I hadn't seen in a long time. A look of awe and pride, not unlike that of a motherly figure doting on those she cared for. It made me feel good and safe. After that, my eyes surrendered to the sleep the booster made me desire so much.

97

Fourteen

I **HAD** no idea what was in the booster Eileen gave me at Lucas's suggestion, but I woke up feeling brand new. The air filling my lungs had a sweeter edge, and every ache in my bedraggled body had fled. Even the knot of dread in my heart had vanished without a trace. If it wasn't for the memories, I'd have sworn the past years of my life had been erased like magic. It was bliss, there was no other way to describe it.

That's not to say fear didn't linger over my head, like a ten ton boulder being held by a fraying rope. More accurately, like a good sized magical ruby tied to a god intent on my capture. Those fears and worries still squatted in my mind. A colony of unwelcome vermin in a freshly renovated home. All the same, the deep seated fear from years of knowing my day to day life could end in an instant, had faded. The bone-weariness that came with that weight, gone. I felt free.

I sat up and noticed Eileen had left me a change of clothes. Ones that fit me better and hadn't been torn apart. There were many options to choose from in the generous pile; from soft skirts and simple shift dresses to pants and cotton shirts. I caught myself trying to select one of the shift dresses, out of habit. As a Maid of Rorric, dresses were the only allowed clothing. If they could even be classified as dresses. The dresses of a Maid were fancy garments, mostly made of sheer, light colored fabrics trimmed in glittering threads or opulent beading. Except for during our "women's time", when we wore sturdier and simple fabrics, dark in color, that served as an indicator to Lord Rorric. Not to be touched. Unclean. There was no pretending our time had come either. Servants checked us daily. Like I said, our bodies were not our own.

Instead, I picked some dark brown canvas pants with utility pockets, and the largest white long sleeve shirt. I wanted to hide my body as much as possible. Control who saw what. The private room suited my needs for dressing without the anxiety of being discovered. I couldn't have anyone seeing Lord Rorric's mark on my chest; the only thing that could identify me. The reasonable side of me knew Elden and his leaders were looking for me, with good intentions. That side knew it would be beneficial to let them know who I was, especially because of Noumenon.

The rest of me wasn't so sure. Hux's caution, the mistrust of people I developed at Galter, and the newly born need to protect this little haven won out. I couldn't tell them. Not until the time came I felt certain I wouldn't be betrayed, used, or tossed out. That my presence wouldn't bring danger in their midst.

Tell them or don't tell them, either way there were major costs to consider. Hence, I kept waffling it over. The decision whether or not to, would torment me as long as my identity was fake.

I dressed quickly, leaving off the makeshift binding, just in case Eileen came back in before I finished. The clothes fit near to my liking, although the pants sat a little lower on my hips than I'd have liked. I'd ask for a belt to ensure they stayed up. Other than that, the beautiful healer had a good eye and good instincts. After putting on fresh socks, I decided to keep wearing the boots Hux gave me. I told myself there was no reason not to, they were good shoes after all. Though, deep down, a small part of me needed them because they came from Hux. I couldn't explain it, it made no sense with how angry I was with him, but I had to have them. In a last minute decision, I rummaged about for some scissors and cut a piece off the discarded binding, using it a tie off a braid I hastily wove my coppery curls into. Finally, I felt ready to face my new home. Hefting my provisions bag onto my back, I headed out of Eileen's office.

The big space outside Eileen's office was nearly empty this time. Smaller groups of people lounged around, mostly older folks. Lucas, easy to spot with his lanky height, stood halfway across the room, talking with the slightly taller Eileen, he waved enthusiastically when he saw me come out, "Hey Ann." I waved back, feeling a little awkward that he was being so nice, acted like he's known me forever rather than a few hours.

"How are you feeling?" Eileen asked when I joined them.

"Great. That booster is something else."

"Right? There's no doc like Eileen. She's the best." Lucas quipped. His body tightened a little as he dove into a memory, "Man, I remember my first booster. I felt like I could single handedly take on Lord Rorric's beasts afterward." He flexed his lean arm muscles, easily seen because of the sleeveless black shirt he wore with khaki pants. I couldn't help but laugh at his analogy, and the lighthearted display. "You have a nice laugh," he commented.

I brushed a stray strand of my hair behind my ear nervously, hugging my body with my other arm protectively. Compliments were almost as difficult to take as being touched. Coming from a prison that I'd been forced into because of my beauty, went hand in hand with compliments. When those compliments came from poisoned lips with grabby hands, they weren't so nice.

"Hush," Eileen smacked his abdomen with the back of her hand. She was highly accurate at reading unsaid cues, "You're going to scare the poor thing."

"I'm okay. Really. It's fine." I fibbed. It should've been, but it made me a little uncomfortable. Lord Rorric spoke in compliments doused in poison and tinged with threats. My body was used to reacting in conflicting ways to compliments because of it. He was pleased as long as we complied bodily.

"I'm sorry," he bowed, "I'll behave myself on our grand tour. I promise."

"Grand tour?"

"Yep, I have been charged with giving you the grand tour of Sanctum," he beamed crookedly and spreading his arms wide.

Eileen leans in and whispers to me, "It's a big honor. Even when you volunteer for it, right Lucas?" she added at a normal, and teasing, tone.

Lucas blushed at Eileen's insinuation, though it didn't delay him any. He turned and offered me an elbow, "Shall we get on with the tour?" He added, "is this okay?" The question was more directed at Eileen. She gave a slight shake of her head and he dropped his elbow, slightly dejected. His hands found their way into the pockets of his khaki pants that were ripped at the knees. Once again his pure heart shone with his want to be chivalrous. It was endearing.

I mouthed a silent thank you to the healer. She understood me best of all out of anyone part of The Rising, so far. The thanks was for more than just saving Lucas from making me uncomfortable; for making sure I was comfortable. It covered everything she'd done for me since my arrival; the clothes and the booster. Everything.

"Hey Ann," she added before we left, her eyes serious, "Let me know if there is anything I can help you with. Anything at all. Even if it's just a good ear." I promised I would, and that I'd check in later.

I fell in step with Lucas, and we set off on the grand tour.

"So this here," he motioned with a wide sweep of his long arms, "is the community room. Pretty much just a big space to hang out in, do projects, and what not. Most people hang out here a lot. This, the meeting room, and the supply space make up this level."

"How many levels are there?"

"Four, this one being the main one. The only one with two entrances." He stopped in front of a door, opening it. The room had sparse decor, just one long table at one end with seven mis-matched chairs all on one side. "This is the meeting room, where all the important discussions take place. Where our founders make all the big plans and decisions for us. You'll probably come here in the next day or two for orientation and get assigned a job. Everyone has a job."

The idea of having to meet with the founders sent nervous bees swarming in my stomach. They were the people I really had to watch myself around. My new nerves must have shown on my face. "Don't worry, Ann. You won't get a job you can't handle. You get a say. Unless you get in trouble, then you get a nasty job," he held his nose in mock disgust. I smiled meekly at his mistaking my nerves being over a job. I wished it were that simple.

He closed the door and we moved on, going down a hall, and stopping at another door. This one was marked *Supply*. Before opening it he pointed across the space to a gray door next to a set of metal doors. "Those over there are the stairs and elevator, but the elevator is off limits. For emergencies only." I'd only heard about elevators before, and my curious side felt crushed I couldn't check it out. "This door here, is Supply. As the label says," he added sheepishly.

He opened the supply room door. Directly inside there was a counter with a window. A minute later, Trevor popped up from behind the counter. "Oh it's you, doofus."

"Be nice, snot brain," Lucas jabbed back. "I'm showing Ann around."

"Duh, I can see that. Since you don't really need anything, I'm gone." He disappeared further beyond the counter, yelling, "It's nothing Mom! Just dumb old Lucas showing the new girl around."

"Trevor's Mom, Dina, runs supply. Anything you need that isn't food or medical, you get from her."

"I thought Prue was his mom." On the short trek down she certainly had acted like it.

"Nah. Prue's everyone's Mom," he smiled a beat before ushering me from the supply room. I got that. There were girls that took on that role among the Maids sometimes. More often than not they were the ones that were there the longest, or had a natural motherly way to them. They never lasted long at Galter, their nurturing countenances made them less desirable to Lord Rorric. He didn't want mothers, he wanted toys.

I noticed yet another gray door at the end of the hall we were in. But we didn't head that way. Instead, Lucas took us to the door to the stairs. "What's behind that door?" I asked, curious why he'd skipped it.

"That's for later," he winked. "It's the best part of the grand tour." We entered the stairwell, going down one flight. He opened the door, but didn't move to go in. "This floor and the next are the bunks, or quarters. If we keep growing we'll need to open up another floor. Families and women on this level, men on the next one. Families get living quarters, and singles older than eighteen without family here get bunks. Sometimes we get kids that show up without their families, they get placed into family units. Each level has showers in the bathrooms, private showers."

Private showers. Those two words sent me into a swift daydreams of steam and bubbles, with no one to see. I hadn't had a private shower ever. No family in my village had anything more than a standing tub, and most weren't connected to running water. Water had to be pumped from the well at the center of the village, or brought in from rain barrels. Even then, with what little water Lord Rorric let the villages near Galter have, it was strictly rationed.

Then, when I was a Maid, there was no such thing as privacy.

We moved on, down another two flights, this time entering the door we came to. Right away I knew where we had entered. The big space was dotted with tables and chairs, all different sizes and shapes. Long counters lined two walls, one being interrupted by a window next to swinging doors. No one was in the room, but I could hear people chatting in the background, their muted words often hidden behind the sound of metal clanging.

"This is the mess hall, and that," he pointed to the window, "is the kitchen. Meals are at 9 a.m. and 6 p.m., unless by special chit." He explained that some people with medical conditions or that missed a meal because of a meeting or mission got waivers for meals, or extra meals. It depended on the situation. I realized I had no idea what time it was, and hadn't since I left the fortress. Time hadn't mattered much over the past several days. My stomach rumbled at the thought, anticipating when the next meal would be.

I'd been at Sanctum less than a day, and I already had things to look forward to.

Lucas led me through the center of the room, which was the only clear path to be seen. When we came to the far wall, I understood why the path was there. A pair of double doors marked *medical ward* were the only things on that wall. This was where Eileen cared for multiples of patients.

Out of respect for any sick or injured people inside, we skipped entering and headed back up to the main level. Excitement laced Lucas's steps as we went. The time had come for the "best part" of the grand tour of Sanctum. By the time we got to the mysterious door, he practically vibrated with excitement. His high spirit infected me, and I couldn't help but feel a little excited too.

The door led into a long tunnel, another door sat at the end of that.

Lucas put his hand on the door handle, trilling his tongue to impersonate a drum roll. "Ta-da!" he exclaimed when he opened the door. He had been right. That door hid the best part of the tour. A large, open, grassy area, edged by forest greeted my eyes. The lawn had several planter boxes filled with growing vegetables, covered by camouflaged canopies hanging high above them to keep them hidden from the air.

Several people dotted the space. Some worked in the garden, others lounged in the warm afternoon sunlight filtering through the canopy. Children scampered about, playing with each other while the adults watched on.

"This is spectacular," I breathed as we exited the building. I turned in amazement, taking in everything. I noticed the door we came out of was green and sat in an ivy covered natural stone wall. At the foot of the wall were piles of green leaves.

"And safe," he said pointing at the piles of leaves. "Those are canopies, like the ones over the gardens. We have lookouts in the forest. First sight of drones, they make the call and the canopies go up, all the way to the tree line, giving cover to everyone as they make their way back inside."

The set-up was thoughtful and effective, a testament to the precautions The Rising took in protecting their home. Time would tell if my joining them would destroy them.

Fifteen

ELDEN MET us as we walked back through the building looking like he'd gotten little sleep. I wondered if his position in Sanctum was to blame, or if it was something he suffered from because of something in his past. It wasn't a hard conclusion to come to. This world wasn't merciful to anyone.

"Well, Ann," he swept his arms around, "what do you think of our Sanctum?"

"I think," I looked to Lucas, his chocolate eyes intent on me, "it's more than I could hope for. I'm looking forward to living here." My gaze fell back on Elden. His face took on an uncertain mask. The good feelings that dared to sneak into my mind sank, becoming leaden knots in my stomach. He didn't have good news.

"We're looking forward to having you here," his returning smile didn't quite reach his eyes.

"I feel like there's a but coming," I called him out on the air he gave off.

"No but, I swear. You're welcome to stay here, Ann. We don't turn away people in need. It's just the other Founders have a few questions for you. A few things to go over. If you'll come with me," he gestured, inviting me to go with him. "Lucas, Dina needs help in storage." Lucas groaned at the order, likely from having to deal with the precocious Trevor, and trudged away.

Elden's reassurance didn't make me feel any easier. The secrets I kept from them weighed me down. Did they suspect Hux and I hadn't been entirely truthful? Nausea settled in as I followed Elden to meet with the rest of the Founders.

He led me to the meeting room, where four others sat at the long table, waiting. After inviting me to sit, Elden joined the others. The Founders were made up of two men and two women, not including Elden.

During the tour, I'd learned the five of them started Sanctum mainly as a sanctuary. It still was. The sanctuary naturally evolved into a rebel hideout as it grew. As the need became more and more dire. As the unrest in their hearts grew.

"Ann," Elden invited, "let me introduce you to my fellow Founders." He introduced the four others in the room, running down the table from left to right. Bea, a plump woman in her fifties with short, graying brown curls and blue eyes. Her features were round and soft, implying a soft-spoken motherly type. She had scarring peeking out from under the collar of her long sleeve shirt, and blue gloves adorned her hands. More scars peeked out from between the shirt sleeves and gloves. I wondered about the scars, how extensive they were, and just how she'd gotten them. Next to Bea sat a string bean of a man, bald with sharp stone colored eyes under overgrown gray eyebrows. Kent. Something about him, despite his hard angular features and slight build, told a story of a man with grit. Scrappy and not to be trifled with. The two sat connected, their hands intertwined and resting between them on the table. Husband and wife, or at least in a relationship.

Al, the oldest of the bunch, sat center of the table. His shoulder length, white hair pulled back into a ponytail. Green eyes danced behind thick rimmed glasses, broken and taped together in several places. His hair was the only clue to his age, as everything else about his appearance told another story, one of a man years younger. His ruddy, terracotta skin glowed and it was easy to see he was exceptionally fit for his age.

Lastly, in the seat next to the empty one beside Al, was Dolly. Small and full of fire, she looked it too with her golden brown hair pulled in a tight ponytail and warm amber eyes set against warm sepia skin. She didn't let her diminutive size hold her back, physically or vocally. I doubted she'd have trouble holding her ground against any opponent.

With a timid hello, I picked one of the rickety wooden chairs and sat. Elden, instead of joining the other Founders on the other side of the table, sat in the chair next to me, groaning from exhaustion as he did. Being the youngest of the group, his role in Sanctum was more active than the others, going on runs and scouting missions. Leading by example appeared to have taken a physical toll on him, yet he refused to slow down.

"Ann," Al didn't hesitate to begin the moment I was seated, "Firstly, on behalf of the rest of the Founders, welcome to Sanctum." His voice was smooth, like aged whiskey.

"Thank you. It means a lot to be here."

"I'm sure. We live in a scary world, that's quickly becoming worse.What we provide here is a safe place that might someday prove a template for rebuilding. We hope."

"Me too," I fidgeted with my hands. "Elden said you have some questions?" The Founders exchanged uneasy glances. My nerves spiked at what I saw as obvious distrust in me.

Time dragged slowly with nothing being said while they floundered silently for their words. Hardly a minute passed, but it felt an eternity before Dolly spoke what the others wouldn't. "Frankly, Ann, we have concerns about your travel partner, Sly. From what Elden reported, his reasons for not staying aren't clear, making us wonder where his allegiance lies."

A silent breath filled my lungs with heavy air. My eyes widened with the knowledge I held. True, their suspicions weren't pointed directly at me, but that didn't stop the guilt of my secrets from welling up my throat.

"What is it you know Ann?" Al coaxed, reading into my reaction.

"I have no love for him is all," I covered, hoping they bought it. "He's nothing more than what he says he is. A coward that wants to be left alone. He has no allegiances," I spat, my lip curling against the sour taste the memory of Hux's rejection to help with what really mattered.

"Whatever his place in this world, he cared enough to bring you to us," Bea interjected. She didn't even know the man, and she defended him for the sole reason of his escorting me to them. "That has to mean something."

"No, he just wanted me out of his hair," I rolled my eyes and scoffed. Bea only gave me a look that said she disagreed. "He found me vexing."

"Are you positive he poses no threat to Sanctum?" Al leaned forward, locking eyes with me.

"Only because he isn't willing to step up with the rest of us, I can't say he isn't a threat. Anyone not willing to fight is accepting how things are, which is as bad as siding with Lord Rorric, in my opinion. But, he wouldn't do anything to bring trouble to your door. That I can say with complete certainty."

Relief swept over the faces in the room. That didn't mean they were done with me. The Founders still had to lay out some rules they wanted me to abide by. There were only truly two basic rules in Sanctum: contribute where you can and keep the peace. Of course there were other rules. Rules and laws were what kept any place running smoothly. Those they didn't emphasize.

What they did emphasize was a rule they laid out for only certain female inhabitants of Sanctum. Stay within the boundaries. Young women of certain ages, and of course of certain appearances, were not allowed out of the base on runs or scouting missions. Their safety, the safety of Sanctum, depended on them not being seen by Lord Rorric's minions and machines.

I offered no argument there.

"Do you have any questions for us?" Al asked when they were through explaining what life in their home was like.

There were so many questions I had about living in Sanctum, none they could answer though. But, there was one question that stuck in my mind ever since the location of the base had been revealed. "How do you avoid detection?"

"What do you mean?" Kent leaned forward, removing his hand from Bea's and clasping it to his other.

"Well, I was pretty shocked when this place turned out to be right under where Sly and I made camp. What keeps it from being seen by drones that might have heat sensing equipment?" I didn't know for sure whether or not Lord Rorric's drones had that feature, but Hux's own device hadn't seen anything. That left me curious.

"We're pretty deep underground," Elden explained. "Plus we have heat deflecting material lining the ceiling of the top floor. Trust me, Sanctum is very secure."

I swallowed and nodded, "Good." My curiosity was sated with that answer, but I wasn't entirely sure how safe they really were.

After my meeting with the Founders was through, Bea showed me to the women's bunks. The singles bunks took up a third of the floor, with family units taking up the rest. There were at least twenty-five sets of bunks and ten simple cots arranged in neat rows, each one made up with a pillow and blanket. Along with the simple bedding, the bunks taken were adorned with personal items, making them easy to spot.

"We try to keep it quiet in here," Bea said as we walked between rows of beds, some of which were still occupied. The schedules kept in Sanctum tended to be regulated. They preferred their people inside after dark. Sometimes that wasn't possible. Raids took time, and scouting missions happened as needed. Still, they tried to make sure the comings and goings of Sanctum happened during daylight hours. Of course, there were exceptions. Like when they found me. Otherwise, protecting the residents demanded a loose curfew.

Picking a bunk proved harder than I thought it would. The people of Sanctum were still strangers to me, my trust in them still fragile. Before I decided to just take the next available bunk I saw, I spotted Cordee sitting on the edge of a bunk near the back of the room, lacing up her boots. An empty bunk sat across from her.

I didn't know her that well, only interacted for those few moments after we met. Still, I knew her better than most of Sanctum. That made me more comfortable sleeping near her. If I had the option, I'd bunk near Eileen. Her calming presence had already made a huge impact on me. She, however, tended to bunk in her office, or in the larger medical wing when the bed in there was occupied.

"Cordee," Bea quietly called out to get her attention. She looked up from her task, her brown hair slipping from its place over her eye to reveal gruesome scarring encircling the outer edge. The revelation made it clear why she was allowed on missions, despite her youth. Despite being pretty. Lord Rorric never would have wanted her, so his men left her alone when they came to reap Maids from the villages.

As soon as she realized the shiny puckered skin had been revealed, she swept her hair back in place. Her eyes darted nervously at me, anticipating a reaction. She wouldn't get one from me, at least not one she expected. The scar around her eye gave her freedom that I never had. To me, the scarring made her more beautiful.

In my head, though, I wondered what caused them. I hated thinking that someone had done that to her on purpose. To save her from a life in Galter with no autonomy. It wasn't uncommon for young girls to be disfigured by their families. While the notion kept their little girls safe, it was barbaric. A sad and cruel indicator of the world we lived in. One I wished on nobody. Even though I envied those that were safe from becoming Maids, I was grateful to my parents for being good enough to not harm me. That sort of trauma, even done with good intentions, had to be just as scarring as what I went through in Galter.

Cordee must have seen the question in my eyes. "It was an accident," she bit out uncomfortably. "A dirt clod fight gone wrong when my brother threw one without realizing it contained a rock."

"I'm sorry."

"I'm not. Even though I hate it, and the piteous looks it gets me, it turned out to be a blessing in disguise. That and the fact I'm not super feminine."

"Yeah," I agreed, a lump in my throat. "I'm glad it wasn't on purpose, though. That's what I was worried about. I didn't mean to make you uncomfortable by staring."

She shrugged her strong shoulders, "It's okay. Most people do. I don't like it, but I'd rather explain than continue to get stared at." She reached to finish tying her boots, nodding toward the bunk near her, "You going to bunk with me then?"

"If that's okay."

"Of course it is," Bea answered for Cordee.

"Yeah, sure. No problem," she confirmed and stood, though she gave the older woman a sour glare. Cordee wasn't one to let others speak for her. "I've got to get going, though. Broadcast duty again, and I need food before I go."

Cordee's mention of having broadcast duty roused my curiosity of how others found Sanctum. The one time I saw the broadcast hadn't been the best experience. The broken Holo-caster and Hux complicated it. I didn't get to see or hear how to find the rebels. Luckily, I hadn't needed to. Discovering Noumenon had helped me and led me to where it wanted to go had changed the journey. Made it less stressful. Not that it allowed Hux or I to just skylark our way across the land. Far from it. We still were on our guard, just in case the stone failed us.

I dropped my pack on the bunk across from Cordee's, "Is broadcast duty hard?" I wondered whether or not I'd be allowed that task ever. I recognized Lucas's voice from the brief broadcast I'd heard at Hux's workshop. If I ever was on a broadcast, would my voice be recognized? "I'd only heard one before trying to find you guys. The holo-caster was broken, so it kind of sucked quality wise. I couldn't see much, not even the knotted snake lasted long on the screen."

"Wow. Really? You got real lucky then." Bea looked shocked at my admission. I knew the news would be shared with the other Founders next time she saw them.

"Yeah," I offered lightly. If she knew the reason why I'd found them so easily, she'd probably drag me by my ear right back to the meeting room. As it was, I was prepared to have to sit through another interrogation because of what I just said. "Why do you say I got lucky then?"

"Finding us," Cordee explained. "We don't give out our actual location in any broadcast. Just locations of dummy sites where our guides frequent to bring in newcomers waiting at them."

"I guess I did get lucky then." Cordee shrugged off my response. Bea, on the other hand, eyed me with new suspicion that told me another meeting with the Founders was in my future.

Sixteen

THE STEADY, repeated chiming of bells pulled me from my dreams. The women's bunk room was still shrouded in darkness, the muffled sounds of protests to wake soon overtook the fading chimes. My bones didn't hold any of the complaints I heard coming from some of the women scattered in the dark. Mine were all too eager to start my first official day as a member of The Rising.

The bunk lights slowly illuminated as the women rose from their pillows. Cordee grumbled next to me, her eyes clamped shut against the new day. The puckered scar around her eye socket was on full display, shining and angry even though it was long since healed, her curls splayed wildly over her plain bedding, until she turned and aggressively covered her face with her pillow.

She didn't have to rise with the rest of us. Cordee didn't return from broadcast duty until late into the night. The short time I spent with her in the broadcast room, which was little more than a closet tucked away in the back of the kitchen, surprised me. What they did there wasn't what I'd expected. The broadcast didn't go out live, they were pre-recorded and looped, then new ones were recorded as news came in or as meeting places changed. Someone always had to be in the broadcast room to switch and reset recordings, and to make sure the feed didn't mess up. It wasn't a hard job, but one that required constant watch.

I stifled a laugh and shook my head as I slipped on my boots, made my way out of the bunks, and followed the stream of bodies to the mess.

The line for food began before the stairs even ended. The majority of Sanctum's population seemed to stand in it, waiting for their turn to get breakfast, many still wore remnants of sleep ether in their faces.

There wasn't a single face near me that I was familiar with as I watched the crowd. My nerves spiked, even though I knew there was no reason to be afraid of anyone there. Still, I felt naked, as though they could see through the lie I lived, my hands pressed to the spot under my breasts where Lord Rorric's mark felt like it burned through the clothes I wore. Then I spotted a familiar head of disheveled long blond hair several feet ahead of me, poking out over the rest of the crowd. He was jovially engaged in conversation with those around him, stealing a beanie from someone next to him. Moments later, a mess of red curls popped up and down, a small hand moving along with it desperately reaching for the tattered old hat. Seeing Lucas torment Trevor like a little brother made me laugh.

He danced about in a circle, taunting the precocious boy with his hat, only to stop when he noticed me watching. His face beamed at me over the crowd of hungry people. There was no hesitation on his part to drop the hat, unceremoniously, on Trevors head, who complained loudly at the shenanigans, and pushed his way through the line to me.

"What are you doing? You're going to lose your place in line."

"No biggie," he replied with a lopsided shrug that matched his crooked smile. "I'd do anything to escape the little terror."

"Trevor can't be that bad," I stifled a laugh.

"You've never had to live with him."

"Oh?" I knew Lucas wasn't related to Trevor and Dina, so his response had me wondering.

He swept a hand through his long hair, as though suddenly aware of his disheveled look. "I lived with him and Dina for a year after I got here, so I guess in way you might say he's my little bro." He passed a look back over the line, watching the little red head for a moment or two. Trevor waved, then raised his middle finger at Lucas while grinning from ear to ear. Despite how much they annoyed each other, they cared. His explanation shed new light on the way he and Trevor interacted. The families made in Sanctum were some sort of miracle in this world where many were torn apart.

"It makes sense now," a light laugh came out with my words.

"What does?"

"The way you two are."

The line moved swiftly, before I knew it we were before the serving tables being offered dense grain bars, pemmican with dried berries, and a small mug of water. True survival food, not too different from what many in the villages survived on during lean and hard months, which lasted longer and longer as Lord Rorric's seemingly eternal rule stretched on. I thanked the dark haired woman that served me with a nod and followed Lucas through the mess.

He settled us at a mostly empty table, a rough hewn wooden thing that had been chipped and scratched within an inch of its life. You could get a splinter just looking at it. He wasted no time digging into the dense protein bar that I could only bring myself to pick at. Nerves hadn't managed to steal my appetite until the pemmican landed in my hand. I'd been spoiled by the savory homespun meals Hux packed for the journey. I longed for just a sliver of the dried fish, and felt guilty for it.

Even though my stomach twisted at thought of the fatty, chewy square of protein, I was grateful for it and would eat what I could. Keeping a community this size fed couldn't be easy when everything was traded, grown, or stolen for a place that few knew about.

"You get used to it," Lucas said when he noticed my bird-like picking.

"It's not the food," I half lied taking a small bite, but not being able to hide the grimace it brought to my face.

"You sure about that?" he laughed.

"Not just the food. This is all strange to me still, and I don't know how long I'll be welcome here."

Lucas's brows knitted together, "Why, though? I don't think anyone's going to kick you out at this point."

"Bea seems suspicious of how I found you guys is all. I told her and Cordee last night I never saw any coordinates on a broadcast. Me and

Sly stumbling on you guys was pure luck." *Luck and a magical stone guiding me,* I thought to myself as I picked at my nails.

"Nah. She's more bark than bite. Besides she rarely is up and about this hour. She survived a fire before coming here, but it left a lot of scars. Not just physical ones." That explained the marks I'd seen peeking from her clothing during the meeting, but that only led to more questions about them.

As if summoned by her name, Bea appeared behind Lucas. Her unkempt curls were piled high on her head, wrapped in a scarf and her face haggard as though she hadn't slept. Her appearance only affirmed what Lucas just told me about her.

"Ann," she yawned coldly. "You're requested in the meeting room."

"Is there something wrong?" Lucas asked over his shoulder.

"The Founders have a few more questions is all. Nothing for you to worry about Lucas," she replied curtly.

"Yeah, okay. Let me finish up here and I'll be there," my voice fought to keep stable.

"Don't be too long," she yawned again leading me to wonder if my confession had been part of what kept her from sleeping. She shuffled away without another word.

A knot formed in my stomach, I'd been in Sanctum less than twenty-four hours and already was causing problems.

Lucas turned his face to me, his eyes wide. "Uh, I think you might be right about Bea."

Those were words I didn't need to hear. I buried my head in my arms on the table before me and groaned, "They're going to kick me out." I didn't know what I would do if the Founders decided I had to go, didn't know where I would go. There wouldn't be very many safe places for me to disappear to. I hated to think it, but returning to Hux with my tail between my legs might be my only option.

A touch on my hand jolted me back, heart racing and palms slick; my body conditioned that a touch I wasn't expecting could be harmful. Only Lucas sat before me, not Lord Rorric. "Sorry," he looked down sheepishly, "I forgot about the touch thing."

"It's okay," I brushed my hand through my curls in an attempt to put myself back together.

"Don't sweat this meeting with the Founders. I'm sure they won't kick you out. But, on the off chance they do," he pulled his gaze from his lap, his warm coffee eyes firm, "I'll go with you."

"I couldn't ask you to do that."

"You don't have to. You can't be out there alone. It isn't safe."

Floored didn't begin to describe what I felt then. Lucas barely knew me, yet he was willing to give up his home, his safety, for me. I sucked in my lip, and twisted my fingers, "I think I'd like that."

Seventeen

THE NUMBER of people living in Sanctum boggled my mind. The population fluctuated as people came and left, almost daily. There were days where I hardly saw anyone. Then there were days where there seemed to be way more people than could possibly live there. The busiest days were when groups returned from missions. I couldn't keep up half the time. Thankfully, that wasn't my job.

After my second meeting with the Founders, Al made me a floater, putting me wherever I was needed most. At that point I was thankful to even have a position in Sanctum. Bea pushed for some sort of contingency in that matter. How I'd lucked into finding myself right above it didn't sit right with her. In the end she was outvoted, Al determining that I had just been extremely lucky and no action was needed.

I enjoyed the rotating jobs, I never got bored with the same thing day in and out, although Eileen seemed to snag me into her services a lot more than others. At least my assignments never took me from the safety of Sanctum. The very thought of being outside of the community left my stomach in tight knots.

A group had just returned from an information heavy mission, that's what Elden said anyway. Though I was pretty sure they were on a man-hunt. Maid-hunt. According to rumors, everyone still looked for the missing Maid. Me. It had been over a month since my escape, and weeks since I'd joined The Rising, and still the excitement over my escapade still had the place buzzing. Every night I went to bed with the hope the next morning would be the day the search would end. Maybe then I'd feel a little better about revealing my true identity. I figured in a few more weeks everyone would presume the Maid had died. It'd be safer then.

I'd been assigned to booster duty, once again working with Eileen. She tasked me with handing out the rejuvenating concoction to the returning members, they didn't need Eileen's supervision since they'd used it before. According to her the first one could be a crap shoot, and it wasn't best to do them alone. I enjoyed the task. I got to see everyone reuniting with their friends and loved ones. Anything that brought a shred of light into a world where darkness reigned was worth seeing.

I spotted Prue's silvery hair across the crowd mingling between the trees. A tall lanky man with peppery black hair leaned over her tiny frame, his long arms enveloped her, holding her tight and kissing her. My heart sang for her. I knew how worried she'd been about her husband, Gerry. He'd been on a mission for a long time, over a year from what I understood. A mission so secret, she didn't even know where he was or what he was doing.

He spun her around, stopping with his back to me as I approached. Even though I tried to not interrupt their reunion, she heard me. I swear she could have heard an acorn drop a mile away. Her hearing was bat like. Prue's sweet face peeked out from the side of the tall man, a big smile on display. She looked like a kid that'd been told they could have all the sweets they wanted, before dinner.

"Ann, I see you have booster duty."

"That's me. Booster girl." I laughed. I worked with Eileen more often than not. Not that I minded. I enjoyed working with the healer, and I trusted her above anyone in Sanctum, even though Lucas was proving to be my closest friend.

I spent a lot of my free time with the tall, blonde man. His light and easy personality was refreshing. The consideration he put into every move and every word he said warmed me. Although, I often felt he sought more than my friendship. I simply couldn't allow myself the closeness, I couldn't get over my recent past enough to. Those were hang-ups that took time, or an act of a god, to reverse.

"Here, meet my husband. Back from his mysterious mission, finally." She looked up at her man, love shone from her eyes. She obviously thought the world of him. "Honey, I want you to meet Ann."

Prue's husband turned his head, and my world slowed down. I recognized him even before he finished the turn. He'd been a servant at Galter. I'd seen him in passing more than once during my assigned times with Lord Rorric. Those were the only times Maids saw servants that weren't female. Even then, we weren't allowed to interact with them. The only men in Galter allowed to interact with a Maid were Lord Rorric and his guards.

Gerry's face morphed from friendly greeting to shock as his mouth dropped and eyes bulged when he laid his eyes on me. With a deep gasp, one lanky hand flew to his mouth as he pointed at me with the other. He staggered back a step and fell to his knees. "She's the Maid."

"I, I don't know. I'm not. I'm Ann, not a Maid." I tried to confirm my false identity, deny the truth spewing from him, but my voice faltered on the stone that suddenly lodged in my throat. My arm slipped and the basket under it was sucked away by gravity. The patches became worthless the moment they hit the ground, and a few bottles of vitamin infused water cracked from clanging together. Precious booster drink seeped into the ground, disappearing forever. I stared at the mess, as if the answer to this situation lay there, and fought the tears that wanted to spill. I wanted to seep into the porous ground like the booster did. I needed to escape, run, but my feet wouldn't obey. I was frozen to the spot.

"Ann. Ann. Ann," the name pulled me out of my head. Elden stood before me now, his dark hand waiving in my face. We'd gotten the attention of everyone near us. They all stared. Bewildered looks and whispers saturated the air. I'd just been outed, made a liar. This wasn't good. I had to persuade them all otherwise. A near impossible task. They had every reason to believe him over me, years of trust built between them rather than mere weeks.

"I swear, she's the Maid," Prue's husband accused in the background. He sounded like he was a million miles away.

All I could do was shake my head. I didn't have words. My foot fumbled back, I tried to retreat before everyone's accusing eyes burned me. I bumped right into someone in the process. Panicked, I looked over my shoulder and saw Eileen. Her serene face was a welcome sight compared the accusatory glares from everyone else.

She grabbed my hand in hers. Once again, her touch brought a calm to my center. A morsel of courage that I needed to face this. Only a morsel. Just enough to keep my feet firmly where they were instead of fleeing into the trees and never coming back. The tears broke beyond the dam I tried to build. My hands covered my face to catch the tears flowing from my eyes, a lame attempt to hide the shame I felt for being a liar. For being outed. "It's okay honey. It's okay," Eileen's voice soothed in my ear. "Elden, let's take this to the meeting room. Go get the rest of the Founders. Prue, bring Gerry."

Everything was a blur as Eileen gently guided me from the garden, the faces we passed melded into one another. I was near completely unaware of what was happening, moving only through the guidance of Eileen's hands. The tunnel enveloped us, and soon enough we entered the main part of Sanctum. From there, Eileen steered me straight to the meeting room.

It wasn't until we entered the room that my panic finished setting in, snapping me out of my daze. I wanted to crumble, and I did. Rather than taking one of the seats, I leaned against the wall, sliding down to the floor. In the pocket of my pants, Noumenon became a weight anchoring me to the spot. It reminded me all of my secrets were about to be exposed.

Eileen sat next to me, rubbing my back while we waited for the others to arrive. The comforting gesture did little to relieve the trembling that had invaded my limbs.

Prue and Gerry, who arrived moments after we did, sat in chairs across the room from us. Their faces were mirrored masks of my own worry. Something else featured in Prue's face that I hadn't seen since I met her. Uncertainty. That was my doing. My fault. She no longer felt certain about my presence here. That made me feel worse than I had in a long time. I crossed my arms over my knees and hid my head in them, contemplating my next move.

The hinges of the door squeaking drew my head out of hiding, my eyes meeting Prue's. I looked from her to the Founders filing in. Elden entered last, he wore the same look as Prue, without the accusing undertone. He was worried. He closed the door behind him and leaned against it, instead of taking his place, the weight of his decision pressing him against it. Elden was an easy man to read once you got to know him. Right then, I could tell his thoughts shadowed my own, that this was his fault. After all, he had approved me to come here. A decision that more than likely had been born out of the excitement of having a man like "Sly" join them. Big and intimidating. Strong looking. Instead, he got me. Only me, useless to aid the achievement of their ultimate goal. Just another mouth to feed. Knowing him, though, even if he knew this would've happened, he would have made the same decision. He had a huge heart, and genuinely loved people. He'd have given the shirt off his back to anyone that needed it. Even in a snow storm.

"What is this meeting about?" Bea asked the second she sat in her designated seat, rubbing sleep from her eyes. Since my second meeting with The Founders, I learned Bea had terrible insomnia, my perceived threat hadn't played a part in her lack of sleep. Her nights were spent awake. More often than not she napped throughout the day, having to be woken for meetings.

Elden pushed his body from the door and sauntered forward, "We've found the Maid. At least that is what Gerry says." His eyes shifted to me briefly, "There's some debate about it."

"It's either we have or we haven't. I don't see how an identity can be debatable," Kent chimed in.

"It's her. I swear. A million percent," Gerry affirmed emphatically.

Al shifted in his chair, intrigued and wary. "Where is this girl then? I only see established community members here."

"That's the problem, Sir, he's identified Ann as the Maid," Elden clarified nodding towards me. Part of me cringed at the gesture, as though it were a brand readying itself to join the one already seared onto my flesh.

"What do you have to say about that, young lady?" Dolly quipped, her quick eyes landing on me with a heavy dose of scrutiny.

As the rest of the group all looked at me, my body wanted to shut down. The icy fingers of fear scratched at me. The truth scared me almost as much as Lord Rorric did. Even though I hadn't been in Sanctum for very long, I loved it there. I loved the people. The friendships I'd formed meant so much to me. I didn't want to lose them over the lies I'd been holding in for my own sake. For their sake. If I lost my place, I was done for. I knew I wouldn't make it on my own out in the world, not while I was being hunted. I didn't know what to do. I hated thinking it, but I wished Hux were there with me. He would've known what to do. He wasn't though. That bridge had been burned.

"I don't know." I looked to my legs, ashamed I couldn't admit the truth.

"You don't know?" Al asked accusingly from the center of the table. "How could you not know? You have your memory, yes?"

Tears began to fall again. I felt too ashamed, too embarrassed, to speak anymore.

"What about the brand?" Gerry piped up. "If she has no mark, then I'm mistaken. Simple as that. Although, her face is not one to be mistaken as any other, not when she was Lord Rorric's favorite." The reminder knotted in my chest. I never wanted to admit that to myself, it was too painful to do.

"Now, that's not fair," Eileen defended me, "I can't let you ask this girl to lift her shirt to show everyone whether or not she's been branded. You all know how intimate a place that brand is left. Elden, you know as much as me about Ann's personal space thing. We can't ask her this." She was a saint.

Elden sighed, running a hand over his dark curls. "I don't see how we can't at this point. Ann isn't answering our questions. We need to know if Gerry's right. And if so, why she's been lying to us. As much as I hate to put Ann through something she's not comfortable with, we need to know." There it was. The confirmation that even Elden had seen the crack in my lie that Gerry's return had caused.

"A compromise then," Eileen proposed. "She can show me. Right, Ann?"

I thought about it for a heartbeat. There was no way they were going to trust me if I didn't allow Eileen to inspect me. Maybe I could work something out with her. She'd understand. Wouldn't she? I managed to nod in agreement as I tried to think of what I could say to persuade her to help me.

"No. Eileen is too fond of Ann. We've all seen the way she's favored her since her arrival. Her opinion is biased." Prue jumped into the conversation, ready to defend her husband's judgment.

"You don't trust me, Prue? You really think that I'd lie to everyone?"

"Well, no. But..."

"You'll both look for the brand then," Al broke up the argument. Prue and Eileen continued to stare at each other. The rift made me feel even worse. I hated they were fighting because of me.

Without another word, everyone except Prue, Eileen, and myself filed out of the room. As they left I caught a glimpse of Lucas pacing outside the door, his brows furrowed as his eyes locked with mine for a brief moment before it closed. I wondered if he would still be willing to leave Sanctum with me when he learned the truth about me, that is if the Founders decided I couldn't stay. Or would he feel betrayed and abandon me as well?

Somehow the meeting room felt more crowded with everyone else gone. The air hung thick with tension. Eileen and Prue were at odds and my nerves threatened to suffocate me with every second that brought me closer to revealing the truth. Time was up. With tears clinging to my lashes, my fingers began to fumble over the buttons on my blue shirt. I had to reveal the brand seared into my flesh no matter how much I didn't want to.

"Ann. There's no need," Eileen stopped my hands.

"Yes there is, Eileen! We need to know the truth!"

"We will, Prue. Just not in a way that will traumatize her more. Can't you see the pain she's in?" Eileen stroked my hair and looked me in the eyes, "I know you're the Maid." I sucked in a breath, trying to keep the tears at bay. Of course Eileen knew. She seemed to know everything.

"What do you mean? You know? And you kept it to yourself?" Prue accused the healer. "Did she tell you when she first arrived?"

"She didn't tell me, not with words anyway. Her actions were glaring clues though. Her fear of revealing her skin. The way she shies away from contact most of the time. Her dislike of being complimented. The far off, terrified look that comes into her eyes, lost in her past."

"I'm sorry," I gulped, my gaze adverted from the two women and became glued to the floor, ashamed of the lies.

"But to keep it from us!"

"I'm sure she has her reasons why she lied. It's not my place to tell, either. I knew she would in time. When she was ready."

"Then why even agree to this? Make everyone leave and waste time."

"To give Ann some time, space, to be ready for this, pick one. Anyone can see she's overwhelmed here. I thought you'd have some semblance of sympathy for her, having lost your daughter to Lord Rorric."

My head whipped up, eyes on Prue in a moment. The fury that laced her features broke into a million shards of pain. Tears began streaming down her cheeks, a torrent of pain and loss. "Your daughter is a Maid?"

"I just hoped she was the Maid everyone is looking for," Prue sobbed. "My Angel."

The memory of my first few weeks as a Maid swept through my mind like river rapids. The rush slowed when my memories landed what I looked for. Angel. I remembered her. She was just as cherubic as her name, round face with big, sparkling blue eyes and full lips. The lightest blonde hair curled around her face. I saw the resemblance between her and Prue once I looked for it. She was just as kind and fierce too. When Lord Rorric tired of her she met her end bravely, championing her freedom even in death.

"I'm sorry," I hugged Prue. "I remember Angel. She..."

"I know. I just hoped, until Gerry came back and told me."

The glass on the door rattled along with the rapping on it. The others thought we'd had enough time. In a way, we had. In my mind, I'd never be ready. It was best to rip the bandage off, though. There was no sense in delaying any longer.

Prue composed herself, wiping the tears from her eyes and onto her skirt. Eileen ventured to the door, waited a beat and looked back at me. The unsaid question. Are you ready? Only as ready as I'd ever be in this moment. My head nodded twice, and I kept my head bowed. My eyes studied the floor, learned every crack and divot, while the sound of the others entering the meeting room marched to my ears. Their uneasy shuffles matched the fast rhythm my heart had taken on. Chair legs groaned against the floor and under the added weight of new occupants. Someone coughed uneasily. I memorized the sounds, just in case this was my last hour in Sanctum. They were proof that people can come together and rule themselves. At least I knew that it was possible.

"Did you see the brand?" someone asked.

"No. I did not see the brand," Prue answered, a sadness in her voice that tells me she was still thinking on her Angel.

"Then it's settled," Elden interjected, relieved. "She is not the Maid. Gerry must've been mistaken. Perhaps his road travels wore him out too much."

"No," my voice came out meek as I raised my head.

"No?"

I stood, rooting my feet to the floor, and wiped the remnants of my tears from my stained cheeks. My eyes scanned the assembled people, gazing each one in their eyes. My breath hitched in my chest. "My name is Grainne. I was a Maid of Rorric. I escaped the fortress, Galter, and became determined to find you once I learned of your existence as I fled. To fight for a better world. I'm sorry. I'm sorry I lied. I was afraid. Afraid of betrayal and being used. Afraid of being turned away because I was a danger to you all. I just wanted my freedom."

"What about Sly?" Elden asked. "Did he know?"

Thoughts of Hux filled my head, warming me. Angering me. "Yes. He advised me to lie. Only because he thought it best, until I was certain of you. He was only looking out for me, like he did from the moment I fell exhausted and sick on his doorstep."

"How are you a danger, other than being who you are?" Eileen asked. It almost sounded like a prompt, like she already knew. There was no way she could though.

"There's more than that. Your sources were right," I recalled the brief bit of cast I heard in Hux's workshop. "I stole something from Lord Rorric. Something that means he will stop at nothing, and never stop trying, to find me. Probably kill me and whoever harbors me, just to get it back. Without it, he is weaker."

Eileen moved in front of me, her eyes questioning. "What is it?"

Noumenon sang from my pocket as my fingers grazed the fabric shrouding it. It wanted to be freed from its new prison. Exposed. My hand wrapped around it, drawing the wrapped stone out. I presented it in my flattened palm, discarding the fabric. Noumenon flared once, responding happily to getting what it asked of me. "I have Noumenon. It's a ruby holding the stolen powers of the Fallen Lords." The room collectively gasped. The news rocked everyone to a point they could have been knocked from their seats by just a feather.

Elden approached me, his coal eyes shining, "Grainne. How could you ever think we'd reject you for this? This is the key we've been waiting for." He smiled broadly and began to clap, "Let's hear it for Grainne!" The room erupted in applause, every face lit by a spark of hope. For the first time since coming to Sanctum, I felt almost completely free.

There was only one thing keeping me from total freedom. The even bigger secret I kept from these people. The one that wasn't mine to share. I couldn't even imagine how they'd react if they learned the rumors were true. One of the Fallen Lords lived. Some of them had met him, but he wanted nothing to do with their resistance.

I held my tongue. I wouldn't betray Hux, even though his betrayal through abandonment made me want to.

Eighteen

THE FOUNDERS DEEMED it wise to keep the news of Noumenon contained to those that were in the meeting room that day. The people would be protected through ignorance of its existence in their walls.

Not only did I tell them about the stone, I relinquished it to them. The weight of it no longer nagged at me from my pocket, I felt freer without it. Revealing two of my three secrets lifted the pressure from my shoulders.

Al, in turn, handed Noumenon over to Eileen for safe keeping. Even though she wasn't a Founder, they trusted her. She'd tried to protest it, claiming she had as little clue what to do with it as they did. In the end, though, she gave in. Her office was one of the most secure rooms in Sanctum after all.

I couldn't think of a better place for the powerful gem to be kept. Something about Eileen having the stone felt right to me.

What couldn't be hidden even if we tried was who I really was. That bit of news spread like wildfire. Becoming Grainne, the former Maid, made me instantly popular. Everyone wanted to hear my story. Everyone wanted to know the girl that escaped Lord Rorric. Answering their questions posed no problems, at first. It didn't take long for it to get overwhelming, though. The constant attention and demand for mine in return was wearing.

There were those, like the Founders, Eileen, and Cordee, that weren't affected too much by my revelation. They treated me as they did before, perhaps a little more reverently at times. Prue and Gerry, they began to look on me as a connection to their daughter. I told them all I could about my experiences with Angel, leaving out the ghastly details of being a Maid. They didn't need to hear that. I couldn't mar her image in their minds with those experiences.

Then there was Lucas.

I found quiet comfort in Lucas. His cheerful attitude kept me afloat and my mind off of the sword hanging over my head. Best of all, he took the news of my lie in stride. It slid off his back like water off a duck. He didn't make a big deal of it, or hound me with questions. He merely accepted I was Grainne, and did everything in his power to make sure I was still comfortable in Sanctum.

The more time I spent with him, the more I knew he felt more than the budding friendship between us. I wasn't entirely sure I did. Or wanted to. Those were feelings I hadn't been allowed. Still, he didn't mind accompanying me into the trees beyond Sanctum's little yard. Under their canopy and verdant foliage, I felt my best. Safe and free. So many of my late afternoons were spent beneath them, lying in a patch of grass and watching the branches dance in the breeze, the rich deep smell of the earth and leaves washing over me. Occasionally I'd get caught in a downpour of green and white when the winds plucked leaves and blossoms from the plants and showered them on me. It hearkened to when I believed in good magic and frolicking freely in great big fields of wildflowers. A time when the only thing I had to fear were scraped knees and the ire of my mother when I left my chores undone. When I was young enough to think nothing bad could ever happen to me. Things were simpler then.

We lay together on the forest floor, as far from Sanctum as we could get without getting in trouble, just watching the sky peek around the leaves and branches. The day was warm and pleasant. Lucas's hand bumped mine and I didn't shy away. I'd gotten a lot better at accepting being touched. It had taken a long time to get to a point where I didn't fear it. I no longer feared they'd speak of vile things, or that they were going to hurt me. Not as much anyway. Being fully healed would take a lot longer, if it ever happened. I knew I'd always be haunted by my time in Galter.

My eyes flicked from the treetops to Lucas at his touch, a gut reaction. He slept. A gentle snore vibrated in his chest, and from his lips a droplet of drool slid a little further down his chin. I couldn't say that I was always good company when he joined me. My eyes on the patches of sky and my head in the clouds. Or thinking on Hux. Despite my best efforts, and better judgement, he occupied a space in my mind almost constantly.

Ever since I'd been outed, I couldn't help wonder what he was doing from time to time. If he regretted leaving me with strangers; his choice not to fight. I wondered if he only stayed away because of pride. Part of me missed his quiet and steady demeanor. His dimpled grin and sleepy brown eyes. The gentleness in his calloused hands. I missed him, even though I barely knew him, and even though I still simmered at his cowardice. My head reeled from the contradiction.

Lucas was so different from that. True, he had the same patience as the old god when it came to me. Yet, at the same time that kindness felt like something else, something more human and much easier to bear than the fiery emotions Hux brought out. Lucas was a bundle of energy, and ready to help. Ready to fight for what he knew was right. Light compared to Hux's storm. Sleeping, though, he had the look of a child. Innocent and untouched by the evils of our world. Seeing him like that, made me realize how much he meant to me. That perhaps I felt a little more than friendship towards him.

My hand found it's way to Lucas's ruddy cheek, lighting there softer than a feather's touch. He didn't startle awake. I didn't want him to. A light smile lifted the corner of his mouth and a pleasant wordless mumble came forth. Perhaps, I thought, it wouldn't be so bad to open myself up more to him. He made me feel lighter than I should, like there really was a chance at a better world for all of us.

My chest constricted at the idea of being more than friends, sending signals to my brain to throw guards in place. I told it no. The time to keep people at bay needed to end. The longer I kept myself locked away from feeling for anyone, the harder it would be to do it. Most of all, Lucas deserved to be let in, to be the first I let in. My eyes stayed locked on Lucas's face as my hand fell away from it and landed in the prickly grass between us. The grass scratched my hand as it slid along until contact. Our fingers grazed. This time I pulled back as if his hand was molten, a knee-jerk reaction. No. Change had to happen, or else it never would. I sucked in a heap of air. I could do this. I wanted to. My fingers crept over his hand slowly and snaked around his fingers. His warmth seemed to fill me the second my fingers locked onto his. I didn't explode, or feel the need to retreat. A moment to be savored, I shut my eyes and allowed the warmth chase away the demons in the corner of my mind.

A squeeze on my fingers jolted my eyes open.

Lucas's dark eyes shone in the thin light, hues of amber coming forward to mix with the earthy brown, and a crooked smile spread across his mouth. "Hey," he drawled sleepily.

"Hey," my cheeks flushed even warmer. A slight embarrassment twinged at the back of my mind. "Sorry I woke you."

"It's good." He gave my fingers another squeeze and turned his gaze up to the tree tops. Relief swept the awkwardness from my heart. He didn't make a big deal of it, like he knew this day was inevitable, if he was patient. I should've known he wouldn't. Lucas was that way. His go-with-the-flow attitude was exactly what I needed then, and made holding his hand a little more normal.

We lay there in comfortable silence, enjoying this new connection, and listening to the sounds of the world around us. Gray squirrels leaping over boughs rustled the leaves on the trees. Birds flitted about their day, unleashing their birdsong. In the distance, I could make out sounds of the camp. Laughter. The moment was beautiful.

Run.

The word sounded like an alarm in my head. An urgent warning from no one. Nowhere. I thought my mind must've been playing tricks on me, trying to get back to the status quo. I brushed it off and there was silence again. Absolutely no sounds from anywhere. It was like the world just stopped.

A sudden low chittering broke the quiet and reverberated deep in the trees, it shook the ground. The warmth growing inside of me was quickly snuffed out by ice taking over my veins. The calm rhythm of my heart sped up ten fold, fluttering like hummingbird wings. There was only one thing that made that sound. Lord Rorric's beasts.

Run, Grainne.

Lightning coursed through my muscles and I bolted from the ground, pulling Lucas with me. We had to get out of there before the danger I knew was coming reached us.

"Whoa, what's wrong?" Lucas's words stumbled like our rushing feet.

"We need to get inside. We need to get everyone inside now. One of Lord Rorric's beasts is out there!" I pointed wildly toward the trees behind us. My words lit a fire under Lucas. He cursed as his stumbling shifted into movement with purpose. The need to survive.

The creature crashed through the trees behind us, bringing the chittering closer and closer with every step. It was gaining. I prayed the beast chasing us came alone. That would be the only way we had a chance of staying safe. How everyone stayed safe. One beast was manageable, we just had to outrun it. More than that, we had no chance of getting back to warn the others.

Our legs pumped harder as the chaos drew closer and closer. Fear kept me from looking back, I didn't want to know how much the creature gained on us. *Keep running, I'm coming,* the voice in my head promised.

Glimpses of Sanctum's little yard came into view. We only had to last a few minutes more. Relief swelled in my chest, and then my hand was empty. A blood curdling scream shook the trees, sending birds flying from their hiding places. The wrenching sound halted my escape. I looked back, trembling in anticipation of what I knew I would see. It was worse than anticipated. Lucas lay under the mirrored beast, his legs mangled; bleeding and broken beyond any simple healing. The monster vibrated over him, the bloody drool dripping from its maw scented the air with a coppery tang. It raised is razor like clawed paw and waited, taunting its prey. Taunting me.

"No!" my scream came out mangled and desperate. The beast moved its unseeing focus off of Lucas and snarled at me. I swear it smirked because it knew it found its target. What it had been sent to find. Me.

"Run, Grainne!" Lucas gurgled through his fear, his hand weakly reaching out towards me, urging me to save myself. I could only shake my head in response. I didn't want to leave him this way.

The beast roared as it stepped forward, flecking me with droplets of spittle mixed with blood. Its massive paw came down on Lucas's chest with a sickening crunch. An inhuman scream, a peal of death, rattled from my friend. My insides twisted, knotting like snakes. Tears fell like rain. My devastation roiled over into blind, stupid rage. I became a feral animal and charged at the beast.

Before I could take more than a few steps, my path was blocked by a large figure wielding an enormous ax. The glowing blade emitted a hellish heat. His free hand stretched behind him, stopping me from my suicidal attack as he turned his head. Hux. He wore a frightening mask of fury, his eyes glowing blue. "Get out of here. Run. Leave the beast to me," he snarled, his face grave.

I obeyed, though my heart was torn at leaving Lucas, and sprinted towards camp screaming at the top of my lungs. At least I could warn the others, and Lucas wasn't alone. My warning screams startled stragglers heading into the tress to investigate the ruckus. "Turn back, get inside! Run!" No one hesitated to heed the call. The fear in my voice made sure of that.

We stampeded into Sanctum's mouth and filed into the main space. My feet didn't stop there. I needed Eileen. If there was even a fraction of a chance that Lucas survived the beast, she would be the one that could save him. She had to, I couldn't lose him.

I burst into her office and the fire in me ebbed, the power keeping me upright and moving failed me. I collapsed into Eileen's arms. "A beast. Lucas." I barely managed to say the words, exhaustion and grief almost succeeding in stealing them away.

She leapt into action, grabbing an already prepared basket of bandages and salves she kept for emergencies. Even in her haste, she moved with grace. Her calming demeanor instilled confidence that there wasn't any injury or sickness she couldn't defeat. It didn't take her long to have what she needed. We were out the door in moments, running again. People dove out of our way on our mad dash to the camp exit.

A group of men waited at the door leading to the yard. The air was heavy with anxiety, fear, and the need to survive. From beyond the door came the noise of Hux battling the beast. He bellowed over a loud snarl from the beast, their battle cries bled into each other. The sounds continued for long minutes, each grunt and clamor stabbed at my soul. I needed to get to Lucas, but we couldn't leave with the fight so close, not until it was safe. The longer it took, the more likely he'd be dead. He couldn't be dead. Not after I'd made the decision to give him a chance, admitted I felt something for him too; even if it was only a fraction of what he felt.

"Who's out there?" a panicked voice rang out over the din. I wished I could tell them our only chance of survival was. Instead I said nothing.

The door groaned against what could only be described as a wave of energy that pushed against it, tendrils of it seeping through the cracks that were strong enough to unsteady the gathered crowd's feet. The beast screeched a high and desperate yelp, followed by eerie silence. A heartbeat passed. Still nothing. I couldn't wait any longer. My arms pushed their way through the men and I forced the door open despite their protests, against their pulling hands trying to keep me in. They were afraid. I knew they thought it was too soon to be sure the danger had passed. They were probably right. There was no way of telling who won the battle in the yard, the odds were against Hux. I didn't care. Lucas needed me.

Outside, the air sparkled. Tiny, glittering particles floated down around Hux's tall figure, his ax, now dull, hanging from his left hand. That arm dripped with blood, his blood, from where his shoulder had been torn by the beast. Hux stooped down, lowering the limp form of Lucas from his good shoulder to the ground. Five feet from them was the beast, its body mangled and disintegrating into nothing, being carried away by the breeze, like mirrored snow.

I knew what had happened. Hux used one of his sonic bombs.

My knees met the ground when I reached the pair of men. I barely acknowledged Hux, focusing entirely on Lucas. I needed him alive. One good look at him was all I needed to know I didn't get what I needed. His ruddy cheeks paled, his usually warm eyes were empty, and his chest was completely sunken in. No breath. Gone. I fell over him, anointing his body in the torrent of tears that blinded me. Lucas was dead and it was my fault. This never would have happened if I wasn't in Sanctum. If I hadn't given the Founders Noumenon, the stone would have kept us hidden from the beast.

I was so gone in grief that I barely sensed the hand lighting on my shoulder. Through my tear laden lashes I looked up to see Hux stooping over us. He appeared just as broken as I felt. He didn't have to say anything. Something in that moment magnetized me to him and without realizing what I was doing, I found myself sobbing into his broad chest. The ax thunked to the ground. Strong arms enveloped me, comforted me. I just wanted to melt away.

"Take him to the infirmary," Eileen ordered the men, her voice thick with grief.

Without freeing me from his arms, Hux turned. I heard his heart stop for a moment, and his breath hitched. The arms surrounding me loosened. I looked up to Hux's face, his sleepy eyes widened and his jaw hung. I peered over my shoulder, hoping to catch a glimpse of what left the god-like man in such shock. His gaze was locked directly on the ice blue eyes of Sanctum's healer.

"Oh my," Eileen breathed out heavily, just as shocked as Hux. She said one word through the hands cupping her mouth, "Hux."

"Orah," the name fell from Hux's lips in a sighing prayer as he fell to his knees before Eileen.

The men behind the healer exchanged silent glances. It was obvious they were as dumbfounded as I was. My head tried to wrap itself around the past fifteen minutes, but it refused to finish. Everything spun faster and faster until I felt like I was stuck in a tornado. The turmoil over-whelmed every part of me, and the world went dark.

Nineteen

I CAME to on the cloudy bed in Eileen's office, hushed voices arguing beyond the door. My head swam with flashing memories of the afternoon. Lucas sleeping, squeezing my hand when I took it in my own. The sound of the beast crashing through the trees. Running. Lucas screaming. Hux, his shocked face looking at Eileen. No, not Eileen. He called her Orah, one of the Fallen.

The revelation felt like a dream, something too fantastical to be real. But it happened. No amount of wanting could undo it. Lucas was dead. Hux came back. And a dear friend had been revealed to be more than she said. It seemed there were more secrets and deceptions in Sanctum than any had realized. Fingers were being pointed, and I feared they'd land on me once more for my part when I left the haven of the bed someone had lain me on.

There was no avoiding it though. Malingering in the medical office wouldn't change what lie beyond its doors. It would only delay the inevitable accusations and grief. The weight of both threatened to keep me down, smother me in the folds of the lavender scented bed. Fighting against them, I got up, feeling as though my body had been replaced with stone, and slogged to the door to face whatever would come at me.

A tense breeze rushed through the opening, fueled by the hush that had fallen the second I came into view. Judgement. Pity. Despair. Anger. Relief. All of these were displayed across the grim faces gathered in the common room. I'd been ready for it, for the torrent of emotions I'd meet once leaving the medical room, or at least I thought I was. Until my eyes fell on the small figure of Trevor, wrapped snugly in the warm arms of his mother, tears staining his freckled cheeks and soft whimpers coming from his trembling lips. Dina was a mirror of her young son. They'd lost a man they considered a brother, a son.

It gutted me.

Every ounce of thready resolve I had left finished crumbling as Bea approached me, her face stern despite the glisten of tears clinging to the corners of her eyes. "I, I'm so sorry," I managed through struggling breaths.

Her arms wrapped around me, surprising me, as she shushed my apology. "There, there, dear. It's not the time for such worries. Not yet."

Despite the truth bomb landing in their laps, the people of Sanctum put their people first. Lucas was priority. The community needed to mourn before exploding into chaos over the two Fallen Lords in their midst. To them, he held more importance. They intended to honor him, his memory, their way, as soon as possible.

That was the way it should have been.

We were given the rest of the day to mourn and prepare for Lucas's final goodbye, which would take place at night, as their traditions called for. The Founders wouldn't ignore those to keep their rules intact. The news of the Fallen Lords would be dealt with the following morning.

Orah, invited me to help prepare his body, gave me the chance for a private goodbye. Though I was sorely tempted just to have time with her, to ask her the questions burning in my mind, I couldn't bring myself to do it. The loss pierced me too deep. The light he brought into my life had been extinguished under the paws of the beast. The attack played on repeat in my mind. Lucas's mangled, terrified cries. The crunch of his bones. The bloody snarling maw of the beast. They all swirled together to torment me. Guilt, anger, fear, and sorrow boiled in my veins to a point I couldn't keep it together for more than a few minutes. Handling his corpse, cleaning and dressing it, would have broken me completely.

All I wanted to do was run through the forest and hide until nightfall. The Founders, though, had banned outside activities that weren't necessary for the foreseeable future. I didn't blame them. It was only a matter of time before another beast, or multiple beasts, came at us. We were still hidden from drones, thanks to the camouflage canopy being ordered up, also for the foreseeable future.

I needed to be alone. With the outside off limits there wasn't a place in Sanctum to do that. There were people everywhere, gathered to comfort each other and reminisce. Standing alone in the middle of the common room felt suffocating, crippling even. I couldn't take all the eyes on me.

Then my eyes fell on the one place I knew no one would be, the elevator. The mystifying contraption was practically as off limits as the yard, but I didn't care. Hiding away from the pity and sadness that filled Sanctum sure felt like an emergency to me. Rules be damned.

I marched across the common room, ignoring the apologies of everyone I passed, and struggling to hold in the flood that was coming. At the wall, the heel of my palm slammed against the button next to the elevator, a gentle ping announcing what I'd done. Another sounded moments later when the doors slid open to reveal the small gray transport lined with an aluminum railing. Squaring my shoulders, I stepped inside the box and turned to find Orah waiting behind me. Her lips moved, as if to speak, then clamped together; her eyes saying what she didn't need to. *I'll leave you be.* She kept her gaze locked on me until the doors slid closed between us.

The moment the doors shut I leaned against the gray barrier, sliding down as another onslaught of memory ravaged my mind, flashes of the brief happy moments before, and gruesome time bending replays of the beast standing over Lucas. The sound of Lucas's body being broken under the monster's massive paw. The death peal in his shuddering breath that followed. I bit into my fisted knuckles to muffle the screams that came with the memories.

My guilty mind tortured me, bringing more tears. I'd cried so much already, I thought I'd shrivel up and die when they ran out. I lowered myself into a ball on the floor, and closed my eyes, waiting for my grief, my guilt, to kill me too. I didn't expect my sobs to give way to a fitful sleep.

Rough fingers stroked the side of my face, jolting me awake and upright. Being touched while unaware still threw major red flags for me. Part of me feared they came from Lord Rorric, I assumed I always would.

When the panic subsided, I saw Hux crouching before me. He looked worse for wear, still disheveled from his fight even though he'd been cleaned up and had his arm bandaged. The concern that etched his dark eyes clawed at my heart. "I'm sorry."

"What do you have to be sorry for?" I sniffled.

"Touching you. You weren't responding to your name." He adjusted himself to sitting next to me, his head tilted to one side as it leaned against the wall.

"Oh," I drew my knees in. Him being there, in that moment, felt awkward. I'd spent so much time being angry with him, certain I'd never see him again, that I didn't know how to respond to his company. I did know, however, I was grateful. If it wasn't for him, not just Lucas would have been lost. I'd be dead, or back in Galter. The beast wouldn't have stopped with me either. It would have torn its way into Sanctum and ravaged anyone in its path.

My eyes misted at the thought of my friend.

"You're beating yourself up for nothing," Hux commented, to which I shrugged. Lucas being dead was on me, no matter what he said. I'd brought the beast to Sanctum. I'd given up Noumenon. "You are. That young man," he paused, not knowing what to call him.

"Lucas."

"Lucas dying is not your fault. There is only one person to blame. Rorric. Trust me, I've spent too many years to count fighting my own guilt. It took a lifetime to understand you can't bear responsibility for things out of your control caused by someone else. Understand?"

"I guess." I didn't really. I just didn't want to talk about it anymore. I tried changing the subject, "You came back."

"I never really left," he admitted. "I got as far as the edge of the blacktop and changed my mind. I couldn't leave you, so I activated the tracker in your bag remotely and figured the rest from there. I've been living in the forest since."

"You're telling me you've been here the whole time?" I wanted to be mad at him. He could have just came back and joined us. He and Orah would have recognized each other and set things in motion sooner. We could have been well on our way to figuring out how to stop Lord Rorric instead of mourning the loss of a friend. I just couldn't bring myself to blame him further. My head was too wrapped in blaming myself for Lucas. "Don't tell me you had that ax in that pack of yours. There's no way it would fit."

"I did," he nodded, amused. "It breaks down."

My mouth formed a silent *O*. Of course it did. "What about the lookouts? How did you evade them?"

"I'm good at not being found," he joked.

"I'm glad you did," I admitted, looking at him. He stared back, a half-cocked smile bringing out his dimple. My heart stuttered, despite my best efforts. It didn't feel right to feel that way in this situation. It didn't make any sense. I'd just opened myself up to the possibility of caring for Lucas. Allowing myself to have those kind of feelings so soon after, how could my heart be so fickle, so quick to patter for someone else? Let alone someone who made me so mad most of the time I'd known him.

"Me too," his hand reached for the hair that strayed into my face, but he stopped himself. I pushed the copper lock back myself, and gave him a weak smile.

Something else nagged at my mind. It had been Hux I heard in my mind, warning me the beast was coming. "Why did I hear you? In my head?"

"It's almost nightfall," he avoided answering my question, reminding me again of the day's horrific event. It was almost time to say goodbye to Lucas.

"I should get going then," I let the avoidance slide. That was an answer that could wait. The funeral was more important. I stood and pushed the button marked for the common room. After a few moments the elevator opened to an emptying room, everyone was headed towards the tunnel for the funeral. Stepping out of the elevator I stopped and turned. Hux shouldn't have to sit out because he didn't know Lucas. He had the right to be there too. After all he brought Lucas's body back to us. Besides, if I was honest with myself, I wanted Hux by my side. Something about his presence made me feel stronger, kept me from completely breaking apart. I needed that. I turned, placing a hand on my hip, "You coming?"

A quick smile, then a solemn face, "Yeah, of course." Hux stood and joined me to walk to the tunnel. Together we moved in silence through the community room to join the rest of Sanctum in remembering Lucas.

Once night fell, the entire population of Sanctum ventured out into the yard. There was no fear of beasts or drones, knowing the danger they posed meant nothing while we grieved. It wasn't likely Lord Rorric would send anything else this way for a while. He probably didn't know about his pet's demise yet.

We filed into the darkening forest with lanterns dimly lighting the way. The Founders headed the procession, leading their people as they should. I lingered at the back, with Trevor and Dina, just before the men bearing the wooden craft Lucas lay in. I wasn't sure where they had stored the small boat, I hadn't seen anything like it in my time at Sanctum. It was possible they spent they day building it.

Orah, walked with me. She'd been asked by the Founders to stay by my side. Every now and then I'd look over at her tall dark figure and wonder how I'd missed the truth. There'd been little clues, more subtle than the ones she used to peg me as one of Lord Rorric's Maids. Mostly, her interest in Hux when she was giving me the booster.

Sometimes her blue eyes, filled with sorrow, found mine in the low light; but she didn't say anything. She was hurting as much as any of us, and the weight of her discovery only added to that. I understood the guilt that came with being outed by someone else. The shame that threatened to bury you being exposed caused. It ate at your soul.

The procession ended at a river's edge, where the Founders entered the water and the rest of us formed two lines leading up to it. The men carrying Lucas stayed back, waiting for their part in the ceremony. Orah joined Elden and the others, ushering me into the water with her. The water was cold with a current just slow enough to not sweep us along with it. I barely felt it, numbed from our loss.

When everyone was in place, Al called for the boat to be brought in to the water. The pallbearers carried the boat low, so Lucas could be seen by the people as they passed. Many of his friends tossed trinkets or flowers in the boat with him, saying tearful final words of farewell. As the boat passed Trevor and Dina, the young lad tossed his beanie in with a sobbing, "Goodbye, brother," before burying his face in his mother's side.

The Founders, Orah, and myself, formed a circle around the boat once it was placed into the water and the pallbearers had joined the others on the shore. In turn, each one placed an item in with Lucas, saying something about his life, and poured some of their lamp oil onto his body.

After they'd all taken a turn, Al turned to me, "Grainne, Lucas grew very fond of you in the short time you have been with us. I know he was a large part in your adapting to Sanctum, and finding some peace after all you've been through. It would mean much to us, and to him, if you had the honors of sending him off."

His words moved me. Through the tears misting my eyes, I approached the boat. "I don't have anything to give him," I said through quiet sobs.

"You don't need to," Orah comforted. "Being your friend was gift enough for him."

I nodded, a knot forming in my throat. Words failed me. Nothing I wanted to say seemed right. I thought about meeting him, the grand tour he gave me, and our final moments together under the trees. The warmth of his hand in mine, and the lazy smile that spread over his face when I let my walls down just before...

I suddenly knew the perfect words, "Thank you," I said, bowing to kiss the bow of the boat. The Founders parted, making way for the current to carry Lucas down river. Giving the boat a little push, they sent Lucas on his final trip.

As the boat passed Al, he set the wooden craft ablaze. I cringed into

Orah, hiding my face against her at the sight of Lucas's body going up in flames. A new batch of heavy sobs raked my body.

Gently, Orah guided me to shore, where I received many condolences from the gathered crowd. I only wanted comfort from one person though. Hux. My source of strength now that my light had been dimmed with Lucas's absence. He wasn't waiting in the crowd though. I only caught a glimpse of him walking back towards Sanctum, his head hanging low.

Twenty

"LET'S take stock of what we have going on here," Al called the meeting to order. This had to be the biggest meeting I'd witnessed since Elden and his crew brought me to Sanctum, not that I went to a lot of meetings. Every adult gathered in the community space. Every adult. The events of the previous day were monumental. We lost and we gained. It affected everyone. "Lord Rorric knows where we are now. He's taken from us and he knows we have an advantage. We have his Maid," he gestured at me. "We have the source of his extra powers." The room murmured excitedly in response to that revelation.

"But he doesn't know what else we have. Two of the Fallen Lords are under our roof right now. Two. He thinks they are dead. But this leads me to wonder, what the hell?" He gave a pointed look at the two god-like beings in our midst. The room's attention fell on them, looks of awe and accusation. I understood how they felt.

"Orah, you've been living here for years, almost since the beginning. You know our mission, what we hope for. Yet, you parade around as a simple healer? And according to Grainne's full story, Hux has been hiding from the world. She offered you a way to get your powers back, and you refused! Are you oblivious to the plight of the people? Or do you just not really care about anyone except yourselves?"

A majority of the heads in the room bobbed in agreement and a discontented murmur drifted through the assembly. I'd have been surprised if one hadn't. These were the only two beings in this world that could take on Lord Rorric. All they had to do was release their powers from the stone. Take a stand.

"You don't understand," Orah countered. "Not one bit. What you're asking of us is a lot more complicated than that. Not a single human knows the whole story, which has been completely bastardized as it's been passed through the generations. Don't you think we want to help?" she gestured at Hux and herself with sharp hands.

"Then why don't you?" a small voice raised above the crowd. Moments later, Trevor shoved his way through the grown men standing like sentinels. Defensive and questioning. "Why don't you?" he repeated once he got past the wall of men. The little sneak had found a way into the meeting. It didn't surprise me. Trevor was crafty, and itched for a better world. He hated he that was too small to fight. That was why he joined in on many simple, short missions.

"How did you get in here? This is not a meeting for kids," Elden chided his little protege. His words countered the twinkle in his eye. Deep down he was proud of the kid. Trevor was a future leader.

"You let me on raids and scouting missions. Those are far more dangerous than a meeting. I think I should be allowed here too. And, it's a good thing I crashed. No one is asking the right questions. You just want to be angry at them for doing exactly what we're doing. Laying low until the time is right. Right?" The kid's earnest emerald eyes shone up at Orah and Hux, full of hope. He wasn't the least bit disenfranchised by their lack of action. He saw himself in the presence of greatness.

"Smart kid," I heard Hux whisper to Orah. He kept his eyes on Trevor, they beamed with appreciation for the kid's insight. He took a step forward, taking the floor. "I'm not going to waste my breath appealing to you lot or going into a very complicated reason why we did what we did. I'll boil it down the bottom line. We can't, not in the way you want us to. Our hands are tied. Before now, had we even tried, Rorric would have gotten the rest of our powers."

"You once told me powers must be freely given by their true

owners," I jabbed back at Hux. "Are you saying you just gave him yours?"

"No," he shook his head darkly. "That's different. Powers can be taken and stored against will, not possessed. Possession requires them to be gifted. The stone can suck the powers out of someone's body against their will. Rorric can, or could use the stone and access the taken powers for brief amounts of time, a few days at most. He can't keep them. It would be too much to bear and would kill him because they weren't freely given directly to him."

"Well, we have the stone now. What are you waiting for?" Trevor piped up again. He was going to make a great leader someday.

This time, Orah answered the lad, pacing the floor. "While we could release our powers now and be what we once were, it would still make no difference. Rorric bound us against him, even going as far as cursing the powers in the stone with the same binding. He tricked us by stealing droplets of our blood through minor accidental injuries. He formed a bloodstone with them, making it impossible for us to move against him. Our blood protects him from us and our powers. Repels us, if you will. If we manage to resist and attack him, we will be inflicted with our blows instead." I remembered the bloodstone now that Orah brought it to our attention. Another bragging point of Lord Rorric's, though he never said why it was his favorite piece of jewelry. A dull black stone wrapped in a simple leather cord he wore as a necklace, and he almost never took it off. I thought it was an odd choice of jewelry to be proud of. There was nothing spectacular about it.

Orah stopped her pacing and took a deep breath. Her icy eyes began to mist with memory, "That's what happened to Blix. A kill shot from her light bow." Orah's head hung in fresh mourning when she brought up Blix. I wanted to comfort her, make her feel better the way she did for me. From the way she spoke of Blix, I could tell she loved her deeply.

"It's also what allows him to draw our powers from Noumenon for just a small time longer than he would have been able to otherwise." Hux added. "We just can't take him on like we should be able to. Not without getting ourselves killed in the process. We had to hide, for things to be set in motion of their own accord. We had to wait for Grainne."

Hux referred to the way Noumenon came into my possession, opening a new round of questions pointed at me. "Why her?"

I relayed that part of my story, the night I escaped Galter. The room hushed as I told them how Noumenon had called to me, enticed me to take it. When I got to Hux's theories of the gem leading me to exactly what it wanted, and protecting me from sight, my heart lurched. Emotion laced my words as I fought the guilt of Lucas's death from overbearing me. Not having Noumenon on me in the woods that day would always haunt me.

"You see," Hux interjected as my words began to fail me, "she's been key. I don't know why Noumenon chose her, but it has. I firmly believe defeating Rorric would have never been possible without it doing so." His words struck at my core. *There was a reason Noumenon chose me.* I just believed I was in the right place at the right time, not that it was a conscious decision made by an inanimate object.

Those were thoughts I didn't want to deal with. Not then. I filed them away.

The room shifted. The accusations hanging in the air morphed into a rain of shameful understanding. Even for me. When it came to Orah and Hux's situation, the disdain I felt slipped away. My heart broke for them. For Hux. I was awful to Hux in the beginning, and fought against the inexplicable draw he had over me. I had clung to the idea he just didn't care enough. That idea confused me the longer I spent in his company when his actions showed me another side of him. I was also too stubborn to admit I grew to care for him in the short time we journeyed together. He had been the first person to show me kindness with no ulterior motive in years. I was too tightly strapped onto my high horse to see anything dealing with Lord Rorric as anything but black and white. Either with him or against him. The idea that such powerful beings had their own limitations and barriers didn't even cross my mind. That made me misplace who I was really angry with onto Hux.

Life wasn't black and white. At least not outside of Galter.

Just like that, I understood completely. Their hesitation to reveal themselves and help didn't come from not wanting or not caring. It came from fear of failing us; not being able to help us they way we wanted them to, if we knew. The way we needed them to be there. Orah took that and adapted to be someone who could help in some way. She became Eileen, a healer that had no expectations slicing away at her confidence. Hux hid away, whether from shame or fear it didn't matter. They both just needed assurance.

Assurance. The word carried my mind like a current at sea to memories of Lucas. It had been his patience and constance that led me to heal just enough to trust again. Hux needed a Lucas. They both did. Someone who made them feel okay about not meeting expectations, feel accepted for who they were now.

I finally accepted how I felt about him in that moment. I cared. I had from the get go, despite all the fighting against it. In accepting it, I suddenly became connected to him. I needed him like air.

My feet carried me out to meet Hux in the middle of the floor. My fingers twined into his. When I lifted my gaze to his face, he looked down at me and I saw it for the first time. He was terribly broken, just as much as I was. Neither of us could be fixed, not easily or quickly. For the time being, we just needed to be supported. Understood. His eyebrows furrowed together over sad and bewildered eyes, shocked by my turn in attitude, no doubt. "It's okay," I told him.

"What?"

"Help us as you are. Every man counts, boundless powers or not." My fingers tightened around his, anchoring the weight of those words. "You're a brilliant tinker, that's who you are now. We cold use one of those."

"Thank you," the corner of his mouth lifted microscopically, his dark eyes shone gratefully. I could tell he didn't just mean for my vote of confidence in him. For giving him another way to help Sanctum and everyone in it. He thanked me for not hating him anymore.

I couldn't help but release a few tears, which I allowed to roll down my face without humiliation. "Thank Lucas," I choked out. I sent a silent one out into the heavens to him myself. He helped me more than I realized. He'd been brought into my life to open me up, and help me heal. I wanted do that for Hux.

Twenty-One

A WEEK WENT by with no other sign of attack. The community relaxed, believing the beast coming had been a fluke. There were a handful of us that still felt wary; me, Orah, Elden, and Hux included. We were on guard all the time, holding our breaths for the next shoe to drop. We knew Lord Rorric too well to do otherwise. With our encouragement, plans were set in place in case of another attack, and for an emergency evacuation if it turned out the sour feelings in our stomachs were right.

The new precautions proved highly unpopular among the people. Only those assigned to yard duty were allowed outside. The canopy stayed up at all times, and no one, except lookouts and scouting parties, ventured beyond the tree line. The restrictions were harsh, but necessary.

Hux became an engineer for Sanctum, revamping many of their systems and creating new devices for them. He'd even managed to hobble together a couple of surveillance drones. Lord Rorric's had been his invention in the first place, so it was fitting he made them once more to benefit us. Back when they all ruled peacefully together, the drones were used to see where their help was needed most. Lord Rorric corrupted that when he took over and used them as weapons against the people. Hux's tool to help became Lord Rorric's tool for control, one he wanted to remedy.

Orah continued her work as Sanctum's healer, though she could use her limited powers to help now that she didn't have to hide them. Only when necessary, though. Al insisted her healing capabilities were not abused. They'd gotten by just fine without the magic before. They would be just fine without it. Orah appreciated the confidence in her as a person.

Not one person in Sanctum bothered either of them to do more than what was humanly possible. They lived among us without the pressure of their pasts.

The extraordinary healer also took me on as her permanent helper. The people were going to need someone to care for their sick and injured if and when they took back what was theirs. When Lord Rorric was gone. Even though I was thrilled she thought so highly of me, I still tried to convince her I wasn't the best choice to be a healer, "Orah, you do know this is a terrible idea, right?"

"So you keep saying," she laughed, laying a large strip of gauze over the sticky mesh she'd just set out. We were making patches, pain relieving and booster. My arms were sore from grinding herbs into oblivion all morning. "Yet, you are doing a remarkable job."

That was easy for her to say. So far my duties had been administering already made patches, giving out medicines when needed, and putting bandages on scraped knees and minor cuts. I didn't have the training to diagnose they way she did, and I didn't have it in me to handle major injuries. I didn't want to hurt anyone, even if it was to help them heal. "Yeah, at being an assistant. Giving out meds and bandages. If I were given a real task, I'd fail miserably. I couldn't even help with Lucas."

"No one would have expected you to either. Death is hard enough in a small community like ours, let alone the death of someone that close to you. I shouldn't have asked you to. Grief and guilt clouded my judgement. The beasts were my fault," she hung her head and rubbed her arms, growing quiet.

I studied Orah, baffled by the slight retreat into herself. How could she even think the beast attack was on her shoulders? "You aren't responsible for Lucas, Orah. If anyone is to blame I am. Lord Rorric was looking for me. You didn't see the way the beast seemed to grin when it realized the scent it had was mine."

"No, you're not," she echoed the sentiments I'd heard from countless others. Not one person had blamed me for the beast appearing at our doorstep. Despite their attempted comfort, I couldn't bring myself to believe them. Not entirely. "Anyway," she paused while spreading a hefty layer of crushed willow bark and charcoal onto the patches being made, looking at me pointedly. "I have no doubt I made the right choice. It's not just easy things you're doing. I've seen how kind you are to everyone. How good you've been for Hux. Healing is as much about caring as it is the physical aspects of medicine."

"But," I began to protest further.

"No buts. I know what I'm talking about. Even if..." she cut herself off.

"Even if what?"

Orah ignored me, continuing working on the patches, "Could you hand me the scissors?" She wasn't going to get out of that started statement that easily. There was something she was keeping from me. It wasn't just those words that made me think so. All week, she'd been watching me closer than usual, and not just because she'd taken me on full time. I caught her staring quizzically at me at times; with adoration others. When we were with Hux, she never said a word that didn't steer the conversation back to us.

"Only if you tell me what you were going to say," I threatened as I grabbed the scissors and held them to my chest.

An exasperated breath flushed from Orah's lungs, "I see what Hux means by you being doggedly annoying." Of course they talked about me. I was the cause of their exposure, the person that brought them back together. The reason they agreed to step up. She put down the roll of gauze in her hands and led me over to the bed, sitting on it next to me. The lavender scent of the bed washed over us, adding a hint of calm to my restless need for an answer.

Orah's blue eyes pierced me while she looked for the words she wanted. Finally, after a minute, she found them, "Did I tell you about Blix?"

"Ummm, what does that have to do with what you were saying?" The turn she took the conversation in confused me.

"I'm getting there. Blix is relevant, trust me," she shifted in her seat, sending another puff of lavender in the air. She might have done it on purpose to calm me more, I wouldn't put it past her. "Blix was fierce by definition, and in contrast to her softness. Everything about her was soft, from her ash gray curls to her violet eyes. I could get lost in her eyes," she sighed. "I loved her, and she loved me. She's the reason I love lavender so much, it reminds me of her. But, to get back on track, it wasn't just a feeling. Our love was deeper, strengthened by our twin flame."

"What's that?"

"A twin flame is the connection between two meant to be together. That unmistakable pull two people have, that draws them together through time and space. It changes you, and completes you. It burns hot and passionate. I was lucky enough to find the one I called my twin flame. Many go their lifetimes without ever finding theirs. Some, it is said, do not have one.

It is possible to love someone without it, and love again after losing it. Most do not, only because that love pales in comparison to what they had."

"I'm sorry, about Blix. It must be lonely to lose someone like that. The one you share a connection that deep with."

"It is very difficult. I'm sure you've seen it, or heard of it before. Every living thing in the universe has one they are connected with. It's not just a phenomenon of my people."

"Like when someone dies of a broken heart? Or, when someone chooses to live alone after their loved one dies?"

Orah nodded. "When we see our twin flame with someone else, it hurts just as much."

Her story was sad, but I still didn't see what it had to do with what she was going to say. She needed to get on with it. "What does it have to do with this?" I motioned between us, indicating the conversation taking place.

'Everything," she took a deep breath, readying herself for the reveal. "What I was going to say was, even if you aren't connected to someone as their twin flame, you have a way of touching them deeply. It's not just Hux you help by just being there."

"I don't follow what Hux or my skills as a healer have to do with all the twin flame talk," I admitted, feeling dense. The dots just didn't come together.

"I think you do. I think deep down, you know all too well what I'm getting at." Orah went silent after that, silencing me from trying to pull any more information from her.

I scratched my head in confusion, staring at her without a clue to what she talked about. So, I thought about her story, about twin flames. I definitely didn't feel that deep connection with Lucas. I cared for him. I might have grown to love him if we'd gotten the chance. But it wasn't an instant pull when we met. Not like with. . .

Oh.

Oh.

I realized I'd felt that instant, undefinable feeling with someone. A pull that, no matter how mad I got at him, I couldn't get him out of my mind. Could not write him off. It made so much sense now. My eyes widened, and I let out a breath, "You mean Hux is my twin flame?"

"Atta girl. I knew you knew it. And, yes, Hux has told me he felt it. It's why he couldn't really leave when you found us here." Orah smiled brightly, her teeth gleaming against her dark skin. "Hux has been waiting for you for longer than you can realize."

"I. . ." a large boom shook the room, cutting me off. Another one soon followed. Then another, and another. They kept coming. Lights flickered with each resounding blast. Each one felt and sounded closer. It wasn't long before chaos erupted outside the medical room.

Orah and I stared at each other as another, closer, explosion rocked Sanctum, sending supplies flying off the shelves and causing dust to rain down from the ceiling. We both came to the same conclusion at the same time, "Lord Rorric."

"Grab one of those bags and fill it with bandages, salves, meds, pain patches. Anything we can use."

"Right," I jumped into action. I would be learning if I could handle this job in a trial by fire. Literally. "We need to get to the infirmary."

"No. We're evacuating Sanctum. There's another facility a few days travel from here already standing by as backup. We'll treat as we go, until we stop to camp." Orah followed suit, doing what she instructed me to do as well. We worked quickly, heading out the door in a matter of minutes.

Chaos ruled once outside of Orah's office. Citizens of Sanctum streamed like panicked fish, this way and that across the community space. We opted to head for the closest exit, the stairwell. Explosions continued as we pushed our way around clamoring people. After long minutes we made it to the door that led to the stairs. Just as Orah was about to turn the handle, it opened. Out poured a stream of dusty, coughing people.

"This way's blocked," a short bald man gasped between coughs. "The grate is covered by debris."

Going out the yard way definitely wasn't safe either then. I feared we were trapped. "What are we going to do? There's no way out."

"Yes there is. There's an old emergency exit we closed down, at the back of the infirmary. Too many kids were sneaking off and getting lost. It's a long tunnel, with a lot of turns, and comes out five miles away in dense woods."

Before heading towards the abandoned exit, we stopped in supply to grab survival kits. Dina, Cordee, and Trevor worked tirelessly handing out anything they could to the people streaming in. Sanctum would need every last item they had to be taken with us. Orah took a supply pack, heavy with equipment and rations, and handed me the medical bag she carried. I adjusted the one I already had so I could carry both easily, while keeping my mobility. I had to be able to move to help.

We made our way down to the infirmary, gathering lost and scared people as we went. Elden and Al were already there, surrounded by dozens of others, taking turns swinging heavy objects at the doors. As we got closer I could see why. Heavy padlocked chains sealed off the double doors leading into the emergency exit.

As the two Founders tired out, they handed off their tools to other able bodied volunteers. We watched with anxious hope for more than ten minutes with no progress being made. Another explosion rocked Sanctum, close enough to scatter debris with the dust, and eliciting panicked screams from the gathered crows as they ducked to the floor.

More and more people filtered in, the space was getting crowded. The air hung thick with the fear that coursed through everyone's veins. It was a real possibility everyone would be lost if the doors weren't opened soon.

A commotion towards the back of the crowd caught my attention. I turned to see Hux, sporting a minor cut over his left eye, leading a group of injured people up to the waiting crowd. Two small children clung to him like a giant teddy bear.

I pushed my way through the crowd, wanting to help with some of the injuries while we waited for doors to be freed from the chains. It would probably be the last time we weren't moving for quite some time, according to what Orah told me about the tunnel beyond the doors.

"You're here!" Hux exclaimed, relieved when I approached. He put the kids in his arms down, who immediately began searching in the gathered crowd for their parents.

"I came with Orah," I said, immediately squatting to look at a young girl who cradled her wrist. "What's your name?"

"Mina. I fell," she sniffled.

"That's okay, Mina. I do that too sometimes," I told her with a warm smile. I began looking through my bag for some large bandages to wrap her wrist in and make a sling out of.

"What's going on up there?" Hux asked.

"The doors are chained shut. They've been trying to open them since before I got here, which was ten minutes ago." Without a word, Hux made his way to the front of the crowd, offering his help with the chains. Before I could even finish slinging the girl's arm, the crowd erupted in a collective sigh of relief. Hux managed to easily free the door. So much for treating as many wounded as I could.

I tied up the sling, and handed Mina a handful of bandages, "You think you can be my helper while we walk?" She nodded, eyes big as saucers and a smile wide as the moon. "Great. I want you to hand these out to anyone you see with scrapes or cuts, okay?"

"Yes ma'am," she took off with her haul. Some nearby kids overheard the job I'd given her and clamored at me wanting to help too. I obliged, giving each a few bandages as they took off to the tunnel, also taking time to look them over as I did. Part of me expected to see a bunch of kids covered in them. I didn't worry about the waste too much though. I had plenty, and it kept them distracted.

Hux waited for me at the doors when I finished with the kids. "You know, most of those are going to be used on fake injuries."

I shrugged, "It's what kids do. You didn't have to wait for me."

"I wanted to. Someone has to make sure you don't do anything rash."

"Like steal an all powerful stone?" another boom shook the infirmary.

"Or run off to stop these attacks."

"I wouldn't do that. I'm insane, not stupid." Hux rolled his sleepy eyes at me. "I wouldn't! Besides, according to you, I was seduced by Noumenon into taking it."

"In the middle of a risky escape, right after poisoning Rorric" he reminded. He was right, my escape had been impulsive, and I'd made a few poor decisions since. That didn't mean I was going to give up my freedom now that I had it. There wasn't much that would send me on that suicide mission.

Twenty-Two

ORAH WASN'T KIDDING when she said the tunnel was long, and confusing. We walked for what felt like hours, taking turn after turn in the low light. I could see how people got lost wandering in there. Most of the adults, at some point or another, carried children tired of walking. Thankfully, after walking for about twenty minutes, the explosions began to sound farther away. Soon enough, they stopped all together. At least there was that silver lining.

The trek was made in uneasy relief. Though the bombing had stopped, we'd lost Sanctum, our home, and our need to keep m moving didn't allow for head counts. We were being forced to live in unfamiliar wilderness, for most of us anyway, until we could reach the back-up base many of us hadn't known existed. On top of that, if we'd lost anyone, we wouldn't know until we stopped.

Hux walked at my side. His presence alone calmed the storm of anxiety roiling in my heart. Yet it didn't stop the turmoil from crashing in on me all at once as soon as my adrenaline waned. The weight of it wanted to buckle me to the tunnel floor and pin me there until it was satisfied. My body froze as I fought to stay upright and hiccuping sobs tried breaking my chest.

In the dim light, Hux's fingers sought out my own. His touch pulled me out of the spiral that threatened to demolish me. "It's okay, Grainne. We're safe now."

"I don't think I can move. I'm not strong enough for this," it was almost an admission to myself. This attack proved I'd been crazy to ever think I could last out in the world on my own. My head-strong attempts before now struck me as incredibly dumb. I'd gotten lucky in finding the underwater cave, even luckier when I first escaped Galter. Then again, Noumenon had led me without me knowing.

"You are. You can," he moved into my line of sight. I could barely make out his rugged features in the slowly receding lantern light. "I think you can do anything you set your mind to, master any challenge thrown at you."

"You barely know me," I whispered into his chest. Even if what Orah said was true, if he and I were twin flames, that didn't make up for how little we knew each other.

"True. But, your spirit is wild and fierce and beautiful. That's all I need to know to understand how much fight you have in you. Look at all you've done since escaping Galter. That alone is a feat in itself. Like I said when I met you, you have balls."

A short, dry laugh escaped me, followed by a weighted sigh. He was right, I'd managed to do a lot in a few months time. Yet, I still doubted anything I did had been the right thing to do. Especially finding Sanctum. I'd brought tragedy to their doorstep twice in a short span of time. "Okay."

"Come on. Let me help you," he draped an arm over my shoulder and guided me into walking once more. I felt better with his solid frame supporting me. Warm and secure tendrils of contentment twined their way through me, our twin flames buzzing in them.

As we walked, I couldn't help overhear the others. Listening to the conversations happening, there were dozens of people unaccounted for. No one knew if they went missing, escaping in the woods or through the grate before it was blocked, or if they were dead. They weighed heavy on my conscious, guilt rearing it's ugly head again; threatening to stall me all over again.

If it wasn't for Hux staying by my side and talking me through it, the guilt probably would have eaten away at me until there was nothing left. He kept me distracted by talking, often about my misplaced guilt. I couldn't bring myself to talk about the one thing I truly wanted to, though. The connection that made us twin flames. I felt it even stronger now that I knew about it.

I had a suspicion that Orah wasn't supposed to reveal that to me. Not yet anyway. Knowing what I did about Hux, he wanted to wait until the right time. That certainly wasn't while we had the threat of Lord Rorric breathing down our necks.

It was dusk by the time the last of us exited the long tunnel into a thick forest. Hardly any darkening sky could be seen through the tightly woven treetops. Hints of stars peeked beyond the boughs, but not enough for me to get my bearings. The thick foliage provided perfect cover from the prying electronic eyes of drones, though it would do little against the heat based vision of the beasts, or soldiers on foot.

The caravan traveled a mile and a half further from the tunnel exit. Only then did we stop to make camp. Everyone was shaken and bone weary, more than ready to stop and rest for the night. The plan was to camp until the next night. We'd travel at night, when it was safest. Precautions would be taken to keep us so during the days while we slept.

For many of us, sleep was a long way off. The Founders needed to organize the camp for the night, and find out who we were missing. They tasked Hux with using what little equipment they had to try and make a heat shield to hide the camp from beasts. Orah and I went straight to work helping the injured. Everyone else, everyone that was able to, got to work on setting up tents, fire boxes Hux had made, and comforting each other. The night would be long.

In the low light, treating wounds proved harder than usual. All we had to work by was the light of lanterns. Their soft glow hardly provided ample light for anything, let alone ensuring wounds were properly free of debris, cleaned, and dressed. We worked late into the night, until finally, just before dawn broke, we patched our last patient. By then, my eyes were too heavy to see straight.

· · ·

"There's no way around it, we need the bloodstone." Orah's hushed tones pricked at my ears from across the tent. I couldn't sleep, despite the exhaustion that turned my bones to lead. Two attacks in as many weeks had everyone on edge. Even though our camp was well hidden and protected by a quickly hobbled together heat shield, I felt it was only a matter of time before Lord Rorric's forces found us again.

They didn't know I lay awake, or else they probably wouldn't have even been discussing the bloodstone. That option was taken off the table as far as Sanctum was concerned. We all agreed to it. It was too dangerous for Hux and Orah to go after it. They'd die and we'd be out a healer and a damn good man to have in a fight. What powers of strength he had left were our ace in the hole.

"Orah, that's impossible," Hux whispered back, his tone harsh and desperate. He was shaken just as much as the rest of Sanctum by the bombing that took dozens of our population, including Dolly. The people, the other Founders, had already turned to Hux to fill the role left by the one we lost.

Prue and Gerry were also lost in the attack. I felt their loss more than the others. Although, part of me was at peace for them. They could be reunited with their Angel on the other side.

"We have to do this without it."

"I know," she agreed, defeated. "I just don't know what to do now. I don't think we have another choice now. These people have lost too many people. Their fight is dying. If we can do more, we should. They deserve that. She deserves that."

A heavy sigh, vines of the broken bond Hux and I shared, crept into his voice. I felt them around my body as I pretended to sleep, tying me to him. Connected. My own breath quickened at the sensation. If I couldn't calm myself, they'd figure out that I eavesdropped.

"We need Raidyn," Hux breathed nostalgically after a moment, "he was always the key to getting into Rorric's head. Knew how he thought and could formulate counter-plans. He's the only reason I got out of there in the first place."

"What happened that night?"

I turned to my other side, trying to emulate the motion as one does when sleeping, so that I could hear a little better. This was a story I'd wondered about too. Everyone had. No one knew what really happened to The Fallen when they fell by Lord Rorric's hand. No one except them. Now, I had a front row seat to unlocking that mystery. A one man secret audience. I intended to hear every word.

Hux waited a beat, probably making sure that I still slept, that it was safe to tell Orah his tale. After a heavy breath he began, "When Blix tried the stealth attack and died, when your grief over losing her overtook your sensibilities and sent you rampaging towards Rorric, and he banished you, we thought he blipped you out of existence. Raidyn and I had no choice but to steal our way out of the fortress. He helped me, as you remember I had taken a blade and was weakening fast. We found the abandoned building in the woods. For days, Raidyn nursed me through the worst of it, our plan was to continue on after I had healed up. Unknown to me, he had other plans. He left me a note one night, he was returning to the fortress. He was certain he could collect both stones and get back to me. Fool. He'd set a spell, protecting me from prying eyes. After a week, I knew Rorric had gotten him, shocked he'd kill his own twin. I decided to stay where he left me, on the thready hope I was wrong. I'd been there since, thinking I'd lost all dear to me. Then Grainne shows up, after decades of solitude outside of the rare venture for goods, and I felt it, the awakening of my flame. She's changed everything."

"Yeah, I'd say she has," Orah paused and yawned. "I can't believe Raidyn did that. He always was just as hot headed as his blood brother. A better man, but just as tempestuous."

"If he hadn't gone off..." Hux wished.

"We should get some sleep. It's almost noon. We'll visit this again when we get to the new facility."

I waited with my eyes closed for a long time, tears streaming silently down my face, before I realized the tension that had built up in my body. I sprang upright, gasping when I let go.

"Grainne" Hux mumbled, half asleep already, "are you all right?"

"Just a bad dream." I had enough of those that my response was easily believed. Nightmares about Galter, and Lord Rorric. Lucas. I hardly went a night without at least one. "I'm fine." I settled back onto the ground and listened as he did the same. Soon his breathing evened out and gave way to snoring. My mind began to process what I'd just overheard.

There wasn't a whole lot revealed, but some things about what happened to the Fallen Lords. Especially Raidyn. I had no clue Lord Rorric and Raidyn were actual brothers. Twins at that. I didn't think anyone did. I began to wonder what Raidyn looked like. Did he look completely different than Lord Rorric? Were they identical? That thought shivered my spine more than it should have. Two of Lord Rorric. I could only imagine the impossible conditions we humans would have faced if Raidyn had been just like his brother. Evil. Would Orah and Hux even still be alive if he were?

Admittedly, I'd imagined the possibility of two of Lord Rorric before. I'd done it before. Many times. More than I could possibly count. Every night I spent in his chambers. In fact, I hadn't needed imagine it. I'd seen two of him before. I could still see it.

In Lord Rorric's chambers there was a wall of mirrors. The wall of mirrors that gave no reflection. The only thing to be seen in it, was ghost of him. A being bearing his resemblance but without the malice etched into his face. He called it a prison for his weakness. "I've locked away my good side, my weak side. A reminder of my past. Of what being weak gets you," he'd explained the first time I joined him. Over the years the image changed, became paler and thinner. Though, he was never successful in snuffing out his goodness entirely. He didn't want to. He let that part of him live on, as if to torture it.

I remembered watching that image of him, trying to imagine what he would be like if he had a conscience. His pale eyes haunted me, as if pleading for his existence to end.

Pale eyes.

I saw those eyes in my head now, clear as day. I couldn't stop thinking about them. Pale eyes, as clear as the sky after a storm. I always thought it strange that the embodiment of Rorric's weakness had pale eyes when he had dark eyes that flamed with his sadistic nature. The more I recalled it, the more differences I saw. The being in the mirror was smaller, slighter. Even in chains it moved like it was made of wind. I assumed because it was just a projection. A ghostly image of Lord Rorric.

My mind stopped. What if? What if? My thoughts skipped like a broken holo-cast. Pale eyes. What if?

What if it wasn't? What if it's wasn't a reflection? What if it was a he? What if the being in the mirror was Raidyn? The better brother in a set of twins. The good one.

As the revelation blossomed into being, a flutter stirred in my belly. Something exciting and game changing tickled my fingertips and toes. What if? I immediately wanted to wake Orah and Hux, and tell them: *What if?* That would betray me though. They'd know I listened in on their private conversation. There was always the chance they wouldn't care with news like that. Then again, what if I was wrong? I didn't want to get their hopes up and put them in danger for nothing. That would have broken me.

A mad idea formed in my mind. A brash, stupid idea that pointed to evidence I'd yet to learn my lesson about my own limits. Proof of my reckless decision making skills. I didn't care. If it was too dangerous for Orah and Hux to go after the bloodstone, I would do it, and hopefully free Raidyn at the same time.

So much for promising not to do anything stupid.

My plan set, I quietly rose from my sleeping bag and I tiptoed my way out of the tent. There was no point in dressing, or packing for a long trip. I was looking to be caught. I just hoped I could repeat my escape when I had Raidyn and the bloodstone. I was doing this, or would die trying.

Twenty-Three

WHILE SNEAKING OUT OF CAMP, I barely evaded being spotted by the lookouts. The whole plan would have been ruined if they'd caught me. No one was to leave camp for any reason. There would have been no way of talking them into believing I had permission. Then I'd have gotten in trouble with Orah and Hux, possibly the Founders too. They all but declared me as important as Noumenon in regards to having leverage over Lord Rorric.

The shade of the treetops did little to deter the blazing warmth of the mid-day sun. It didn't take me long to regret making a fly-by-the-seat-of-my-pants decision, again. I craved water, or something stronger to keep my sleep deprived body going. Turning back wasn't an option either. I couldn't risk being caught while sneaking back in, or leaving again. I had to deal with what I had, which was nothing of my own and the nature surrounding me. I needed to keep an eye out for a water source while I moved.

Stopping for too long wasn't going to be an option. I wasn't taking a chance on Hux or Orah waking, finding me gone, and coming in search of me. Even without their full powers, they had the advantage of god-like stamina. Granted there was nowhere I wanted to be more than back at camp, and even though turning back held more appeal than I could say, I wouldn't. I had to do this, even though I didn't really want to. The last thing I wanted was to return to Galter. Only death, or worse, waited for me if my plan didn't go well.

As I hiked through the forest, I worked on formulating some sort of plan. I couldn't waltz into Galter with no idea what to do, not having an agenda wouldn't play out well. There was no magical rock in my pocket to protect me this time. I'd left Noumenon with Orah. All I had to go on was my need to take the bloodstone and find a way to free Raidyn; if it was him behind the mirror. The biggest problem had to be getting the stone. I couldn't just snatch it like I had Noumenon. Lord Rorric almost always had it on. The only time I'd seen him without it was when bedding one of his Maids, it got in the way he said.

My stomach churned when I realized that was what I would have to do to even think of getting my hands on the bloodstone. I had to get back in his good graces and in his bed. Just the thought of it made my stomach sour.

Even then I couldn't just take the stone. He wouldn't allow for that, not with how important it was. I saw no way of succeeding. My crazy idea that I could do this was beginning to seem like the absolute worst idea I'd ever had. It looked like I had to abandon it, and go back to camp after all.

Heavy hearted with the knowledge I had to turn back, I decided I could afford to stop and rest for a moment. I settled under a tall pine with heavy boughs dotted with its conical seeds, using a mound of moss as a seat. I breathed in the earthy scent around me, hoping it would console me that I was at least free. It didn't. That freedom I gained tasted bitter knowing how little help I had actually been in the end. Yes, we had the source of Lord Rorric's extra powers, and two of the Fallen in our ranks. One thanks to me. I also helped a lot with the sick and wounded of Sanctum, and was being trained to do more. All those, though, did little to free us from the tyrant without that bloodstone.

In my frustration, I kicked at the ground before me. Dirt and pebbles flew everywhere as I leaned back against the rough bark with a huff. After resting a few minutes, I figured I'd better head back to camp and hope I got there before everyone got up for the night. I didn't want to be punished on top of being a useless failure.

As I stood, a patch of dark stones caught my eye at the edge of the moss I'd sat on. There were several of them, in varying shades of gray and black, in different sizes. A new idea formed. One that allowed me to continue back to Galter. I would find a stone close enough in shape, color, and size to the bloodstone that it wouldn't be noticed if I switched them. I'd still have to endure a nightmare inducing turn in Lord Rorric's bed, but it'd be worth it to get the upper hand. Yes, switching the bloodstone out was just the ticket to save us all.

None of the stones there were close enough though. I'd have to keep looking while I traveled. I already had a cord of leather that would do, the one holding my hair back in a braid. I undid my hair, sending my coppery curls tumbling about my shoulder, and put the cord in my pocket. Now I needed just one thing. Surely I could find a stone that fit my needs while I traveled towards Galter.

Not having to give up, and having a solid plan put a spring in my step. A much needed one. I had to make up for lost time, even though I'd only stopped for a little while. Each second counted. I continued on my hike, my eyes searching the ground for the perfect stone to fool Lord Rorric with. Once I had one in my possession, I'd make my way to a village in search of one of his bounty hunters out looking for me and get myself caught.

Dawn was approaching, and I still hadn't found a stone or a village. Once again, I felt regret rising in me. I'd walked through the day and all night, getting no sleep at all since before the bombings, only eating berries I'd foraged and drinking a few times from meager streams I'd come across. Good water sources were scarce the closer to Galter one got, thanks to Lord Rorric's hoarding of resources. I needed to stop and rest, badly. If I didn't find what I needed soon, unintentional trouble could find me.

I hadn't been able to look for a stone while it had been dark. Since I had no lantern, I'd relied on the minimal light of the stars and moon to guide my steps. I hated those hours had been unproductive search wise.

It wasn't long after the sun had risen that saw the first signs of village life filtering into the world around me. Most notable a path with obvious wear from heavy travel. I needed to slow down and find a stone before I found the village itself. Or before someone found me. I stopped and began to scan the area for stones. There just had to be one near by. There had to.

I heard the rumbling of hooves seconds before the pebbles on the path vibrated from their approach, sending light clouds of dust into the air which grew as they drew nearer. My heart picked up, matching their pace. Only Lord Rorric's men and hunters rode horses. Time was officially running out to find the proper stone to replace the bloodstone. Frantic, I dropped to the ground. My hands clawed at the dirt and grass, raking up stones and discarding them quickly when they weren't right. I didn't care if I ruined a nail or even broke a finger digging through dirt and stone. My plan hinged on that one small thing. Without it everyone was doomed.

The sounds of the horses got closer and closer, thundering in my ears until they were close enough I could smell the animal's sweat from hard ride and feel the heat from their powerful bodies. Dirt sprayed over me when they halted inches from my body, their heavy breathing became a dire omen of failure. I looked up just enough to see two sets of horse legs, but not enough to reveal my face. I wasn't ready to be caught. Not yet. Not when I was set to fail.

"You there, girl!" a man shouted. "Out of the path, make way."

I inched over to the side, making room for the two horses to pass single file. But, they didn't move on. Instead, with an annoyed huff, one of the men dismounted. His leather dusty boots edged into my line of sight. "I said, move from the path." Sun darkened hands shot down, grabbing my shoulders and yanking me to standing. I tried my best to keep my gaze down. The man wasn't having it. "Do you have no respect for authority, girl?" his rancid breath washed over me as his hand forced my chin up, revealing my face.

"Well, well, well. Look like it's our lucky day, Brand," the man still on his horse gloated when he laid eyes on me. He dismounted then, his face eager with greed glinting in his eyes. Soon, his beef-fed frame joined his companion before me, pulling my face from the other's grip with fat, dirt caked fingers. "This girl right here sure looks like that Maid we've been looking for."

"Lord Rorric's bombing must have flushed her out of the forest. Lucky indeed," Brand grinned, exposing yellowish, browning teeth. No wonder his breath was so rancid, his teeth were rotting away. The sight and smell had my stomach fighting to keep what little food I had down. He stroked my cheek, "No wonder he's so intent on finding this one unharmed. She's lovelier than her images, just look at those eyes, Wally. Like fresh spring leaves." I jerked from his touch, staring him down with venom.

"Feisty too," Wally chuckled. "Must be fun. Too bad we can't give her a go. Lord Rorric would melt our skins." Thinking fast, in a bid to keep my freedom until I had what I needed, I twisted enough to sink my teeth into Wally's fat hand, filling my mouth with the acrid flavor of his dirty, sweaty flesh. Faster than a viper, he grappled at me, giving me no time to even attempt an escape. "Hurry up and get a lead, Brand. We're getting ourselves a reward today."

While Wally held me tight, Brand bound my hands together with a long length of scratchy rope. He tied the other end to his horse's saddle. My capture had come too soon.

I couldn't bring myself to cry. The tears would have been useless anyway. There was no point in crying over something I'd gotten myself into on purpose. I'd meant for this to happen. It just wasn't supposed to happen until I had my stone.

I kept my eyes on the ground as Brand's horse tugged me along, still looking for a stone. I would find one. I had to. I wasn't going to let being tied to a horse stop me from accomplishing this goal. Still, the task proved harder than it would have been otherwise. Most things lying on the ground passed by before I could get a good look at them.

At least Brand and Wally weren't traveling at a break-neck speed. Their moseying pace allowed me to somewhat look. All the while, my brain worked overtime to come up with a plan B. When the dark stone spires of Galter peeked over the horizon, I still had nothing. No rock. No plan B. The heavy hand of dread clenched my spirit, wringing out the last droplets of hope I had. Despair began to settle in. Regret that my rash decision ended in failure. My dumb-luck had finally worn off.

My friends, humanity, were doomed to be snuffed out.

As I hung my head in defeat, I noticed a patch of black stones coming up on the path. Perhaps, just perhaps, there was a shred of serendipity left. I dared one final look for the stone I sought.

A few steps away from the rocks, I stumbled to the ground. My knees scraped against the ground on impact, the stinging sensation made me smile. I liked the idea I wouldn't be returned in perfect condition. My body would be marred, bruised and bloodied. I only wished my other scrapes had left scars, Lord Rorric wouldn't want me then. Orah was too good at her job.

Dust filled the air. When it settled, I had to stop myself from laughing with joy. My fall had been timed perfectly. I landed right next to the patch of stones, and right next to my hand was exactly what I'd been looking for. A black, perfectly smooth and oval stone about the size of a thumbprint. If that discovery was the end of my luck, so be it.

I snatched up the stone and tucked it into my pocket just before Brand had dismounted to pull me to my feet. "Careful, Maid. We can't get our reward if you're harmed. Seems like you need a rest." He cut the bonds on my wrists and hoisted me up onto his horse, climbing up behind me. "Don't be thinking you can escape me."

"You're terrible people, you know that?" I seethed, rubbing my wrists. "Turning your back on the world for riches. It makes me sick."

"Lord Rorric's not all bad. He takes care of those loyal to him."

"You wouldn't say that if you had a daughter," I felt him stiffen at the challenge. I'd said something that struck a nerve.

"I have a daughter."

"I hope for her sake she's never chosen as a Maid. You'll regret your loyalty if that happens."

"Isn't going to. My daughter's not going to be a beauty. I'll make sure of that," he bit his words that were laced with sadness. Fear. They were telling. He didn't really believe Lord Rorric to be "not all bad". He saw the monster he worked for, plain as day.

Bile coated my throat at Brand's implication, "You mean you'd harm her to keep her from becoming like me?" His silence said it all. He would. "You don't have to do that. There's other ways to protect her. The rebels, they'd take her. She'd be safe."

Brand's responding silence spoke volumes. He saw nothing wrong with protecting his child by hurting her, if it kept his life comfortable. Men like him were hardly men. They were selfish cowards.

I shook the hurt fro my heart and focused on wrapping the stone in the leather cord, making the differences imperceivable from the one Lord Rorric wore. The project occupied my mind until we reached the gates of Galter.

Twenty-Four

BRAND AND WALLY pulled me through the heavy doors with a rope, like an animal. Sickness rose and knotted in my throat. My whole body trembled, fighting against what it was being forced it to do; enter Galter. The panic was real. My fight was not. Not entirely anyway. This is what I needed to happen, I reminded myself. I thrashed against the lead, crying uselessly, making my captors think what they needed to. That they'd found me and brought me back all on their own.

"You there," Wally called to another guard soon after we entered. I recognized him. He was the same guard I'd bumped into the night of my escape. The one that didn't see me because Noumenon protected me.

The guard appraised me, a slow smile spreading over his features. A smile of relief. "You found her," he half sighed as he removed his helmet. Beneath was the evidence of his punishment for his part in my escape; a horrific scar marred where his hairline should have been. He'd been scalped. I was certain he wasn't the only one that bore new scars. Others had to as well. The ones that had been on duty that night in particular. This one, this one actually ran into me, and his master likely knew that.

"Where is he?" Brand bit. He'd been quiet since I'd called him out on being willing to hurt his daughter to protect her from becoming a

Maid. Mar her face and damage her psychologically for life. My words hadn't sat well with him.

"The Maid Oasis." The bile coating my mouth dried, leaving a bitter sticky taste coating my tongue. Lord Rorric was in the oasis, unaware of my return, lounging with the other girls who frolicked fearfully for him. My return had an audience. How Lord Rorric loved an audience when he doled out punishments on the Maids. He liked to remind them that their lives were his to control. He relished in the anguish that peeked from the Maids' eyes behind masks of enchantment. Even though he wanted us to pretend we didn't fear him, he craved the fear. The pain.

It was evident even in how he treated the world at large. He lived comfortably in Galter, while most of the populace was stultified by his greed and power. Especially in the villages closer to the fortress. Those villages suffered the worst droughts and shortages. Lost the most girls to his carnal desires.

The thought of being brought back to him in the Maid Oasis froze me. The other girls would suffer watching whatever he decided to do. I prayed I had it in me to endure the little tortures before them and persuade him to take me back rather than render me a pile of ashes.

Wally yanked on the lead again, breaking me from my gorgonized state.

The closer we got to oasis, the less I had to pretend I didn't want to be there. Whether it was from reality settling in or not wanting to let the other girls see me returned, I wasn't sure. Perhaps it was both, or neither. Perhaps regret merely began to haunt me.

I felt all of the regret. More than I had over anything before. It consumed me as Wally and Brand marched me towards the oasis. It nearly broke me the moment I heard the indoor waterfall splashing. My heart shattered when I caught those first glimpses of the other Maids in their forced play, pretending to curvet in the water; doting on the man in their midst. Their giggles and cooing played as melancholy music to my ears.

Seeing those girls, my resolve stopped fleeing, and my broken heart reforged into iron. Every ounce of regret melted away. I was doing the right thing. By stealing the bloodstone I was going to pave the way to saving them from this horrible life we'd been forced into.

The oasis fell silent as we entered. The Maids stopped their games, their bodies stilling and slumping. Some fluttered their hands to their painted lips to stifle sobs. Others gasped audibly. Disappointment and disbelief infiltrated every aspect of each and every one of them. I knew what they thought, my return meant there truly was no hope for any of us.

Lord Rorric, still unaware of my presence, stood with a slow growl. His Maids stopped entertaining him, doting on him, and that wasn't acceptable. His hands glowed orange with his rising anger as he began to turn to survey what had caused them to disobey.

I only caught a brief glimpse of the pure anger painted on his face before he registered my return. The tremble of his snarled lip and the fire in is glowing orange eyes sent waves of fear through me. Then his face shifted into something even more terrifying. A malicious victory glinted in his eyes, darkening to their natural coal as his power ebbed. He clapped in delight with a grin that promised nightmares in my future.

In seconds he was on me, his hand caressing my cheek, "My naughty Maid." I fought against the natural instinct to try to run as he studied me, circled me. His hand trailed over my shoulder while he inspected, stopping to breathe me in. He was rapt, fascinated, his mind turning with what he wanted to do to punish me.

"My Lord," Brand interrupted his process. Lord Rorric's head snapped towards the man, who jumped at the sudden motion. He messed up and he knew it.

"Leave us," Lord Rorric ordered the pair of men. He snatched the lead from Wally, wrapping it around and around his arm and hand.

Brand began his retreat immediately. He knew not to push Lord Rorric. Wally, was dumber. "The matter of our reward?" he asked with trembling jowls, he was stupid but no so stupid as to not fear the man before him.

"You want your reward?" he slid up to Wally, devoid of any emotion that could giveaway what he would do. Wally's head nodded, the sweat beading on his brow shaking off in the process. Lord Rorric's mention of reward stopped Brand's retreat. Greed won out over his sense. "I'll give you your reward."

Lightning erupted from Lord Rorric's fingers and engulfed the men that had brought me back to Galter hoping for riches. Screams of pain tore into the peaceful air of the oasis. Their bodies twitched from the millions of volts of electricity that coursed through them. When his flesh began to char and smoke, Wally fell to the ground and his screams stopped soon after.

But Lord Rorric didn't stop. He continued to send raging lightning into them until Brand fell silent, too. When the cracking light subsided, Brand finally fell in a charred heap. Death had been their reward.

"The only one who will be rewarded with her return is me," he laughed, turning his attention back to me. He yanked the shortened lead wrapped around his hand, pulling me close to him. "Now, what to do with such a wicked little Maid?"

Faster than a striking snake, Lord Rorric's hand seized my throat, his fingers sparking with power as they dug into the tender flesh there. His touch burned and soon the acrid scent of burning flesh drifted into my nose. The searing touch unsteadied me, my vision began to fade in and out.

My eyes shot to the Maids across the oasis. They stood huddled together. None of them held onto to the composure Lord Rorric expected of them. They freely cried for me. For themselves. I'd been a symbol of hope, that escape was possible. Then I came back and ended those dreams.

"I'm sorry," the whisper fought to escape me, but it was heard. They heard me. He heard me.

"What was that?" he crooned, releasing his hold on my neck.

"I'm sorry," I repeated, grasping my throat in relief. The raised skin stung under my fingertips, which came away speckled with blood. I knew I'd scar, but I'd live. That was what mattered. I lived and could still accomplish my mission.

"That's all I wanted to hear." He mistook my apology to the Maids as for him. I'd never been so thankful for his vanity. It bought me more time to do what I came to do.

I swallowed hard against the knot forming in my throat. "Let me show you how sorry I am," I lowered my gaze and looked back up through my lashes, "please."

"Of course, my Maid," he chuckled wryly. Lord Rorric stepped over the charred remains of Wally, lifting his robes so they weren't sullied by the mess. As he left the oasis he gave me one last dark look, "I'm looking forward to it."

I didn't dare move for minutes after he left. Neither did the other girls. We wouldn't until we were sure he wasn't coming back. Only then did we come together in a reunion of tears, hugs, and apologies.

My fellow Maids swarmed around me, full of fear and sadness. I made them a promise, "I'm going to save you."

Twenty-Five

MY HEART ECHOED every step on the stone corridor leading to Lord Rorric's chambers. I kept my eyes fixed on the back of the servant before me, rather than take in my surroundings. I knew them well enough, despite being away for so long. I knew which corners were dark enough to conceal me and where every guard was posted.

The cloak hanging around my shoulders transformed into a noose the moment the gaudy doors of his chambers came into view. My heart picked up, panicked and excited for what lay behind it. Soon I'd have answers to my questions. Was it Raidyn in that mirrored wall? Will I succeed? Will I fail?

Time slowed as the doors swung open, wafting the musk incense scented air of the room over me. Memories assailed my mind, memories of every night spent between those walls. They threatened to steal my resolve, but all I had to do was picture the Maids counting on me, the good people I'd left behind, and Lucas's smiling face to remind myself why I had to do this.

My eyes flicked to the wall of mirrors as I entered. There in the reflection languished a waifish figure of a man, nearly identical to the vile man that put him there. He didn't look up at the noise we made entering the room, but he did hug himself tighter with those twig-like arms.

I let the servant lead me to the foot of the bed. Without looking me in the eye she took my cloak and my slippers with trembling hands, which were spotted as though she were decades older than she was. Gray hairs twined with her dark locks and her eyes were bagged with exhaustion. Her job, though no where near as treacherous as that of a Maid, had aged her beyond her years. My heart twisted for her. One more person added to my list of those I fought for.

As soon as she had my shoes and cloak I climbed onto the bed, decked out in white satin instead of the usual dark colors Lord Rorric preferred. It struck me as odd, but I thought nothing of it as I settled on the pillows. The servant left me there, still not daring to look at me or say a word to me. She didn't have to though. I could practically read her mind. My return had disheartened her too.

I let minutes pass before I dared to even breathe. As soon as I knew the servant was far enough to not hear me, I made my first move. Unwinding my hair from its plait, I released the found stone lashed to a leather cord from it and stowed it under one of the large pillows to wait to be switched. Step one done, on to step two.

While the servant was retrieving Lord Rorric, I wanted to find out if I'd been right. Had to find out if I was right. If the man in the mirror was Lord Rorric's twin, Raidyn. I didn't even bother with covering my gossamer gown with anything. There was no time for modesty. I knew Raidyn had already seen all of me. Seen me at my most vulnerable and damaged. That was if the man behind the glass was Raidyn and not just an image. The cold floor stung my feet as I slid out of Lord Rorric's bed.

I stepped up to the mirror softly. The man's impossibly emaciated form hunched against the wall, his arms clinging tightly to his sides and his eyes to the ceiling. His hair hung in limp greasy strands. My fingers drummed on the surface, making a hollow sound. This would be my only shot to learn the truth. He didn't respond to the tapping, but I said what I needed to anyway, "I don't know if you can hear me. If you can see me. I'm here for you, Raidyn."

His head lolled in my direction at his name, pale eyes sharp and wet. Acknowledging. My body sighed with his response, relieved my suspicion was correct. Raidyn started to stir, "No, stop. Don't waste what energy you have," I said quietly and he settled against the wall like a broken doll. His eyes never left me, though, he studied me with concern, lifting a trembling hand to his throat.

"I'm okay. I'll be okay," I assured him. As much as I wanted to speak to Lord Rorric's weakened twin, time was running short. "Your brother has to be nearly here, so I have to be quick. Orah and Hux are alive and safe. I'm going to do everything I can to get you to them. But first, I need to get the bloodstone. Then I'll do my best to free you."

His slight nod looked painful, as though he barely had the will to move it. He understood. Now, I just needed to execute my plan and figure out how to get us out of there.

"Thank you," I mouthed and then dashed back to bed. Lord Rorric couldn't suspect I knew this secret.

I made it to the bed just in time, barely settling myself against the over-sized satin pillows when the doors flung open. Lord Rorric marched in, arms spread as if in victory. He wore a long, black robe over loose pants, chest bare save for one thing, my next target. The bloodstone.

Under the pillow, my hand sought out the replica I smuggled in by braiding the necklace into my hair and hiding the stone between plaits. My fingers locked around it, buzzing excitedly at the idea of it all. I was counting on him taking it off, as usual, and placing it on the small table beside the bed. There, it would just be in my reach for a slick exchange while he was distracted. For once, taking my place in his bed served my needs.

He slithered over me, slime and spiders inching across my skin. Every muscle in my body tensed. I'd rather have been anywhere but there and my body prepared to fight. *This is for everyone, keep calm. Don't blow it now.* My head ordered, but it did nothing to stop the adrenaline coursing through me. My eyes clenched, conjuring the faces of the people I was doing this for. Orah. Lucas. Raidyn. The survivors of Sanctum. The Maids. Hux. Every face that flashed in my head strengthened me.

Opening my eyes, Lord Rorric's toothy sneer, full of gratification, hovered over my face. My eyes flicked towards his chest. No stone. He already took it off. He wasted little time in moving his mouth onto my skin, lapping at it and leaving a trail of saliva that burned like acid. Bile rose in my throat. *Let him do this*, I told myself, it was the distraction needed for eventual victory over him.

He was so consumed by his lust for flesh that he didn't even register my movements; my hand slid from under the pillow and swept over to the table. Keeping my eyes on him, I hovered my fisted hand over the stone there. It trembled so much I feared I'd botch the switch.

I faked a moan as I set my fist on top and flattened it, to cover any possible sound the action might have made. Next came laying the fake next to the real bloodstone. Another moan, masking the clink of the fake being put on the table. The sound elicited grunts of excitement from Lord Rorric. So far, so good.

A shift of millimeters over, and my hand hovered in place to pick up its prize. In moments, I clenched the real stone in my palm. My hand flew back under the pillow, giving the bloodstone a tight squeeze of assurance before releasing it. It would be my strength to endure what I must.

Then, I finally allowed myself take my eyes off of Lord Rorric, close them against what he did to my body and wait. He'd finish soon enough, leaving me to clean myself and wait for his need to rise again. Only, I wouldn't wait, I'd move on to freeing Raidyn and getting us to freedom.

A new, sharp sensation jolted my eyes wide as searing pain blossomed on my left thigh. Something wasn't right. Lord Rorric had stopped. He straddled my legs and in his right hand he held a slender knife, wickedly silver and dripping with my blood. He'd taken my permission to hurt me to a new level.

I began to thrash, to fight to free myself from under him. His free hand flew out in front of him, fingers splayed. "Be still," he commanded, and my body obeyed. I couldn't move anything but my head. He'd cast his paralytic power over me. Of all the powers he ever displayed, his or borrowed, it was the one that I feared the most. He turned his knife over in his hand once and brought it back to my flesh, cutting a small line across my lower abdomen. "Little Maid, do you think me a fool?"

Through clenched teeth I managed a stutter, "No, no Lord Rorric."

"You must. You lie. Now, tell me. Where is my Noumenon?" he placed the knife against my belly again, just above the belly button.

"I sold it. I needed money."

"Lies," he hissed and sliced into my skin. "Try again."

Tears streamed on my cheeks, and onto the pillow and pooling. "I don't know. I swear." It was a half truth. I didn't know where it was anymore. Certainly, the caravan of survivors had moved on by now. Perhaps they'd already made it to the new stronghold. At least that was what I hoped. I hoped they weren't trying to find me. Although, in that moment, I wished I hadn't got caught on purpose. My mission was proving futile, dangerous. Deadly.

"I think you do know, and I think I do too. I know who has my stone," he seethed before leaning in to press his face against my neck. He breathed in deep, "I can smell them on you."

Oh God. I forgot. How could I forget something so stupid? Hux smelled Lord Rorric on me. Orah smelled them both. He could smell them on me. I felt so stupid to have overlooked that detail. My delusion that I could be the hero was going to kill me.

"Okay, I found Hux a few days after I escaped. The stone led me to him, but he didn't want it. I left the coward where he hid and moved on. I haven't seen him since."

"But I think you saw him much more recently than that, otherwise his scent wouldn't be so strong," the knife sliced into the skin above my left breast. I clamped my lips against the scream of pain it caused. "Plus you smell like her. Orah. My Orah." He inhaled deeply, as if savoring a favorite scent. "Not as much as Hux. She didn't bed you, but you were close to her. You have a thing for power." The sneer on his face looked demonic as he sliced right above the last cut.

My cries sounded foreign to me, like a wounded animal rather than a human. "I never bedded you by choice," I seethed between sobs. I let him think what he wanted about Hux. I'd slept wrapped in his arms, safe and secure, one time before the bombings. Not even on purpose. I'd passed out after a long and exhausting day while talking with him, and woke in his embrace. I never bedded him the way Rorric thought. My remark, though, earned me another slice. This time he ran the slick blade along my right cheek bone.

Hollow, rhythmic thumping echoed through the chamber. The noise drew both mine and Lord Rorric's attention. Raidyn stood at the mirrored wall, hands pounding against it furiously. Soundless screams stretched his already emaciated face and fogged the glass.

Lord Rorric whispers in my ear, a smirk on his voice, "Seems my brother wants in on the party. Your lack of reaction tells me you aren't surprised my weakness is my twin. You knew. Of course you did, the company you recently kept tells me that. He doesn't seem to like me hurting you." To that his knife became a blur, slashing and cutting into my arms, chest, and face. In the air my screams battled with his laughter for dominance. The smell of my own blood clawed at my senses, turning my stomach. All the while Raidyn howled against the glass of his prison, desperate to get free.

I knew I was going to die.

A low bellow infiltrated the din in the room, mingling with my screaming sobs, Raidyn's pounding on the glass, and Lord Rorric's evil laughter. The desperate sound grew little by little, and the air began to vibrate with it. Lord Rorric froze as the noise increased. Fear crossed his face for an instant, something I'd never seen before. The knife in his hand clattered to the stone floor and he snatched the stone from the table. He couldn't put it on fast enough.

The vibrations grew heavier and faster until the whole room buzzed like a bomb about to explode. A brief moment of calm overcame the room, a complete silence that filled every minuscule space it could climb into, and it felt like all of the air had been sucked away. With a deafening pop the door splintered inward, off of its hinges. Hunks of wood and metal were sent splaying across the room. I tucked my neck in best as I could against the paralysis holding me, to try to protect my face. None of it came close to hitting me. One large piece, however, hit Lord Rorric, his body accidentally shielded mine. He flew off of me, hitting the solid bed post and rolling onto the floor. When I thought the worst of the explosion was over I craned my neck, attempting to see what happened.

The dust in the air obscured me from seeing anything much more than a large figure looming where the door used to be and glowing blue eyes. Those eyes set my heart leaping out of my chest. Hux. He lingered in the door, eyes trying to make sense of the chaos he'd created. The dust obscured his vision as much as mine.

As the air cleared, I began make out a slightly smaller form behind him. It had to be Orah. Her statuesque figure was hard to mistake for anyone else. They both took cautious steps into the room, on high alert for an attack from Lord Rorric. I'd seen no trace of him since debris knocked him to the floor. He could have been anywhere.

At least I had the real bloodstone.

A heaviness settled all through me, dark and unnatural, and my body lifted off the bed. My gossamer gown trailed under me, dripping with my blood. I felt sensations of ice and fire, a juxtaposition of being made of lead lighter than air. It meant nothing good. It terrified me, especially as I couldn't rail against the unnatural feeling. My body was still confined by Lord Rorric's spell, who still had yet to be seen.

My head turned back and forth from the figures becoming clearer in the door and the rest of the room. I searched for Lord Rorric, as if seeing him would make this situation any better. He was still nowhere I to be seen.

The invisible constrictor wrapped around me continued to tighten its hold as the dust settled. The wounds from Lord Rorric's attack ripped and twisted, opening more as my body was squeezed. My bones popped and cracked, releasing an avalanche of pain. It was like lightning replaced the blood in my veins, crackling and burning me from the inside. My screams filled the room, pushing out all other noise until my lungs ran out of air.

I couldn't breathe. Panic set in and I searched again for Lord Rorric. Finally, I found him at the far end of the room, his eyes glowing a sinister orange that matched the auras around his hands. One hand he held raised before him, fingers splayed in a message to stop. The other, raised in the air, and clawing in on itself. One hand held Orah and Hux where they were, the other was the force behind the invisible snake squeezing the life out of me.

"Did you really think you could out-wit me? Beat me? You have no power that can match me, no way to get them without this," he nodded his chin down to the fake bloodstone. His voice may have held the confidence of an unbeatable man, but the waiver of his lip and the fear in his eye said differently. He feared them still. "Goodbye," he cackled, raising his clawed hand higher in the air and closing the fist completely. The aura around his hands vanished seconds before he did.

With the closing of his fist, the assault on my body rampaged to completion. The constriction happening to my body devoured me. My skin burned where it tore and stretched as bones pieced through it, and my insides twisted violently until I felt something in me pop with searing pain. In the next moment, I was splayed on the bed again, a broken doll. I bled and convulsed. Every movement felt like a hot knife impaling me over and over again.

"No!" Orah's cry was muffled by blood filling my ears; by the gurgling of blood in my throat, the rattle in my chest. Red streaks and black spots floated across my vision. I barely saw her climb on the bed with me through them. Orah was followed closely by Hux, his large hand seeking out mine. I winced at his touch. Orah's iced eyes melted down her cheeks. Her hands hovered over me, "I can't fix this Hux. I can't unless I'm plenipotent."

"I know," he choked on the words. I knew he stroked my hair. Thanks to the connection I recognized now as being twin flames, I knew the touch of his hands anywhere. They were my calm, my center.

"The pi, pil. . ."

"Shhh," he hushed. "Save your energy."

"Pillow," I finally managed to stammer between sucking in air to steel the pain. "Blll, bloodst, stone."

"What?" Orah gasped, along with frantic movements that jostled the bed. Pain exploded with every movement. Hux's hand remained on me. Water splashed on my forehead. Tears. "Hux! She has it! The clever, stupid girl, I could kiss her."

"What?" he exclaimed without making sudden movements.

"The bloodstone. She has it. She switched it somehow. Get the stone from your pocket now!"

The room was so quiet, so dark by then that I thought I'd already died. As lights swirled in the air, I was certain I had. Until I realized the orbs were their powers released. Blue and purple orbs danced around the blackness that splotched my vision. A burst of warmth, a summer breeze swept along my broken body. The lights and wind died down with a burst of white light then were gone as suddenly as they came.

"Hurry Orah. Please," Hux begged. "Save her, I can't lose her."

"I know, my friend. I know." I felt another set of hands light on my head. Orah's hands. At first it felt like scratching at my scalp, an itch that spread and burned. Then her touch morphed into flame, I felt like I was being burned alive. The cry coming from me could have shattered stone.

"What's wrong?" panic vibrated in Hux's voice.

"I don't know. I'm trying to heal her. I think he left a cast in her stronger than my healing powers. One that damages her more if someone tries to heal her. She needs something drastic. She needs her own powers."

"She can have mine, if she'll live."

"No. Hux, she'll lose you."

"I don't care," he sobbed. His emotion added to the stabbing pain already in my chest. My dying, broken body wanted to comfort him, and I couldn't.

"She needs you as much as you need her. I don't think she'll survive losing you after all she's lost already. I've had my love, and I miss her. Let me go to her. Grainne can have my powers." Those were the last words I heard before blackness took me.

Twenty-Six

I BOLTED AWAKE, heart racing and dripping in sweat. The nightmare of my death seeped away from my mind, leaving a residue of darkness that chilled me to the bone. No, that wasn't a nightmare, that had been real. My bones remembered crunching together, my skin remembered tearing. I remembered the searing pain of my insides ripping to shreds. Yet, there was no trace of that pain left. I felt made of feathers and cool spring breezes; light and pure. Perhaps this was the dream. Death.

Smugness etched into my soul. At least I helped restore Hux and Orah. That light show of their powers released from the stone had to be the best last memory to have. I did that. I'd gladly do it again to save my friends. My people. I'd die for them a million times over.

Only, what happened to Orah and Hux. Their conversation over my dying body played back in my mind, coated in molasses, slow and muffled. The sticky thickness prevented me from getting to it completely. All I understood was the frantic and sad tones that sprang hot tears into my eyes. I wiped them away, inspecting my hands after. The wetness that glittered on my fingertips came back tinged rust. But why? If I were dead, if I became a ghost or spirit, or whatever happens when we died, why were there remnants of blood mixed with my tears? Would a ghost even have tears?

Sitting up, I took stock of myself. My body crusted with my blood, more than I thought possible. The gossamer gown was stained and torn. Other than that, no evidence of Lord Rorric's attack showed itself outwardly. Only the mental damages remained. The wounds were gone. My limbs were intact. As a test of my mortality, I pinched myself, and the small gesture hurt. This wasn't a dream. I didn't exist in a strange state of fantasy-like death. I lived.

How?

Whispering caught my ears. My head turned finding Hux kneeling, head hanging low, by the mirrored prison that held Raidyn. I was surprised to see more people in the room. Elden, Cordee, Al, and two others. I hadn't seen them behind Hux and Orah. Hadn't heard them while I writhed in pain, dying.

Orah lay by Hux's legs, one bloodied hand splayed up on the glass wall where it pressed against Raidyn's hand on the other side, in matching position. Raidyn's form flickered frantically and a he adorned a mask of grief. His mouth moved rapidly, as if in prayer.

I swung my legs over the side of the bed, lowering my feet one at a time to the cold stone floor. Testing my legs, I slowly rose. My footing seemed stable enough. I took a ginger step towards the scene at the mirror. Morbid curiosity pulled my gaze back to the bed I just left, I dared a glance over my shoulder. The white satin sheets were covered with rusty red blossoms that marked where I had lain. There was so much blood, too much for me to still be alive.

I continued on, my feet deftly navigated the wooden debris of the door scattered across the floor. As I went, my eyes wandered, taking in the room anew. Everything looked sharper, cleaner. The walls were etched in a glowing blue, latticed like an iron bridge. I drifted towards the opening where the door once stood. The new bright barrier hummed lightly as I approached, it almost sang. My fingers fluttered towards it, driven to touch it out of curiosity. A moment of hesitation came, leading me to pull back before allowing my fingers to run along one of the paths. I expected heat and crackling. I got ice. A sense of security rushed over me. I knew these magical wires would keep those inside safe.

I allowed my fingers to caress the lines as I walked away, back on path to the trio of beings at the mirrors. Though I knew I wasn't dreaming this, nothing felt entirely real. More surreal. Being in Lord Rorric's chambers, alive, after everything, shouldn't have been a possibility. What he did to me would have killed anyone.

The strangeness of it was highlighted with the group before me. Orah and Hux hadn't been inside the fortress since they were forced out decades ago. Raidyn, in his glass prison, was on the brink of being reunited with his godly family. These were things no one in this world thought would ever happen again. Including the five people from Sanctum that stood by, watching the Fallen Lords with tears in their eyes. Was this a small taste of a future within our grasp? Humans and gods united and bringing Lord Rorric's reign to an end.

My mind wanted to imagine it. The celebrations that would come at Lord Rorric's fall. The dream was a real possibility now. My heart felt too lost now, though, to put too much effort into it. Ruptured by the mourning in the air. That grief kept me from seeing it fully. Recognizing what they cried over took priority to imagining a future.

I pushed past the wall of bodies and got my first real look at what happened. I fell to my knees next to Hux, devastated by what I found.

Orah's body was what mine should have been. Torn and broken, blood seeping from every open wound and every orifice that could be seen. Death rattled in her chest with every strained breath. "Orah," I weeped, "how did this happen?" the question more directed at Hux than Orah.

"She took on your injuries, to save you," Elden sniffled in Hux's stead. "She. . . it was a miracle."

Ghosted memories assaulted me, fuzzy and weak. The muffled conversation between Orah and Hux as they struggled over my ragged body, played again. This time clearer. Orah saved me by transferring her life force, her powers into me. I became her. She became me. We exchanged places. This realization crushed me. "Orah. I'm so sorry."

Her dark fingers, stained red, fluttered weakly into my hand. Her touch was a hint of winter. "Don't. . . be. . . sorry," she gasped. Her hoarse voice strained to come out, "It's not your fault."

"Why? I'm not important. The people need you not me."

He answer came on a rattle in her chest, "Love." With that word Orah became still, her cold fingers slipped from mine and slapped lifeless against the floor. She was gone. Her last word would be the epitaph of her life. Her last act in life had been done for that one thing. Love. As long as I knew her, she acted from love. Until her last breath. Always.

Her gift of life meant so much more than her motherly relationship with me. She acted for Blix, her lost twin flame whom she'd be reunited with. She acted for the people of this world, those needing to be saved. She acted for Hux, the chance to give us what she once had. We could not let her sacrifice be in vain. Her legacy of love had to triumph.

My arms sought out Hux, needing his comfort. Needing to comfort him. Our tears flowed together, a river of loss. A single thud on the mirror joined our grief. I didn't have to look to know it was Raidyn releasing his pain. Orah's death must have been torture for him, knowing he wasn't able to comfort her beyond his prison.

A ray of comforting warmth tickled around my body and I pulled my face from Hux's chest. Tiny purple lights danced in the air. They hit my body and vanished, becoming one with me in bursts of somber joy. I knew immediately it was Orah saying goodbye. She must have held onto a small bit of her power to do this, wanting to comfort us all in some small way.

When the orbs cleared, Orah's body was gone. Only the stains of her wounds remained. A solemn reminder of her and what she did.

Twenty-Seven

ORAH'S TAKING of my death hung over Lord Rorric's bedroom.

All of us wanted to grieve under its crushing weight. Our spirits were zapped of desire to do anything other than that. We couldn't, though. The threat of Lord Rorric still loomed over us. Part of the problem was we'd essentially trapped ourselves in his fortress, in his bedroom, surrounded by ghosts of violence and death. The barrier erected by Hux both trapped and protected us. We needed to face our reality and do something about it.

But first, we needed to free Raidyn from the prison that had held him for decades upon decades.

Freeing him was a puzzle with no defined edges, a game with no clear guidelines. We could only make educated guesses about the rules Lord Rorric set in place for the prison to contain Raidyn. He shared some powers with Rorric, evidenced by the flickering he exhibited while grieving over Orah's dying body. Magic must not have been able to leave the room, or else he could have just teleported out of there. What we did know was what it was, sturdy. There wasn't even a scratch on it from the door exploding.

Still, it wouldn't hurt to try breaking it in the same way.

"Hux," I sniffled. I was hesitant to break the deep silence that had taken residence with us, "we need to help Raidyn."

His head lifted from its sagging position, eyes glistening and rimmed red. He looked as ragged as I felt. "Yeah," he exhaled, nodding his head. "Orah wouldn't want us to delay on her account."

"Magic can't get out, am I right?" Raidyn nodded and flickered to demonstrate. Just as I'd thought. "Can magic get in?" He nodded again. "Couldn't we just teleport him out from this side?"

"It's a good idea, Grainne," Hux sighed, "but we don't have that ability. Raidyn still has that in his possession and he can't use it from his side. And reversing the mirrors won't work. We can't risk it damaging our protective barriers. We don't know if Lord Rorric and his men are waiting for us to remove them, and pounce the moment we do."

He had a point there. A good one. With Lord Rorric's teleporting skill he didn't need the door. He sensed any point of entry open, he'd likely take it. He had to know Hux had Noumenon on him. Getting that back was a priority for him.

“What about Grainne?” Cordee chimed in. “What can she do with healing powers?”

Cordee brought up a good point, I had no clue what I powers I had to work with. I had no idea what my powers were, or what theirs were for that matter. I needed to be asking better questions. “Cordee's right. What do we have? What can we do? Honestly, I have no idea what I can do now. Or you."

Hux chuckled, the corner of his mouth barely lifting. "I guess you've got a lot to learn about yourself now. For now, a crash course." He rubbed his face, his mental exhaustion was clear. We all felt it. "Orah was always what you knew her as. A healer. Her powers were absolutely the most threatening to Rorric. She wasn't left with any remnants of her higher abilities, just low level healing. That didn't mean she lost her touch when they were taken. She was smart, never fully relied on her power when she was healing those in need. She knew what she was doing.

But, her powers also encompassed the other side of the coin. Power of death. Decay. That is what made her absolutely terrifying and saintly at the same time. She always sought ways to heal and understand rather than bring destruction with her touch. It was absolutely a last resort."

Master of life and death. I stared at my hands in disbelief. This power I'd been bequeathed sounded more intimidating, more daunting to have coursing through me than I could have imagined. Flashes of Lord Rorric using such power on the Maid I was introduced with sent a shiver down my spine. I knew exactly what I could do. Suddenly, I was afraid to touch anything or anyone. My arms crossed my chest, hands tucked under my armpits. Holstering my weapons. The move registered another chuckle from Hux, Raidyn shook his head and laughed silently behind the glass.

"What about you? How did you break the doors here? Was that a small fraction of your powers?"

"Before getting my full abilities back, I had a fraction of the strength I possess with them. The door was not that. There's no way I could've done that before. Now, yes. That was a microbomb, another device I'd made to mimic my powers. My last microbomb. Soundless and efficient.

On top of everything, our main abilities, we have excellent hearing and sight. We can speak telepathically to those we are connected with. We're fast. And obviously immortal outside of mortal wounds."

He dropped a lot of information on me, including why I heard him in my head the day the beast attacked. All of the knowledge was almost too much to bear, but I couldn't say no to it now. It would be wrong of me. Disrespectful. I would accept my new mantle, grow into it and flourish. I just wished I had more time to do it.

"We can smash the mirrors," Al suggested.

"We could," Hux agreed, "Even if it's magically reinforced, I can do it." He looked between the rest of the group, getting our impression of his idea. He pulled power to his hands in preparation. It wasn't a bad idea, in my opinion. Raidyn, on the other hand, shook his head fervently. Not a good idea. He mocked hitting the mirror then splayed his fingers out, mimicking shattering. He then pointed to himself and then motioning to the floor, I got what he implied. He'd be stuck in the mirrored room with no way out. Shattering was out.

I didn't think of that. No room actually existed beyond the mirrored wall, just an altered replication of the one we were in. If the mirror broke, the room disappeared. Raidyn disappeared with it. "Doesn't look like a good idea, we don't want Raidyn stuck forever."

Hux nodded once in agreement, rubbing the stubble on his chin. "If only I knew how that bastard put him in there. There has to be a way to make the mirror into a portal. Make the glass pliable. Weaken it without breaking it."

Weaken the mirrors. The phrase vibrated in me and gave me an idea.

"I could try," I offered meekly. All I could do was try, I had no idea if I could actually do it. My powers were completely foreign to me, using them would have unknown results. I didn't even know where to start.

"Huh?"

"The death part of my powers. I can try to use them, weaken the mirror. Decay it, as you say, so it's soft. Weak. Just enough to pull Raidyn through. Magic on this side only."

Hux went silent, dark eyes squinting as he thought about my newest idea. His mind worked over all the variables, building results piece by piece. Like one of his projects. Thoughts connected like wires, ideas soldered together with bit of information. Rejecting parts that didn't fit. Tinkering. "It could just work, if you're careful. What do you think?" He looked to Raidyn, who responds with a shrug and a not completely confident thumbs up.

If I was him, I wouldn't be all that confident in me either. This would be my first time using my new powers. There was an enormous possibility I'd use too much, send the decomposition power too far into his mirror world and reduce him to a pile of ash and bone. Butterflies flitted through my veins at the prospect. Nerves like that could easily make me mess up.

"Are you up for it? It's a bitch of a way to introduce yourself to your powers."

"Do we have a choice?"

"No." Hux gathered me into his arms and rested his chin on my head.

"I'm counting on you to guide me through this. So I don't turn Raidyn into an old man," I said into his collar as if in prayer. He was right, this was big. A trial by fire. I needed to borrow his strength and steadiness to get me through it.

He pulled away and placed his hands on my shoulders. "Anything you need," he assured me, his dark eyes gazing deep into my own. "Elden, you and the others need to move to the other side of the room. Just in case this goes wrong. I'll try to shield you from any stray pieces if this mirror shatters."

The group from Sanctum went to the other side of the room, passing the blood covered bed. Each one eyed the gore with the same look of horror and fear. Witnessing Lord Rorric's wickedness first hand was rough, especially the first time.

With our friends settled a safe distance away, Hux and I were ready for me to test my powers. Together we stood and faced the mirrored wall. The shiny surface gleamed at me, taunting me to weaken it. "Before we begin, it might be good to know glass has a long life. It can take up to a thousand years for it to decompose. It might take more effort that you think in order to weaken the surface. Perhaps even to its breaking point, and we pull Raidyn out just before it cracks."

"Got it. Any idea on how I actually do it?"

"I can't help you there. I don't know the mechanics of how Orah summoned or controlled her powers. My best answer would be to listen to your instincts. Let the powers guide you." Raidyn nodded in agreement with Hux, his long inky hair shaking.

I placed a trembling hand on the glass before me, the smooth surface felt alive under my touch. An equally shaky breath rose from my mouth. Raidyn, placed his hand opposite mine, his mist colored eyes wide, optimistic, and encouraging. The gesture didn't help. It made my nerves worse. "Raidyn, I think I'd feel a lot better if you weren't touching the glass." His mouth formed an *o* and he shuffled back a little. "Thanks," I breathed.

A hand dropped on my shoulder. Hux's eyes were glowing blue when I peered at him. An electric current traveled through the pathways of my muscles and nerves. I felt bolstered, filled with an extra shot of strength on loan from him. He didn't need to say anything, neither did I. But this was exactly the thing I needed to push my doubts away; slay my nerves and try.

All of my focus transferred to the mirror before me. I imagined flowers, wilting and frosted over. The beginning of the cold time of year when everything in nature either hides or dies. Bones of creatures lost, bleaching in the sun. A vibration started in my chest, chasing after the borrowed strength of Hux. They collided into thunder that rumbled down my arm and into my fingers, where it exited and grabbed onto the mirror. I could feel it's solidity, unyielding and strong. As the seconds ticked by without any result, I feared I wasn't able to do it. Then the firmness of the mirror started to weaken.

A new sensation came back at me, like sand and ice clawing at my fingers. A metallic tang coated my tongue and filled my nose. The magic in the mirror sought to punish me for sucking away its integrity. My stomach roiled sending chills coursing over my body, and my head pounded with a heaviness that seemed unbearable. I hated it. If it was just the mirror failing, I couldn't imagine the way I'd feel if I was using this power on a living thing. It would probably kill me. No wonder Orah hesitated in using that side of her powers.

Not sure if it was the magic or the decay of the mirror that made me feel waves of nausea, I came to a conclusion. This power was something to be feared.

The mirror's resistance began to fade further, becoming thinner and thinner. Each unseen layer I shed created energy waves along the shiny surface. The glass groaned, warbled, and shimmied faster and faster as the minutes went by. The sensations continued until a sudden emptiness began to creep in to my hands, just when the surface seemed to flicker like a candle in the wind.

"Hux! I think it's about to crumble. Get Raidyn!"

Like lighting, Hux removed his hand from my shoulder. I felt a distinct change in my power with his gone. It became softer, less energetic. Gritting my teeth, I pushed myself harder. Keeping my connection with the mirror took every ounce of my concentration.

Hux's large form scooted around my side, waited a breath, and watched the mirror's surface fade in and out. Studying its rhythm. When it faded, he shoved his arms in. Raidyn locked his hands around Hux's wrists. Hux's eyes burned brighter as the dying mirror fought against giving up its prisoner. With a deep bellowing groan, he pulled hard.

Raidyn flew out, tumbling against Hux, who crashed into me. We all fell into a heap at the foot of the mirror. My connection with it broke with an audible pop. The mirror shattered, sending fragments and shards flying out into the room. Hux lurched over me, protecting me from the sharp pieces.

As fast as the mirror exploded, the air cleared. Where the mirror once covered the wall was now nothing but the stones beneath. After a moment of silent disbelief, Raidyn burst into hoarse laughter. "You did it! I'm free after all these years. I'm free." His arms wrapped around me tight, "Thank you sister. Thank you."

His infectious joy spread through the space and warmed everyone in the room, easing the pain of our loss, just a hair. It was a momentous occasion, one the people of this world would hopefully note as a turning point in their history. A moment that would be spoken about for generations to come, as long as we succeeded in taking Lord Rorric out of the equation. The small victory felt amazing. At the same time, it served as a reminder that our real fight had yet to come.

Once we had Raidyn out of his prison we moved right to restoring his powers to him. His slender fingers wrapped around the two stones delicately, reverently. He looked like a saint touching a holy relic. A calm smile spread across his face as he touched Noumenon and the blood-stone together. White orbs blossomed from Noumenon, like petals of a flower, and swept into Raidyn's chest. His almond-shaped eyes lit white for an instant as the last orbs entered their rightful home.

The restoration of Raidyn's magic did more than give him back what his brother took. He was completely restored. His long emaciated muscles filled out just enough to deplete the living skeleton look he had since I first saw him. Still lean and long, but strong. The shadows beneath his eyes disappeared and his obsidian hair reflected the light from the barrier. This was the warrior the legends of the Fallen painted. Formidable and fast. He was far from healed, though. The psychological scars from years of imprisonment would lace his soul for what could be the rest of his life.

We all bore unfathomable scars.

Twenty-Eight

"WHAT DO WE DO NOW?" I asked, lying in Hux's lap. We couldn't stay holed in Lord Rorric's chambers forever, protected by the humming magic barrier. It held us like a cage while it protected us like a mother's womb, until we were ready to dismiss it and face him, and whatever else he intended to throw at us. At this point, we had no idea what that would be.

There was also the question of the bloodstone. Had he figured out that the one he wore was a fake yet? Or, did he think he'd won somehow? His enemies were in his clutches, fretting over the dead Maid they came for. We wouldn't know anything until the barrier came down.

That alone felt terrifying, for me at least. Probably for Elden and the other rebels that came with Hux and Orah as well. They were just thrown headfirst into reaching for their goal, with no preparation. The Rising was nowhere near ready to take on Lord Rorric, even with the help of two Fallen. If I hadn't disappeared from camp, they'd still have been months away from any progress.

Hux and Raidyn, on the other hand, were made for this. They were seasoned warriors, smart and powerful. Magic had been in their blood their whole lives. They knew what they were doing. I, on the other hand, didn't. It was pure luck I successfully freed Raidyn. Luck and trust.

Thats not to say the pair them were prepared for the battle to come, they had as much hesitation holding them back as I did. Lord Rorric was not a stranger to playing dirty. Hux and Raidyn knew this all too well. He bested them before, in order to strip their powers from them. They needed to assume he was capable of doing it again.

"We destroy Noumenon," Raidyn replied. "That way there is no chance of it falling into his hands again. And the bloodstone."

"You're right. We can't have any chance looming over us that he could take our powers again." Hux held out the stones in his hand. "They are too dangerous to keep intact."

"Want me to..." I wiggled my fingers in the air. Part of me itched to test out my powers again. The more I used them, the better control I'd get.

"No," he caressed the side of my face, filling me with warmth. I closed my eyes happily, still amazed how easy allowing his touch was. Weeks ago, I'd have shied away from any uninvited contact. "I've got this one." He clenched his fist around the stones, and squeezed until his knuckles went white. When he opened it back up, the two stones were reduced to dust, black glittering with red. He let the particles sprinkle from his hand onto the floor. "What we need now is a plan." We couldn't lower the barrier until we had one.

"The best plan is built on knowing your assets," Raidyn advised, coming to sit closer to us. He ran his fingers in the debris of the stones thoughtfully. "What my brother doesn't know and what he does."

"True," Al agreed.

"He knows we have Noumenon. Had Noumenon," I recalled the demand he made hovering over my body, and the searing pain of the torture. "He thinks I'm dead."

"He doesn't know I'm free," Raidyn added.

"He thinks Orah lives, and we grieve for Grainne. He's waiting for us, me and her, to emerge powerless and beaten again."

"He thinks he has the bloodstone," Elden chuckled. That bit of truth was an unseen tack in the bottom of his shoe. He didn't realize it was there, right under his nose waiting to reveal itself. He was bound to notice it sooner or later, that the stone hanging around his neck wasn't the bloodstone. Just a rock, from a pile of rocks. Nothing special about it at all.

Raidyn stood, holding a pinch of the stone particles in his fingertips. He rubbed them together, letting the dust fall. "So, we let my brother believe his truths instead of the truth." Raidyn laid out our plan in that sentence. We needed to reinforce what he believed to keep the upper hand. I had to be dead. Orah had to live. Raidyn had to be trapped. Hux had to have Noumenon.

I sat up, "How do we do that?"

Raidyn grinned and raised his face to the ceiling, releasing his power across his skin. He became like a star, brighter and brighter until the light was blinding. When the glow subsided it wasn't Raidyn who stood before us.

We were more than tense, having crept our way through Galter with no intervention. It was eerie and jarring at the same time. Lord Rorric could swoop in anywhere, anytime, with no warning. So far, we'd been lucky. Though we knew he waited somewhere, hoping to lull us into a false sense of security. We were too smart for that.

Hux carried me in his arms, pretending he carried my lifeless body. The dried blood still covering me help set the illusion, even though my wounds were healed. For all Lord Rorric knew, Orah had drawn her powers from Noumenon to heal them after I'd died. My healed wounds also set the foundation for him to assume Hux and Orah had his precious stone, when in actuality all we had was a handful of red and black dust that I held tightly in my fist. I planned on revealing it at the most opportune moment.

Raidyn, who could do spell work just as well as his twin, changed his appearance to look like Orah. The facade was more than skin deep. Even his voice and mannerisms morphed into hers. The result was uncanny. If I hadn't seen him transform with my own eyes, or seen her disappear after her death, I would have sworn he was the beautiful healer.

Our rebel friends followed us nervously, keeping a few paces behind. We weren't sure if Lord Rorric knew they were here or not. Either way, they wanted to help despite the danger. Brave didn't begin to describe them, mere mortals going against a being that claimed he was a god. I was beyond proud to call them my friends.

We made it to the large iron and wood doors that led out to the courtyard, the last door before we were out of Galter. We weren't holding our breaths that we wouldn't encounter Lord Rorric at all. It wasn't like him to turn tail and hide when he had the upper hand, or at least thought he did. His arrogance always won out. If we were going to run into him, it would be beyond those doors. We were prepared.

Before moving through the doors, Hux looked down at me, "You got this?"

"Yeah," I responded, even though I wasn't sure I did. "I'll stay perfectly still until it's time." They'd assured me I wouldn't have to do much against Lord Rorric. The heavy lifting would be done by the rest of them, with assists from me if I could manage getting close. I'd use the decaying power to subdue him, but not kill. I wasn't ready to feel a life ebb, not even his. Not even after all the years of abuse at his hands.

He flashed his dimple at me, his sleepy eyes full of warmth. Love. "Okay then, snuggle in. It's time." I followed his instruction, though part of me didn't want to. I didn't want to be blind to what happened out there, but in order for us to have the best advantage, I had to.

I heard the heavy doors open, a draft of warmth washed over me. Immediately, I sensed a change. The air felt prickly, poised with battle. Lord Rorric indeed waited behind the doors.

"Do you honestly think I'll let you leave here with my Maid, Hux?" Lord Rorric's voice dripped haughtily with perceived victory.

"She's dead, not worth anything to you anymore" the lie flowed from Hux easily, he bit his words angrily to sell our ploy.

"She belongs to me, always. A Maid like her doesn't lose her worth in death." Lord Rorric's words sent ice coursing through me. I wasn't even safe from his machinations in death. What did he have planned for me? My imagination flared to life with horrific images. I had to fight to stay still in Hux's arms. "Might I add, how thoughtful it is you fixed her up for me, my dear Orah. Saves me the trouble."

"I didn't do it for you," Raidyn seethed with Orah's voice.

"You can't keep her. I won't let you."

"I could be willing to let you go with her. I just need my Noumenon back."

"We don't have it," Hux referred to his self and the disguised Raidyn.

"Lies. I know you do. She all but confessed."

"We don't. If we did, we'd never give it up."

Footsteps approached from behind. The rest of our group made their appearance. "Oh look, you brought friends," Lord Rorric mocked. "So cute how they think they can fight a god like me."

"Just let us pass, and we won't bother you. You can keep your throne if we can give her a proper goodbye," Raidyn offered falsely to let Lord Rorric keep his position as sole ruler of the world.

"How sentimental, and stupid. You have no position to be making that kind of deal with me. Or have you forgotten my bloodstone?"

"No," Hux replied, his voice cold. "We haven't. We don't care about your stone. Grainne is worth the fight, regardless." He gently lay me on the cool cobbled stones, and stepped over me. It was then I dared to turn my head, my ginger hair falling half over my face, and opened my eyes just a slit.

Raidyn moved like a ghost, joining Hux in his advancement on his twin. Halfway there, Lord Rorric flickered, he meant to teleport away. Seconds later he disappeared, reappearing right in front of me. His claw-like hands reached out towards me. Instinct to preserve myself kicked in, and I flinched. The second I did, I regretted it. I'd made a mistake and revealed our secret too early.

"What's this?" Lord Rorric's voice cracked with surprise. "How is this possible?" he reached for me again, eyes gleaming wickedly. Revealed, I used my feet to try and scoot away. I proved too slow and he was inches from nabbing me. His reach was suddenly blocked. Raidyn, still disguised as Orah, appeared between us. At the same time, Hux came up behind the devil, wrapping his arms around Lord Rorric, keeping him from moving any further. Confused rage rattled from his throat, "You can't keep me from her, Orah!"

"Oh really, brother?" Raidyn asked, dropping his magical facade, and raising a white aura around his hands in preparation to attack.

"You can't hurt me," he sneered back. In response, Raidyn's wrist flicked, a resounding snap followed. Lord Rorric gasped in pain, cradling his own wrist as best he could while Hux restrained him. His coal-like eyes dulled with panic.

I got up, standing next to Raidyn, "I think you'll find they can," I loosened my grip on the dust in my palm, which showered the cobbles at my feet in red and black. "I switched your bloodstone for a regular old rock before you maimed me. Hux destroyed them both as soon as we freed Raidyn."

"And Orah?" he stammered, actual concern hanging on his words.

"You killed her." Hux whispered loudly in his ear. "You killed the one person you actually cared about other than yourself."

"I never touched her! I wouldn't have!" he fought against the hold on him.

"But you did, when you tried killing Grainne. Orah had to take drastic measures to save her, trading her life for *my* twin flame." Lord Rorric's eyes widened at Hux's revelation. He knew that our connection to each other made Hux even more dangerous. He'd stop at nothing to protect me. Avenge me.

"She chose death to let love thrive. To let us beat you. To be reunited with her twin flame." Raidyn added.

"I should have been her flame!" Lord Rorric screeched. "And now, you'll pay for taking her from me!" He let out a low whistle, a chorus of chittering growls filled the air seconds after. He called the beasts.

I stepped back as his five remaining beasts made their appearance from the shadowed corners of the courtyard. He'd had them lying in wait this whole time, cloaked in magic so they weren't seen. His own ace in the hole. Only the members of The Rising had weapons at their disposal, small and sharp, but useless against monsters. We three had our powers. Terror shadowed through me, this was a fight I knew I had little chance in. That Cordee and the others had no chance in. The mirrored monsters would chew us to bits. I wouldn't be fast enough against them even if I tried getting close enough to use my powers on them.

Lord Rorric took the opportunity of the distraction and teleported from Hux's relaxing grip, popping up behind the half circle of beasts that approached us.

I shouted for the rebels to run and hide. After witnessing Lucas die under the claws of a beast, I had no interest in watching more of my friends do the same. "No can do, Grainne," Elden shouted back. "We're in this." I scanned the group of them, and their faces said it all. They were ready to fight and die if need be.

"Keep back, Grainne. Leave the beasts to us," Hux and Raidyn took up defensive stances in front of me, their power auras on full display. Despite his order, I tried to follow their lead, standing out in front of the rebels with us. I'd protect them if I could. My new powers only flickered across my fingertips before fading out. I couldn't hold an aura yet. Still, I prepared myself to defend us.

Four of the beasts clashed with the two men before me, the fifth staying back to protect its master. Not one made a move to come at me, nor did they look like they would go after the others. The beasts focused on the biggest threats. That alone seemed strange, though I didn't think much of it. I was too concerned with Hux and Raidyn. They were sorely outnumbered, there had to be a way I could help.

Hux punched one of the beasts as it leapt towards him, its shiny maw dripping with drool. The beast flew across the courtyard, landing with a crack on the cobblestones, slivers of stone scattered under the impact. It tried getting up, but yelped in pain and collapsed back to the ground, leaving Hux to wrestle with one beast. He grappled with the animal, neither one gaining or losing ground. With his full strength restored, Hux was evenly matched with the beast.

Raidyn teleported in and out, dancing around the two beasts he stood against and using spells to block their attacks. Their growls grew in frustration at every invisible barrier they encountered. They riled more with every blocked attack until they were near frenzied. He spun to avoid the snapping jaws of one beast, while blocking the other with a bolt of energy.

A hot puff of breath came from beside me. Slowly, I turned and found myself staring right into the snout of a beast. I'd been so focused on watching the fight before me, I hadn't seen the fourth beast recover and sneak its way around the courtyard. I threw a panicked look back at the people I wanted to protect. They wielded their inconsequential weapons with shaking hands. Each of them knew they stood no chance against a beast, yet they would try.

"Run, please," I begged them, replaying Lucas's death beneath the claws of one of these monsters. I couldn't bear seeing anyone else die that way. "I can take it alone." The rebels backed up just inside the heavy doors of Galter, ready to aid me if they thought it necessary.

I took a hesitant step away from the beast, readying to run from it; to lure it from my friends. I willed my power to flood my hands, the aura only sparking erratically. It'd have to do. I held them up before me and prepared for the attack.

Yet, the beast made no move. It barely even acknowledged me. It just stood there.

"Why don't they attack me?" I called out, not really expecting anyone to be able to respond. Their focus had to stay on their fights.

"They were Orah's before Rorric stole them, abused them into what they are today," Hux shouted without turning his focus away. "I wasn't sure they'd recognize her power in you, it seems they do." The beasts had been hers at one time. No wonder she felt so much guilt over Lucas. I wished I had known and could have comforted her better.

Hux's revelation about the beasts became a silver lining. There was a chance I could protect the others from them, if they in fact recognized her power in me. If they did, I could control them, take them from Lord Rorric and turn the tides of this fight.

Cautiously, I reached up and touched the muzzle of the great animal, surprised that it's mirrored fur felt soft and downy. The beast didn't react to my touch. I closed my eyes and brought up images of peace in my mind; a still lake, a cloudless sky, a sleeping baby. Hot, smelly breath washed over me. I opened my eyes back up in time to catch the tail end of a yawn coming from the animal as it sat on its haunches.

The snarling behind me ceased at the same time. I looked back to the fight to find the other four had mimicked the one I touched. They were telepathically linked, a hive mind. What one did, the others followed. I smiled, amazed.

In a flash, Lord Rorric was on me. His long fingers wrapping tight around my throat. His eyes lit by the desperate fire of defeat. Somehow, I stayed calm, even as Hux and Raidyn charged from behind him. I held a hand up for them to stop. My other hand wrapped around his wrist, a purple glow emanating from it. I imagined him frail and old, weakening with time. This time there was no foul taste coating my tongue, no eerie feeling of death chasing my pulse. This decay I sent, felt natural.

Slowly, Lord Rorric's grip loosened. His arms flopped to his sides weakly as human aging began to take effect on him. Liver spots and wrinkles appeared over his eternally youthful skin, and his dark hair became streaked with white. His eyes glossed and his cheeks sagged.

Seeing him weakening caused something in me to snap. All the pain and humiliation he'd every dealt coursed through my veins seeking their revenge. All I wanted in that moment was to see him turned to dust, to revel in his suffering.

I slowed the flow of my power, relishing watching him deteriorate. His eyes, frantic and scared, searched my face looking for something that wasn't there. The girl he could control. His fear only fed my vengeance.

"Grainne," Hux softly called and placed a hand on my shoulder, "stop."

"He needs to pay, Hux. He needs to pay for everything."

"He can pay another way. Killing him doesn't make it right."

My head shook, releasing the enchantment of vendetta that gripped my heart. Hux was right. This wasn't right. Killing Rorric didn't make anything better. My power paused, leaving Rorric a shell of what he was; weakened and trembling. He wasn't a threat anymore.

Still, he couldn't remain free. I knew just what to do with him. "Raidyn, can you find me a mirror?"

He blinked away, and was gone for only a moment before coming back with a tall gilded mirror in tow. Hux raced to help him prop it against the outer wall of the fortress. I led Lord Rorric there. He was docile as a lamb, complying with my commands. It didn't feel right, to lock him away with no fight. He had to suffer, if only for the torment he put his own twin brother through. He deserved a long life of suffering, years to reflect on every girl he harmed. Decades to reap the punishment of what he did to our world and the people in it. Millennia to simmer with the knowledge he'd ultimately killed the woman he loved. I wanted to restore him to as he was before locking him the mirror. I wasn't sure I could do it, but I was going to try.

"Hold him for me," I asked of my friends. Each one took an arm.

I positioned myself between Lord Rorric and the mirror, placing one hand flat against the glass surface and the other on his still bare chest. My focus split, sending decay to the mirror and life to the now elderly god. At first, my powers struggled to obey the counter orders, they fought against me. I pushed my thoughts harder until finally I felt them bend to my will. The mirror began to warble and wave as it decayed. Lord Rorric began to struggle as his fight returned with his youth.

Soon the mirror was on the brink of shattering, "Now!" I ordered, pulling my hands in and stepping away. Together Hux and Raidyn shoved him through the shaking mirror surface. The second he was through I grabbed the gilded frame, my fingers grazing the mirror, and rushed life back into the glass. In moments, it solidified again, but not before Lord Rorric managed to get a hand through.

He yanked with all his might, trying to free himself to no avail. His raging screams couldn't pierce the glass. "Goodbye, Rorric," I dropped his title, affirming that he finally held nothing over me. "Hux?" his eyes flashed blue as he drew back his arm. With all his power he punched the mirror. It shattered into thousands of pieces, frame and all. Rorric's hand broke free of his body, falling to the courtyard ground. A pool of blood seeped from the dismembered appendage, that twitched briefly before becoming still.

It would be the only part of him ever seen again.

Twenty-Nine

AFTER THE DEFEAT OF RORRIC, all my body wanted was to collapse and rest. The new power coursing through my veins took a lot out of me. A lot. My body's call had to wait. I had more important business. Business that I'd dreamed of for myself for years that I needed to share with others like me. A promise to keep.

I took off, back into Galter, running as fast as my feet could carry me. Hux's calls after me went unanswered. Nothing could stop me. This task was too important to delay for any reason. Keeping this promise was the most important thing on my post- Rorric list. My feet carried me to the Maid's Oasis. Where I became a Maid twice, something no one would ever be again. Not while I had a say in it.

As I rounded the bend leading into the oasis, the sounds of the waterfall greeted my ears. A row of guards stood at attention around the water. Behind them, the Maids, the former Maids, huddled together trembling. No doubt they were told Galter was under attack, just as they likely heard traces of our fight. The probably listened intently, trying to decipher who the victor had been. Listening for the promise I made earlier to be fulfilled.

A wide smile spread over my face when I spied Rorric's gaggle of enslaved lovers. The girls all stared wide eyed, the horror on their faces fading when they saw me standing before them. Hope dared to bloom there.

The guards took one look at me, and lowered their weapons. Even in my disheveled state, covered in dried blood and clothes ripped to shreds, they didn't perceive me as a threat. A few looked at me with pity. They knew what abuse Maids endured at the hands of their master, and turned blind eyes to keep themselves safe.

A sandy haired guard stepped forward. "Maid, you need to join the others. You'll be safe here until the attack is over." His hand reached out for me only for me to sidestep away. His eyes narrowed at my dismissal. He was one of those guards; one of the ones that didn't care how awful Rorric had been because it didn't affect him. He lived well and that was all that mattered.

"Are we saved?" a small voice rose from the girls. The guard before me shot a look of irritation back towards the group. Definitely one of Rorric's loyal men. I needed to watch him in case he became a problem.

I laughed, "Yes. Rorric is gone." The gathered crowd exchanged uneasy glances. Whispers spread through the girls, wondering and hoping what I said was true.

"Impossible, Maid. Lord Rorric is unbeatable. He has power no one else has," the sandy haired guard scoffed.

Soft steps came up behind me, and the men before me tensed their weapons. Over my shoulder I saw Hux and Raidyn, both with their eyes glowing at the threat the guards posed. I turned back to the guard in charge, "Do not call me Maid. There are no Maids. Not anymore," I sent my power to my hands, which easily lit purple in response. My head shook as I smirked to myself, of course they'd behave once the real danger had passed. At that point I repeated, "Rorric is gone. Myself and the two last Lords, Hux and Raidyn, defeated him for you all. To free this world from his tyranny."

The majority of the guards dropped their weapons and bowed in recognition of our standing. We defeated Rorric, we were to take his place. A few others, the sandy haired man included, hesitated. They had every right to be nervous about the change in power. It threatened their ways of life.

"You can join us," Hux boomed, throwing power in his voice, "or, not. But know this, we will not stand for the cruelty of Rorric to continue on in any form."

"Choose wisely," I added. The threat behind our words had them kneeling with the others. "Now, go. Spread the word as far as you can."

Hux and Raidyn eyed the reluctant guards as they stood and filed from the room with the rest of them. We would have to be careful of men like them as the news spread. Seeds of discord, of evil, were dangerous enough without sprouting. If any of those loyal to Rorric sowed their newfound discontent, it would spread.

Some of the girls followed the guards out, but a handful lingered behind. A girl with sleek chestnut hair stepped forward. I recognized her as a girl that arrived a few days before my escape. "Is it really true, Grainne?" she asked, hesitantly reaching out for me.

"What is your name?"

"Posey."

I let the aura around my hands dim. Stepping up to Posey, I took her hands in mine and looked into her green misting eyes. "Yeah, it is. He's been banished to a place he will never return from." In an instant, her arms were around me, and the other remaining girls began to swarm us, Hux and Raidyn included. That moment, the gratitude and relief that poured from the girls that used to be Maids, made everything worth it.

Word of Rorric's defeat spread fast in the following days. But there was one place I needed to make sure they heard it myself. My village.

I thought I'd never set foot in it again.

The village where I grew up sat a half day's travel south of Galter. As we approached my heart contorted and broke. The land around the village had dried out more that I remembered. Water no longer flowed down the small waterfall the children used to play on, only a thin stream trickled down the slope. The fields of dried grasses no longer grew tall, having given up completely. The scene dampened the excitement I felt about returning and sharing the news they'd waited for, for so long.

It made me want to attempt to use my new powers on the land. To see if, perchance, I could heal it. I couldn't do anything to help the waterfall. Healing powers couldn't conjure water from nothing. That would require more investigation.

As we entered the village itself, I could tell nothing had changed other than the increased evidence of drought. Too thin children still played in the dirt covered streets, caking themselves in a fine layer of dust and sweat. Their mothers would stress later on how to get them clean without enough water. Adults milled about in the hot sun, no work to be done in the dead fields left them with little to do.

My feet needed no reminding how to find my parent's meager home. It was little more than a shack, no real rooms to speak of. Just an open living space with a wood burning stove for cooking and heat, with sparse furniture. More often than not, my father would give up sleeping on the bed and take a spot on the floor near the stove, letting my mother and me share the bed that was barely big enough for one. They both sacrificed so much for me to give me what I needed to grow, only to have it thrown in their faces when Rorric's men took me.

The moment I saw my childhood home tears welled in my eyes. I paused in the dirt road, dust flying in the air marked the abrupt stop. A sigh left me was I looked at the structure. One of the windows was boarded, the fresher lumber contrasted against the graying older wood around it. Parts of the roof had been thatched with dry grass, a simple repair to fill holes in the aging tiles. In the remaining window the same tatty plaid curtains rustled as a slight woman in a pale blue dress walked by them.

My mother.

Hux took my hand in his, drawing my attention to him. I still marveled how his touch never made me flinch, even when it surprised me. Connecting to Hux was natural as breathing, evidence of being made for each other. "Are you ready?" his brown eyes gazed softly at me. No one needed to explain to him how special this moment was for me. I nodded, unable to speak. Together, we took the next step towards the house.

The knock beneath my hand sounded hollow against the old door. It echoed the nervous feeling in my stomach. Feet shuffled inside, soft and light, sending hummingbirds flittering through my heart. The handle turned and I swallowed hard. When the door opened, I felt like I could fly.

My mother stood in the frame, her red hair pulled away from her face had begun to gray in the past few years. Other than that she looked as she always had, younger than her years with bright clover eyes and rosy cheeks. She was beautiful, even with the port wine birthmark kissing the edge of her lips. The slight defect had saved her from sharing the fate I had.

Her weathered fingers trembled to her mouth, her face crumbling with the emotion that spilled down her cheeks. A thick sob broke from her chest, "Oh my goodness."

"Hi, Mom," a choked through tears. Over her shoulder, my father appeared. His haggard face, weary from the harsh living they endured, mirrored hers he moment he saw me. "Hi, Dad." He broke into a smile that lit his sky blue eyes that shone with unspilled tears.

Wordless, they moved at me together. Hux stepped aside to allow them to embrace me. Our quiet tears gave way to laughter as we hugged, warm, secure, and together against all odds. We stood there for ages, arms wrapped around each other and enjoying the unexpected reunion to the fullest extent, before coming apart.

"How is this possible? We never thought we'd see you again," my father wiped away a few errant tears.

"Rorric is gone. He won't hurt anyone ever again."

Their faces wore twin looks of disbelief. "Really? How?"

"It's true," Hux confirmed. They looked at him, as if they just noticed him with me, and their eyes grew wide. He'd allowed a sliver of power to glow behind his eyes and fade, exhibiting he was more than a man as proof of what we told them.

"He's Fallen," Mother stammered a whisper.

"I'm Hux," he confirmed, unleashing his dimples and stretching a hand to them.

Heartily, my father took up the offering, shaking Hux's hand for a moment before pulling the large man into another tearful hug, "Thank you. Thank you for coming back, for saving our girl."

"Don't thank me," he pulled out of the hug and motioned to me. "Thank Grainne. It was her that saved me."

My parents looked back and forth between me and Hux, disbelief once again overtaking them. I called up a fragment of the power residing in me, letting it settle in my eyes, just to help them understand. Their mouths gaped at the display, until finally my mother said, "Well, it seems we have a lot to talk about."

Thirty

THE VISIT to my village invigorated me. Seeing my parents, having their support behind me, gave me the boost I needed to face returning to Galter and take on transitioning to a new world. A better one.

Before I left my village, I tested my powers out one more time. I put my hands in the earth of the fields surrounding the village and imagined life springing forth. The ground hummed beneath my touch. Soon, the dry grasses and dying plants began to brighten, brown giving way to green.

While I focused on the land, Hux went to investigate the source of the waterfall. He found the river diverted by man made canals heading toward Galter. Something we were sure to find in other villages as we visited or sent envoys to help the people recover. He destroyed the canals, blocking them with rocks and logs only he could manage to lift.

The villagers that gathered to watch me work cheered as the waterfall became flush with water once again. Children and adults alike didn't hesitate to clamor up the hillside to splash in the cool water as it refilled the shallow basin, sliding down once it was safe.

When Hux returned, we silently slipped away while the village rejoiced, leaving them with the world blooming around them. We stopped in villages we came across on our way back to Galter, bringing the same gifts to them that we had in mine. Every village we left, we left with the sounds of celebrations filling the air.

With so many places needing a jumpstart of help, it took days rather than hours to reach the fortress. By then, there were already people migrating and gathering outside the gates seeking help from the returned Lords and offering tribute to us for the miracles we had already provided. Thanking us for freeing the world.

We spent months, after that, traveling back and forth between Galter and the surrounding areas offering the same help. Sometimes Raidyn joined us, others he went off on his own doing what he could do best to help. Mostly, it was summoning rains to drought ridden areas that didn't have nearby water sources.

As time passed we began sending people out in our stead. Ambassadors offering aid under our guidance. Guidance we offered as a means to teach the people independence from us. We could have taken control of the world, the way the Lords once ruled before Rorric betrayed them. But none of us wanted to. We had no desire to rule, only to live freely. Of course, we'd help when it was absolutely needed, when we were called on. Other than that, we craved simple lives.

Al and the people of Sanctum were our first ambassadors. They were solid proof that the people could mange this world themselves. The former rebels were more than happy to take on the role. They traveled the villages handing out aid, booster kits I carried on making, and new contraptions Hux invented to help people recover faster.

It wasn't long before they began delegating their jobs to others they found in the villages willing to act as ambassadors. They transitioned, as we hoped they would, from helpers to leaders. They would be the ones to lead the world into a better future. A free one.

There was one thing we asked of them before we left Galter in their capable hands. We wanted to give the world a name after it had gone so long without one. A name to honor those we lost in the process of freeing it; Lucas and Orah.

We called this new world Lorah.

. . .

Raidyn went his own separate way after leaving Galter; after leaving governing Lorah in the hands of our friends. He took off on his own, in search of a new life. He'd missed so much being locked away behind mirrors, he wanted to see the world and help rebuild the far reaching corners. We would miss him, but we knew we'd see him from time to time.

Hux and I went back to where our journey together had started, his workshop. Of course, I had to take my new pets along, despite Hux's protests. There was no way I'd leave them behind. They needed me. Besides, I didn't think they'd do too well with strangers in charge of them. In the end, we came to a compromise. They would stay in Galter, only until we had a barn built for them. All but one of them anyways. Hux allowed me one. As luck would have it, one of the beasts turned out to be with pup, and I, of course, picked her and named her Hope. From the looks of her, it wouldn't be long before she had her babies.

"How long do you think before the barn is built?" I curled up on Hux's ugly green couch, tucking my feet under me. I'd grown a little attached to the beasts in the short time we stayed at Galter. They really were just big babies when treated right, as evident by the massive girl sprawled out before the couch, half rolled on her back and tongue lolled out of her mouth.

"You're impatient, you know that," he plopped down next to me, scratching Hope's burgeoning belly just before. She chittered happily from the attention.

"Yes, I do. And it gets results, if you hadn't noticed."

"I did," he grinned, unleashing his deep dimple, and tweaking my nose. He moved a stray strand of my hair behind my ear, "I wouldn't have you any other way, my Grainne." His dark eyes grew heavy, full of wanting.

"Good," I breathed. My heart sped and my skin warmed under his heated gaze. Since the fight at Galter, we'd spent a lot of time together. We were still getting to know each other, the new us. Hux, ever patient, took his time with me. There was no rush in advancing our relationship. I loved him all the more for it.

His large hand caressed the side of my face, working its way back into my hair. He pulled me forward, gently laying his lips on mine. Electricity jolted over my every nerve, bringing me to life. I never knew a kiss could be so wonderful and pure. It was exactly what my first kiss should have been, not something forced on me.

The intensity of our lips moving together increased, becoming like a fire raging and being extinguished into relief all in once. In that moment something shifted in me, woke from deep inside. Our soul deep connection bound its last tendrils together with our passion. As the kiss broke, I looked into his sleepy brown eyes and saw myself in them. More than myself. I saw us, bonded by twin flames for all of time.

Acknowledgments

Shortly after I started writing *Stones of Blood,* the world became upended. It became my escape from the madness of dealing with the whole thing that 2020 was. A piece of something I held onto and counted on to be what I expected it to be, as much as one's creations can be that is.

I think that sense of limitation the pandemic put on everything was absolutely what I needed to fuel this story, that want for a normal world and feeling powerless against something that affects everyone.

I'm so thankful for all the support I had during this project. To my husband and kids for their unwavering love and willingness to listen to my mad ideas.

To my family and friends that have become my biggest support.

To my beta readers for pushing me to make *Stones of Blood* the best it can be.

To my readers, present and future, your support means the world to me.

I love you all.

Dawn J. Braithwaite is an emerging author from the glorious Pacific North West, relishing in the rain and weirdness found there in abundance. A mild mannered geek with a dark sense of humor, Dawn thrives on nerd and pop culture, and the written word. She lives with her three children, husband, and small menagerie of furry and scaled animals.

Stones of Blood is Dawn's third book.

Also by Dawn J Braithwaite

Of Secrets and Crowns

Like the Moon